WHEN you MAKE it HOME

AUG 2 6 2019

Claire Ashby

When You Make It Home
Copyright © 2014 by Claire Ashby. All rights reserved.
First Print Edition: July 2014

ISBN 13: 978-1-940215-31-0
ISBN 10: 1-940215-31-5

Red Adept Publishing, LLC
104 Bugenfield Court
Garner, NC 27529
http://RedAdeptPublishing.com/

Cover and Formatting: Streetlight Graphics

For Brian

CHAPTER ONE

I FIRST CAUGHT SIGHT OF THEO at his welcome home party. A mob shifted around him, jockeying for a position next to the guest of honor. I lingered near the door to the living room and listened to the joyful words and murmur of good wishes directed toward him.

Someone whispered, "... lucky to be alive."

The doorbell rang, and the crowd parted. For a moment, he stood alone. Tears burned the backs of my eyes. I couldn't see the luck in what was left of him.

Ellie pinched my arm. "Don't stare," she said on her way to the door.

I bit my lip, turning away. But my attention found its way back to him, and I sneaked another look at his arms, surveying the road map of scars trailing away from bandages. My gaze traveled to his face, and I gasped. Theo glared at me with defiant hazel eyes, as if to say, *Go ahead and look all you want; I can take it.* I knew he'd lived through much worse than I had and that my own problems paled in comparison with his. I could use some of his strength. But, of course, I couldn't tell him that.

"What's wrong with you?" Ellie hissed, using the same voice as when she caught me eating the cookies meant for story time at our bookstore.

She steered me into the dining room, and once she had me cornered, she snatched a box of tissues and pushed them at me. "Get control of your hormones. We already went over this. If you want to keep your secret, you can't get all teary eyed.

"I know." I blinked rapidly, waving the tissues away. "I'm not crying. I'm sorry. I don't know what's wrong with me." I pressed my lips together, trying to clamp down on the list my brain rattled off. I had plenty wrong with me. But a party wasn't the time for a self-directed lashing. I could save that for home, after I dispensed a generous share of support to my best friend, who was desperate to give her brother-in-law the hero's welcome he deserved.

Ellie hugged me, and the tension between us evaporated.

"Don't let Theo see you looking at him with those weepy eyes. He gets pissed whenever anyone shows him an ounce of sympathy."

"Deal. But I wish we could do something for him." I hadn't meant to gawk at the guy.

With all the progress updates Ellie had shared with me, I knew far too many details about his surgeries and struggles. Theo often woke up screaming, but no one said whether his cries came from pain or nightmares. That knowledge haunted me until my overactive imagination filled in the blanks. I knew too much about the man, and I'd never met him before today. Worse, all I could do about it was put on a happy face.

I stepped back and reached out to touch the soft cotton of Ellie's new yellow dress. "You look fantastic." The fabric hugged the curve of her belly, erasing any doubt she was pregnant and not just packing on the pounds.

"Thanks." She scanned the crowd. "Jake got back late last night," she whispered. "He picked Theo up at the rehab facility and brought him to their mom's house." The lines around Ellie's mouth deepened. "Jake offered to let Theo stay here, but fortunately, their mom didn't like that at all. Jake's optimistic, but I never met Theo before he deployed, you know? I wish I had." Ellie rubbed her belly. "Theo's quiet."

The doorbell chimed, and Ellie hurried off. I used the chance to slip into the bathroom. I flipped the exhaust-fan switch and sighed with relief that the hum muffled the noise of the partygoers. With trembling hands, I turned on the cold water and let the icy stream rush over the insides of my wrists. I took a deep breath and checked my clothes in the mirror.

My new Marc Jacobs jacket covered the basic black T-shirt that hid a waist-contouring camisole. Skinny jeans and burgundy, open-toed heels completed my look. Almost anywhere else in the country, my outfit would've been perfect for a casual spring evening.

But not in Texas.

Early May, and the temperatures had already soared into the mid-90s. To make matters worse, my jeans fit tighter than they had the week before. I'd expected they would loosen after I wore them awhile. At least the cut of the jacket hid my growing belly. *My secret is safe for another day.*

I licked my lips and swallowed the lump in my throat before rejoining the party. The chatter and laughter had risen to competitive levels. I couldn't face trying to fit in, and I fell back into a trance. Theo fumbled around Ellie's living room, gripping his crutches. One of his arms was heavily bandaged, and he had a thick square of white gauze taped below his ear. But what sent a shiver through me was the sight of his leg. He had only one.

"Come on. I'll introduce you," Ellie said from behind me. She hooked her arm through mine and pulled me along. "Theo, this is my friend, Meg Michaels."

"Hello." He gave a slight nod, shifting on his crutches to extend his hand to me.

Despite the fact that I'd had my eyes on him for most of the last half hour, I'd failed to notice his hit-the-pause-button good looks. Theo's injuries drew attention away from his athletic build, but there was no hiding the tall, rock-solid composure. Close-cropped dark hair added to his dangerous edge. But when his full lips lifted into a smile, I could barely stand still at the unexpected warmth that surged through me. That surge skidded to a halt when his brooding eyes locked onto mine.

Theo cleared his throat.

I reached for his hand. "It's a pleasure to meet you." Did he have any idea how much I already knew about him? My face heated, and I felt like a big dummy while he appraised me as though he had all day. Ellie had disappeared, and I didn't know the proper protocol for socializing with a man I inexplicably felt intimidated by. Not that Theo seemed to mind.

He appeared all too comfortable with silence, but I needed to speak, if he wasn't going to. So I wouldn't have to yell over the noise of the party, I leaned into him, despite the fluttering in my chest that made it hard to inhale. "Would you..." Background music and clatter from the growing crowd swallowed my words.

He angled in closer. "What?"

I kept my eyes on his, refusing to glance at any other part of him. "Can I get you something to drink? Do you need anything?" I cringed at my voice — too pitchy, too polite.

He shook his head and looked past me.

I mumbled an excuse about helping out with dinner, stepped away from him, and fled to the back of the house.

Melinda, Ellie's mother-in-law, darted around the kitchen, yanking covered casserole dishes from the fridge and shoving them in a row along the counter. How had Theo and Jake come from such a trim little woman? Her white hair fell in waves around her flushed cheeks.

"Hey there." I huffed shallow breaths to fend off the strong aroma of browned butter. My stomach clenched.

"Hi, Meg." Melinda's puffy, dark-ringed eyes surveyed the spread in front of her.

"You're doing an amazing job, but don't you want to go sit with Theo?" I wrapped my arm over her shoulders, giving her a squeeze, suddenly aware that no one was looking after her needs. I wasn't qualified for that job; mothers were not my thing. "Tell me what to do. I'm here to help."

"Why did I insist Jake and Ellie give Theo a party?" Her

voice cracked and her lip trembled, but she continued to work, tearing foil off macaroni and cheese, baked beans, and corn on the cob. "Theo used to be so popular. He always wanted his friends around — they were all so wild — but only a few of them replied to the invitation." She slammed her hands down on the table and lowered her head. Her pale-blue eyes were wet and red rimmed, but she held back her tears.

"It's okay. He's going to be fine," I promised, even though I had no clue if that were true. "He's not alone. There are tons of people out there. Ellie invited the staff from the bookstore, and Jake has plenty of wild friends."

Melinda turned to me, nodding. "You're right. You know, I accepted what Theo had been through... how he had changed. But that was at the hospital and at rehab where he was surrounded with guys he could relate to, people who were going through the same thing he was. It's different here." She blinked, and tears slipped in two straight lines down her face. "Every time I look at a young man I think: Theo should be like that. He shouldn't have to go through this. It's not fair."

"It's not, and I'm so sorry." I moved to hug her, but she wiped at her face and turned away from me.

"It's okay. I'm fine." She cleared her throat and squared her shoulders. "Theo needs to eat. He has to keep his energy up. Can you man the grill? I can't do the burgers and do this."

"Trust me, no one wants me in charge of the grill, but I'll go find Jake. Are you sure you're okay?"

She yanked open the silverware drawer and rummaged around, pulling out a collection of serving spoons. "I am. Thank you, Meg."

I ducked out of the kitchen, wiggled my way around the thirty or so people in the living room, dodged conversations with friends, and found Jake and Ellie whispering together near the front door. Jake's hand rested on Ellie's belly, an image I'd seen many times, but today I had to look away.

Watching Jake and Ellie highlighted the loneliness of my pregnancy. I could almost long for Bradley's return, but since he disliked public displays of affection, I doubted he'd be much of a tummy toucher. I had called off our wedding four months earlier, partly because of his business trips. At first, he'd leave me for a few days or a week at a time. But as his weeks away piled up on each other, that feeling of a shared life fractured. The longer he stayed away, the less we connected when he came home.

Especially once I found out he had plenty of time to spend in the company of another woman.

"Hey, break it up, guys," I said. "Jake, your mom wants you at the grill."

As he walked by, he patted me on the shoulder, in on my little secret. When one's best friend gets married, one learns that even the most classified information is going to echo off an extra set of ears. I loved Jake, though, so I was okay with it. Ellie's man was loyal. I'd trusted him even before she did and had convinced her that she was going to lose a good one if she didn't give in to love. In the first year of her marriage, Ellie was already four-and-a-half months pregnant.

That was the best part of my mistake. While I might have gotten my single self knocked up, at least my lifelong best friend and soul sister was preggers, too.

"Hey, little momma." Ellie rubbed her belly, smiling deliberately at mine.

"Shush!" I looked over my shoulder and stuffed my hands in my jacket pockets. "Don't say that." I've never been a self-conscious person, but since my flat abs had exploded into a telltale pooch two weeks before, I'd been nearly hysterical, feeling as if I were wearing one of those "Baby on Board" T-shirts with a big arrow pointing down.

"Sorry, Meg. I just know everything is going to work out for you." The warmth in Ellie's voice triggered a lump in my throat. "Besides, you've always got me to lean on." She squeezed my shoulder.

Scanning the faces in the room, I struggled to breathe. How many of those people thought they knew all about me? I took a step back, but there was no escaping the pressure that rolled over me like a wave pulling me under.

My stomach churned under the unrelenting fear of discovery and the weight of choices before me. The smell of beef cooking on the grill didn't help. Rising bile in the back of my throat overwhelmed the familiar metallic taste.

"You don't look good." Ellie came to my rescue, as always. "Why don't you lie down in my room for a while? I'll cover for you."

"Are you sure? I'm supposed to be helping you." I took a deep breath, determined to pull myself together, but prickling sweat popped out on my brow.

"Let's go." Ellie put her arm around my waist and led me away from the crowd. I looked over my shoulder. Theo was eating from a plate on a TV tray, carefully chewing each bite. Melinda sat next to him looking calm and composed.

After Ellie left, I kicked off my heels and hung my jacket and T-shirt over the chair of her antique vanity in the far corner of the room. The ceiling fan, set to low, spun in lazy circles. I lifted my hair in a twist and looked down at my body. The camisole that used to conceal my belly accentuated the protruding bump. I couldn't deny the obvious.

There *was* a baby on board.

I tugged the hem of my camisole up over my bump and tucked it under my swollen breasts. The snug top stayed where I'd left it. I couldn't believe someone was in there. Before, every choice I'd ever made was calculated. A few random decisions had changed everything.

The bedroom door banged open, and I jumped, expecting Jake or Ellie. Instead, Theo lumbered in on his crutches and slammed the door behind him.

"Excuse me, do you mind?" I tugged my top in place to cover myself, but Theo's gaze took in my bare skin. He watched my movements closely and locked the door. For some reason I flushed and grew warmer as he came closer to the bed. *Could he want to trap me?* Of course, the thought was ridiculous.

I was pretty sure my small, five-foot-five-inch, exhausted, knocked-up self could plow through a one-legged boy covered in bandages if I wanted to get out of there badly enough. The thing was—I wanted to stay.

"Give me a break." He hobbled to the king-size bed without looking at me then propped his crutches against the wall before falling back onto the mattress. "You think you can hide in here all by yourself?" He hauled what was left of the lower half of his body onto the bed. A flash of pain crossed his bronzed face. Closing his eyes, he lay back on the striped navy sham. He ran his good hand through spiky hair the same tawny brown as the week-old scruff on his face. "Hit the light on your way out," he barked.

"Hey, I was here first, and I was just about to rest there. Ellie told me I could." I smacked a hand over my mouth. "Wait... I'm sorry. That was rude."

Theo lifted his head off the pillow, squinting from the overhead light. He peered at me in a slow, thorough inspection that left me fighting not to squirm.

"Well, Jake told me I could crash here. Turn off the light and come on." He patted the bed next to him. "Forgive me—I didn't notice you're expecting." He rolled his eyes.

The breath shot out of my lungs, and I wrapped my arms around my stomach as if I could hide the truth. "Stop looking at me," I said, making my way to the light switch.

Although he'd draped his tan, muscular arm across his forehead, I sensed his eyes tracking me. I pictured my belly growing with each step, the truth transparent. I switched off the lights. The sun was on the other side of the house, and fading afternoon light glowed in the room. I went back around the bed and paused, not sure I really wanted to get in with this hostile-looking guy who had spent recent years surrounded by sand and weapons.

Theo glared sideways at me. "Don't flatter yourself. I'm not about to make a move on some pregnant chick. Either get in or get out—I don't care."

My mouth fell open. "Oh... you think I think..." My voice quivered, so I stopped and tried another tactic. "I don't..." More quivers. I forced out the only response I could manage. "Whatever." I snatched my heels off the floor, ready to go home.

"Wait. What are you doing?" Theo scrubbed his hand over his face. "Don't go." His tone softened. "I shouldn't be alone right now." He was giving me those big, puppy-dog eyes, but I could see his smirk.

"What? Now you want me to stay?" No more quivering. The words flowed when the focus was on him. "What's with you?" I itched to make a run for it, but even so, he intrigued me.

"Cut a guy some slack, will you? My social graces are rusty."

"Oh, please! I've been warned not to give you anything that might resemble sympathy."

"I don't want your pity." A spark flared in his eyes. "Are you always this sassy, or is your condition playing with your hormones?" He had a full-on grin, his white teeth gleaming.

His audacity got the best of me. "Shut up, or I'm going to take your crutches when I leave."

My threat only made Theo roar with laughter, infuriating me more.

"You're a *bad* girl, teasing a hurt man. Just get in bed—you look tired. I'll leave, if you really want me to."

I gave in because he was right: I was worn out. "No, don't go." I dropped my shoes, went to the bed, pulled back the covers, and climbed in, staying as far away from him as I comfortably could. "Let's call a truce. I'll stay over here, you stay over there." I settled the plush bedding around me and rolled over to face his direction. The visible side of his body was flawless.

"Fine, but you better not snore or I'm going to flatten a pillow over your head."

I stifled a giggle. "You're not at all what I expected."

He jerked his head toward me, eyeing me suspiciously. "What did you expect?"

"I just thought a war hero would be nice." I yawned.

"I'm not nice enough for you?" His voice, low and smooth, did nothing to hide his amusement.

I relaxed, sinking in the mattress. "No, you're a total asshole."

The bed shook with his laughter. "Well, at least you're honest, but don't call me a hero."

I heard the smile in his tone, but my eyes were closed. *I really should have just stayed in bed today*, I thought, drifting off to sleep.

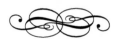

My eyes were open before I realized I was awake. Theo, bathed in moonlight, lay stretched out on top of the covers next to me.

"You don't have a ring on." He searched my eyes.

"I gave it back when I cancelled the wedding. Bradley wanted me to keep it..." I looked at my bare hand in the dim room. My ring finger felt naked without the karat-and-a-half, princess-cut diamond. Sometimes I still caught myself rubbing the area, searching for the phantom ring. "But I couldn't."

"So what, you didn't want a shotgun wedding?"

"Wait. Bradley's not the father." I cringed as soon as the words left my mouth.

His eyes twinkled in the moonlight, and he grinned again.

"So you *are* a bad girl."

CHAPTER TWO

IN THE DAYS FOLLOWING THEO'S welcome home gathering, I constantly replayed the strange moments we'd spent together. After he'd called me a bad girl for the second time in one night, I'd bolted from the bedroom and called out goodbyes to everyone I passed on my escape to the front door. Sure, I hated what he'd been through, but the way he looked at me, and the way he talked to me, left me raw and exposed.

I had my own problems to sort out. But like a good book I couldn't put down, I wanted to know more about Theo. What was his story? What was next for him, with his body — his life — forever altered? I thought about interrogating Ellie or Jake, but I didn't. That would only attract attention to my curiosity. Anyway, I wasn't sure of my motives. Maybe I needed a mental diversion. Sooner or later our paths would cross again, but I didn't expect us to gravitate to each other. I certainly didn't anticipate him being drawn to me.

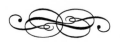

"I smell bacon." Steve's warm voice came from behind me while I was setting up a display in the cooking section of The Book Stack. I snatched a copy of the newly released *Bacontarian Diet*

and spun around to face him, catching my hip on the corner of the immense repurposed dining room table.

The sensible part of me held steady, even though I twitched to chuck the book at him and bail. "Check out my Father's Day gift display." I kept the book level with my belly. "Doesn't this cover make you hungry?" I tossed him a bar of bacon-like soap. "That's what you smell."

"Soap? Now that's original. I can stink like bacon all day." Steve sniffed the bar and scrunched up his nose. "Some things are not meant to be. Think these will sell?" He cocked his head and gave me the inquisitive, younger-brother-by-seven-minutes look that reminded me how thoroughly he trusted me.

My throat tight, I barely hung on to our conversation. "Sure, but not as well as the bacon gum, bacon-flavored toothpicks, bacon Band-Aids..." I tapped the items as I listed them. "Or my personal favorite..." I reached for the little red-and-white rectangular box and shook it. "Bacon jellybeans!"

"Nice ensemble. I never knew such a vast array of porcine novelties existed. I can't help myself." Steve took the box of jellybeans, opened it, rattled out a handful of bacony beans then tossed them into his mouth. He studied the label, chewing away while I waited for his verdict.

"Not bad."

My stomach rumbled loudly enough to catch Steve's attention. He looked down, and I sidestepped to stand behind a stack of cookbooks.

"You skip lunch again?" His brows pulled together, and I heated under his inspection. He read me too well.

"I'm about to head to The Tavern." The words rushed from my mouth.

He shook out another handful of jellybeans. "Have a bacon bean," Steve offered, his mouth full.

I flinched at the smoky whiff of pork on his breath. "I'll pass. You better pay for those. They're six dollars a box."

"Ha! Put it on my tab." He strolled away, loose limbed, all easy and light. Keeping a secret was bad enough, but keeping a secret from my twin felt like a tumor growing inside. If I told him some of the truth, he'd want to know all of it. And in the details, his heart would break.

The Tavern, located on the opposite corner from The Book Stack, was my go-to place for a quick bite and a reprieve from work. That day, I passed through the big wooden doors and inhaled sharply. The restaurant was packed. Tuesday Night Trivia—always a good time to skip The Tavern. I slipped past the "Wait to be Seated" sign, which didn't apply to regulars, and shouldered through the crowd to an empty, high-backed booth in the front corner.

My favorite waitress, Karen, spotted me. "Hey, girl! Having the usual?"

"No." The usual was the healthiest item available: a grilled chicken salad with lite vinaigrette dressing. I smoothed my skirt, wiggling to adjust the bite of fabric sinking into my sides. The last time I had a lapse of self-discipline, I ended up pregnant, so at this point I figured I might as well live a little. Even though I knew the menu by heart, I grabbed one from behind the napkin dispenser. "I'll have this..." I pointed to the chicken tender salad, justifying that the pile of greens canceled out the fried parts. I flipped the menu over. "Oh, and some of those." I tapped on the shiny photo of potato skins, and my mouth watered.

"Diet Coke?"

"Lemonade."

She smiled broadly, jotting down my order. "I can tell it's one of those days when someone is willing to eat what they're not willing to say out loud." My mouth fell open, but she laughed and sauntered away before I could change my order.

The usual was safe. I should've stuck with the usual.

With my back to the windows, I sat facing the crowd of people stopping in on their way home from work. The Maroon

5 song was loud, but the talk was louder. Stools circled the restaurant's high-top tables, and booths lined its main walls. In the heart of the room, beneath stained-glass lights, an oblong bar pulsed with human activity.

In a precise row sat five men, dressed casually in cotton clothes in tans, grays, and greens. They were well built, well groomed, and well received by the flock of women huddled around them. Although not in uniform, the fit and handsome group had the look of military. But in their current location, they stood out in an ocean of black and navy wool-blend suits, starched white shirts, and colorful silk ties loosened just a tad.

In the middle of everyone sat Theo.

I couldn't take my eyes off of him. Neither could the tall, lithe brunette chatting with him. Her electric-blue top left three inches of perfectly taut, tanned stomach exposed, and her ample breasts fought against the shimmery fabric. Theo appeared completely enamored of her; his gaze trained on her boobs as if he'd never seen anything more tempting. And who could blame him? She radiated youth.

I never worried much about my age, but something about being twenty-four, sitting in a bar, single and pregnant, watching a chick who was rocking the barely legal look flirt with the man who'd been haunting my thoughts... well, that left me feeling past my prime. Done with people-watching for one night, I switched to the other side of the booth for a view with 100% less cleavage. I zoned out, staring at my bookstore, and I thought about work, my favorite distraction.

By the time Karen delivered my order, I was ravenous. I sucked down my lemonade and plucked the fried chicken strips out of my salad, dipping the chicken into creamy ranch dressing, moaning as I savored it all. After finding food repulsive for so long, I was suddenly infatuated with eating. The flavors and texture of most anything I put in my mouth tasted richer and more delicious than ever. So, there I sat, almost making out with my fried chicken strips, about to dive into the potato skins, when Theo fell into the seat across from me.

"Slow down, blondie. No one's going to steal your chicken."

"Don't start with me." I scooped up a potato skin covered in — yes — bacon from my plate.

He also helped himself to a potato, not bothering with a plate or fork. Or my permission.

"Why don't you dig right in?"

He nodded at my belly. "That thing is growing well on all this fried food."

I nodded right back to the cigarette tucked behind his ear. "Yeah, and you're the poster boy for good health and wellness." I pushed my plate away and folded the napkin in my lap.

"No." He leaned in closer and spoke in a firm almost-whisper. "I'm not well, *and* I'm not all that good either."

I tensed. Maybe I'd pushed too hard. Ready to apologize, I met his stare, but his lips stretched wide in a grin.

"Don't stop pounding food on my account." He winked and scooted the plate back in front of me. "You're pretty hot when you stuff your face."

A rare feeling bubbled up inside of me, and I laughed — something I hadn't done in far too long.

His attention lingered on my open mouth; a flicker of mischief flared in his eyes.

"Look at that, Grumpy Girl knows how to smile." Theo appeared pleased with himself. "So you're still hiding your condition?" He gestured at my long, elaborately tied silk scarf.

I cleared my throat and reached for the lemonade. "Yes, and I plan to for as long as I can."

"What's the big deal? What do you care what anyone thinks?"

"Because assumptions are made when a girl ends up like this." I resisted the urge to place my hand on my stomach. "You don't understand." I lowered my voice and glanced over my shoulder. "The timing is awful. Everyone's going to think my ex is the father." I fished a twenty and a ten from my wallet and tossed them in the center of the table. "And then what?" My volume pitched higher. "Do I give details of my sex-life mishaps? I own a bookstore... I'm the go-to girl for information.

Can't you hear the jokes? *Doesn't she know how babies are made?* Trust me, it's bad all around."

"So let them assume. You shouldn't have to answer to anyone."

"Easy for you to say." I sat back and let out a long sigh, but I appreciated his concern.

Theo raked his fingers through his hair. "What's your ex think?"

"Bradley doesn't know." I hated how the truth sounded like a confession. My pregnancy didn't involve Bradley, but if he knew, he'd treat it like a problem he could solve. "He's been out of town for several months. He got a promotion, proposed to me, and then we bought a house. Right after we moved in, his new boss assigned him to a quality-control plant in China. It was his dream territory, and he said at the time he'd only be on site for two weeks every quarter."

"He was out of the country when you dumped him? That's brutal. I've seen what that does to a man."

"Hey, look how fast you've switched to assumptions." My voice was louder than I'd intended. "It's hard getting left behind." I twisted the napkin in my lap, shredding the edges.

"That's not a good enough reason to call it quits."

"Sometimes at night, I'd call his room, and a woman would be there. He swore nothing was going on, but why was she always there? Worry consumed me, and I couldn't let it go."

"So, was he guilty?"

"I don't know, but I was in the middle of planning our wedding, and he was preoccupied whenever we talked. I couldn't take the uncertainty anymore. I called off the wedding, took my condo off the market, and moved home."

"He didn't come back for you?"

"No." I swallowed against my dry throat. Bradley was not the first one to forget about me.

"He sounds like an idiot." Theo's words pleased me. "So just like that, no more house, no more wedding?"

I nodded slowly, and I could almost hear the next thought click into place.

"Where'd the little one come from?" he asked.

"Nice try, buddy. I've given you enough dirt for one day. Your turn."

He lined up the salt and pepper shakers to the side of the napkin dispenser and straightened the menu behind it. "My turn?"

"You got me to unload intimate details of my life. Now talk." I leaned forward. "What's your story?"

Theo studied the room around us, and when his eyes snapped back to mine, they cut into me, exposed and restless.

I knew that a roadside bomb had ripped him away from the life he wanted and pushed him back into a world that was no longer his, and I marveled how he could handle it all. Or maybe he couldn't. I clutched the edge of my seat. My breath was trapped in my lungs, as if exhaling might blow away any chance to connect with him.

The moment passed, and Theo returned to his guarded self. "No secrets here." His voice betrayed none of the rawness his eyes had held seconds earlier. He held his palms open, his face lifted in a blinding, openmouthed grin. "What you see is what you get. End of story."

I smacked the table. "Yeah, right," I said, and he chuckled. I glanced out the window to the bookstore and inventoried the things I had to do. "This has been delightful, but if that's all you have to offer, I must get back to work." I slid to the edge of the booth.

"Okay, I'll come with you."

"That wasn't an invitation."

He shrugged, a gleam in his eyes. "I need a book."

I glimpsed his comrades lining up at the bar. The brunette moved to the seat Theo had previously occupied and busied herself flirting with another guy.

"What about your friends?"

"Nah, we don't have to invite them." He positioned his

crutches then heaved himself out of the booth. "Let me say my goodbyes."

At the entrance, I turned back in time to see the brunette help Theo put his backpack on. The gesture appeared oddly maternal, but then she slipped a folded napkin into his pocket, ruining the illusion. Theo laughed at something she said, and he turned to his friends, who got up to give him back-clapping hugs.

Then he lurched toward me, and as I held the door, he thumped by. Theo stopped on the sidewalk in front of The Tavern. A neon Guinness sign buzzed in the window, casting a green glow across his profile. Theo pulled the cigarette from behind his ear, lighting up. I went to the crosswalk and pressed the button. He wobbled over as he puffed on the cigarette clenched between his lips.

"What's with the face?" he asked, speaking from the corner of his mouth.

"That's nasty."

He took a deep drag and removed the cigarette from his lips. Squinting at me, he exhaled; a bluish-white plume of smoke billowed into the night. He shook his head, smiling.

"Um... what's so funny?"

He smirked. "It *is* nasty." He dropped the cigarette on the ground and stepped on it with what appeared to be a brand-new Nike shoe. I pictured the mate alone in a box somewhere. Theo reached in his pocket, removed an almost-full pack of cigarettes, and tossed it in the trashcan by the light pole. "You happy now?"

"You're quitting? Just like that?"

"Just like that," he said with confidence. His hands opened and closed, clenching the grips on his crutches. "Just something I picked up in the sandbox, anyway."

The light changed, and I turned to walk across the street, trying to go slowly enough for him to keep up.

He trailed behind me and let out a low whistle, the kind that captures the attention of anyone in earshot. "Girl, you are working it in those heels with that short skirt." His voice sailed to me. "I never knew pregnancy could look so *hot*." The words sent a heat wave up my legs, not unlike a caress.

I *knew* he could move faster.

"Hush," I hissed, stopping under the storefront awning to The Book Stack. "If you want to come inside, you have to take an oath to honor my secret. This is my place of business. My brother doesn't know about any of this, so lay off the jokes."

"Sorry, sorry." He held up three fingers on his right hand, his good hand. "Scout's honor — your secret is safe with me."

I marched over to him — right into his personal space — and mustered the meanest look I could offer. "If you betray me, I will make you pay." The last thing I needed was my cover blown.

"Hey now, everything's okay." His pupils dilated, ringed by browns and mossy green flecked with pale gold. "Relax, I'm not going to hurt you." Kindness entered his voice, and he shifted his eyes toward the door of the bookstore. "Trust me."

I went to the door and opened it wide. "Come on in." When he hesitated, I sighed. "Are you going to make me beg now?"

Finally, he moved his crutches forward, taking a step. "I won't make you beg." He stood at the threshold, filling the doorway, surveying the surroundings. Once he finally moved past me, I followed, and the door slammed shut behind us. He was in my territory.

The Book Stack had been my grandfather's business, a gift Steve and I inherited after college graduation. Anyone could be envious of our hand-me-down career, but running an independent bookstore in the midst of Amazon's world domination required more cunning than luck.

Steve charged around the information desk, hand outstretched. Theo shook his hand.

"Hey man, that was some gathering the other night. I'd meant to thank you for your service, but you were so popular, I didn't want to monopolize your time. It's good to see you again."

Theo nodded. "Thank you." Theo looked past Steve at the towering rows of books. "This place is great."

I tried to see it through his eyes: an eclectic collection of furniture filling a large main floor, crammed with books. Of course there were bookshelves too, but my grandfather had supplemented them with any solid-wood furnishings he could acquire. He'd transformed every piece of furniture into a bookshelf or display. There were armoires with the doors wide open, revealing rows of colored spines. We had a scarred cupboard, an antique rolltop desk, large oak cabinets, even an old kitchen table with mismatched chairs—for the person who had to stop, drop, and read. Every surface fostered volumes. My grandfather envisioned himself a gatekeeper into the endless journeys one could find inside a story. He believed the bookstore was a sacred honor and a responsibility.

And he passed that duty on to Steve and me.

"Do you mind if I browse?" Theo asked.

"Have at it. I have to finish up my files for the night," I said. "Make yourself at home."

"Hold on." Steve's hand hovered above Theo's shoulder but didn't actually make contact. "I'll help you get settled in the coffee shop, and I'll bring you whatever you want. We have magazines, too." Steve waved toward a china cabinet full of magazines, and if I could've reached out and snatched a copy of Vogue, I would've rolled it up and knocked him right on the head.

My chest got all tight, and for a second, I regretted bringing Theo over.

"No thanks, I prefer to roam." Theo readjusted the straps of his backpack and headed down the center aisle of the store.

"Don't be an ass," I mumbled to Steve.

"Hey!" He threw his arms in the air. "What'd I do?"

I caught up with Theo at the intersection of the two main paths of the first floor. "If you get bored, you can find my office in the back."

"Sure thing." He scanned the gothic-lettered signs that hung on wires from the ceiling, and he headed toward Nonfiction.

The second I got to the back of the store, I rushed through my office and into the bathroom to freshen up. My reflection caught me by surprise. I looked flushed and full of expectations. "Stop," I said to my face in the mirror. "Don't pretend. Life is going in a different direction now. There's no future with this guy." I knew that was true, but it didn't matter; I wanted him to like me. I shook out my hair, pinched my cheeks to bring some color to them, and applied a fresh swipe of soft-pink lipstick. Satisfied, I returned to my desk.

My eyes fixed on the computer screen, but my mind fixed on Theo. I switched the security camera views to find his location in the store. He wasn't in the magazine aisle or the coffee shop. I finally spotted him in the travel section. Was he ready to leave again? Sure, I was sneaky to spy on him as he moved about in my turf, but even with that guilt thrumming through my veins, I zoomed in closer.

The phone rang, and I jumped. "Hello."

"Hey, you sound funny." Ellie cleared her throat. "Is everything okay?"

"Theo's here," I answered, as if that explained everything.

"What's his deal?"

"What do you mean?" The sound of a baseball game filtered through the phone, along with Jake's voice shouting for his team.

"He doesn't say anything about himself. He's living this great big tragedy, and back in a town where he's hardly spent any time in the last three years." Theo had left Travel. I flipped from camera view to camera view, until I found the one that captured him. He moved unsteadily on his crutches to the register, a book tucked under his chin.

"Well, that's all I know, too. Jake and their mom are adjusting to having him around. He's barely been home since he finished basic training four years ago. Jake says Theo's different now. His whole world has been turned upside down overnight. Any woman who gets involved with him is going to have a lot of drama on her hands."

"What's that supposed to mean?"

Ellie dropped any pretense that she wasn't referring to me. "Don't take on his problems."

"Okay, point taken." Theo headed in my direction, and I switched off the security camera monitor. "I better go. Call you later?"

"Wait! Don't forget we have our ob-gyn appointments tomorrow morning." Ellie's words carried a warning tone, probably because I'd skipped out on our last appointment.

"I didn't forget." I heard Theo walking through the storeroom, and I swiveled in my chair to wave him in when he appeared in the door. "I'll pick you up at nine. Promise."

I hung up and went to close the office door. The lock let out a satisfying click as Theo shot me a questioning look.

"So I can take my jacket off." I tried to ignore the fluttering in my chest. "I can't have anyone charge in here and catch me pregnant."

"No, you certainly can't risk that," he said with a clear note of humor in his voice. He lowered himself onto the one non-office-like piece of furniture in the room: a gingham-upholstered loveseat.

He scrutinized me while I undid my scarf and hung up my jacket. I wore a thin black camisole. Goose bumps rose along my arms.

"Do you always wear black?"

"No, but it works when I want to minimize." I slipped off my shoes and sat next to him. He always managed to end up facing me with his good side, and I had to wonder if this was deliberate.

"What's this?" He picked up a framed photo of Ellie, Steve, and me.

"I have a mild obsession with fairy tales." I gestured toward the framed illustrations that hung all around my office. "That photo was taken on our annual Fairy Tales Forever Day. Steve and I were Hansel and Gretel, and Ellie was the witch."

"She's not a scary witch," Theo said, inspecting the photo closely.

I smiled. "She's not. She should've dressed like Sleeping Beauty or Little Red Riding Hood."

Theo set the photo back on the short file cabinet next to the loveseat that I used as a side table and glanced around my office, taking in the artwork. "I thought fairy tales were for children. You have a gloomy collection."

"Gloomy? Philipp Grot Johann did these for the original Grimm Brothers. They're beautiful. Haunting and dark, yes, but also hopeful."

"You have so many of them," Theo said. "Have you been collecting for a while?"

"No." I grinned sheepishly. "I cut them out of the book."

"You cut up a book?"

"Sure. Books are meant to be used."

"What did you do with the rest of the book? The pages of words?"

"I saved them for art projects and displays. Don't worry. I'll get the most out of that book." I pointed to the bag in his lap. "What'd you get?"

Theo took out *The Complete Poem Collection of e.e. cummings.*

"I wouldn't have pegged you for the poetry type."

"I'm not. My dad was." He smoothed his hand across the cover. "He read poems to Mom after dinner when I was a kid." Theo laughed but sounded sad. "I'd think about those nights when I was over there, trying to remember some of the lines."

His pain was palpable, and I desperately wished I knew him well enough to give him what he needed. Maybe a hug or a bad joke. But everything I thought of seemed too pathetic to offer.

He cleared his throat. "But I'm not going to slice out pages of this and go frame them."

"That's okay." I laughed. "You can still have a greater bond with that book than the words on the pages."

"Yeah?" He looked at me skeptically.

"When you find the poems you remember, mark them. People can be so uptight about writing in books, but trust me. There's something special about coming back to a spot you cared for and seeing a thought or memory you left behind."

"Are you familiar with e. e. cummings?" Theo asked, and

when I nodded, he handed me the volume. "Show me. Mark it however you wish."

I searched the contents and found the page for my favorite e. e. cummings poem, "[love is more thicker than forget]." I reached for a pencil from my desk and held the tip an inch from the page.

"What are you waiting for?" His voice was low. "It was your idea — write something."

"Are you sure? I've never messed with anyone's books besides my own."

"I insist." His face reflected the same curiosity I felt about him.

Placing my palm over the poem, I traced my hand. The lead made a scratching sound as I followed the path of my fingers. With tiny, precise script, I jotted down the date and a message along the outline of my hand: *Remember these words. Your friend, Meg.*

"Thank you," he said, reviewing the message. He closed the book and returned it to his backpack.

A comfortable silence settled between us. I may not have known what to say, but for once, I was fine not saying anything. My quick glances progressed to an obvious stare.

Theo was even nicer to look at up close. I shifted my sights higher and met his calm eyes, surrounded by thick, dark lashes. "So... you hit it off with that girl back at the bar." I wasn't even sure where I was going with the line of conversation.

"Huh?" He rubbed his chin. "Oh, the girl with the abs? You think she was into me?"

I cringed at the word "abs." *I'm going to miss mine.*

"Is there anyone special in your life?" I asked.

"You mean a girlfriend? Not lately."

"Did you date when you were deployed? Is that even possible?"

"Sure, sure. I've dated a soldier or two."

I gave him a doubtful look.

"What? I'm not scared of a strong girl. Women with guns are hot."

"So that's what you're into: chicks that pack heat. That might be harder to find around here."

He held my gaze. "Actually, fraternization is in violation of General Order Number One."

"That sounds serious."

He nodded. "Oh, it is. Anyway, find me a nice, soft lady who's scared of spiders, and I'm there. No guns required."

"When's the last time you went out with someone seriously?"

"College. We were together for almost three years when I left for Iraq."

"Can I ask what happened?"

His mouth tightened. "I guess it's my turn after all. Home didn't quite feel like home after fifteen months in Iraq. I didn't anticipate that." He chewed on the corner of his lip. "When I was growing up, we had this gigantic oak tree that would spit acorns all over the front yard. Jake and I would battle with the acorns. He'd peg them so hard I'd get bruised. When I was gone, a storm came through and ripped the tree right out of the ground. So every time I pulled up to the house, I felt like I was at the wrong place." Theo turned to me and seemed to realize he'd skirted the question. "Apparently, that's how my girlfriend felt about me.

"They needed more guys in Afghanistan, and that's where I wanted to go all along, so I stepped up. That's it, really. And if you want to know the truth, she dumped me after I shipped out."

"I'm sorry."

"Nah. People drift apart." He shrugged. "It happens. We were young."

"How old are you?"

"Take your best guess." He tilted his head, his expression serious.

"Maybe... twenty-one?"

"I'm twenty-five."

"Not quite a baby anymore," I teased.

"Not quite. Speaking of babies..." His hand hovered above my belly. "May I?"

For a split second, I didn't know what he was asking. Then I nodded.

He placed his hand on the slight curve of belly. Meeting my eyes, his smile erupted with pure joy. "Wow," he whispered, his hand circling my stomach. Theo's caress sent heat racing through my body. It was the first touch I'd received from a man since the day my baby had been conceived, and I craved more of it.

"My turn?" I raised my hand.

"What, you want to touch me?" he asked, his voice a low rasp. "Go ahead. Put your hands anywhere." He spread his arms, palms up.

The look in his eyes pulled me closer to him, to the welcoming heat that swirled around him. With his invitation, I reached for the top of his head, sliding my fingers through his dark hair. It was cut short, close to his head, and felt like velvet. My hand trailed down the side of his face to the rough scrape of stubble. Our shoulders brushed and my every nerve quivered, achingly aware of him. I leaned into him. My palm skimmed down his neck, my gaze dropped from his eyes to his wide mouth with those delicious-looking lips, and I knew I was in trouble. Especially when I saw that he, too, was eyeing my mouth.

But instead of a kiss, he encircled my wrist lightly with his massive hand, pushed it away from him, and dropped it onto my lap.

"You need a TV in here." He shifted away from me and focused on the wall across from us. And with that, the mood screeched to a halt.

I looked away, overwhelmed and tired. "A TV would be nice, except I'd never get any work done."

"I get the feeling you work too much."

"Yeah, I'm ready to call it a day." I stood and moved to shut down my computer.

Theo zipped up his backpack and adjusted it on his

shoulders. He clenched his teeth, making a muscle on his neck pop out as he struggled to stand. He teetered momentarily before stabilizing himself with his crutches.

"Can I give you a ride home?" I offered.

"Sure, why don't you come hang out and watch TV with me?" He sounded casual, but a wariness had settled between us.

"Maybe some other time." I pushed my tired feet into my heels, shrugging into my jacket. "I've got to get out of these clothes."

"We'll swing by your place so you can change. It's not even nine o'clock. Live a little. My mom's friends stocked the fridge. You can catch up on your eating and relax."

Why did he keep pressing for more time with me? Maybe he was lonely. I knew I was. But I didn't really care *why* he wanted to hang out with me because I knew that, regardless of his reasoning, *I* found him more and more captivating. I picked up my bag and took a deep breath.

"Okay, let's go."

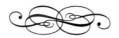

Theo waited in my car while I ran inside to change. Stacks of boxes crowded my condo, even though I'd moved back in months earlier. When Bradley and I had moved to our house, I had meticulously unpacked, and kept at it until I had every little thing right. Six months later, when I moved back alone, I was sick of the whole process. I'd eventually get to it, so why hurry? Instead, I made my bedroom a haven and didn't pay attention to the rest. I hardly noticed the boxes anymore.

Rushing to my room, I considered what to wear. Sweatpants — that wouldn't be overdoing it, and my pink ones were pretty cute. Nothing felt as good as cotton and elastic at the end of the day. I pulled my hair up into a ponytail and slipped on my favorite black hoodie that also helped to veil my condition, in case I ran into anyone in the parking lot. Finally, I was comfortable.

I practically skipped on the way back to the car.

"You ready?" Theo asked, when I bounced into my seat.

His glorious smile made me shiver from head to toe. Oh, I had other things to focus on than a man with his own troubles, but I grinned back at him and said, "Absolutely!" Then I threw the car into reverse. We drove in silence, me lost in thoughts about him, and him lost in thoughts about who knows what. My sidelong glances uncovered no clues; however, his presence was comforting.

The lights blazed behind every one of Melinda's windows.

"Is your mom home?"

"No, if I'm not here when she leaves for work, she turns on every light. It's annoying, but she ignores me when I tell her I can find my way in the dark."

"Oh, your mom is great. She's thrilled to have you home." *Instead of dead.* I shuddered.

Theo struggled to get out of the car. I leaped from my seat and rushed to his side. With one hand on the car door, I reached out to him. "Let me help—"

"No." He twisted away from me and then stumbled, bracing himself against the car. He bowed his head. "I got it." A muscle stood out on his neck.

I stalled by digging through my purse for a stick of gum I knew I didn't have until he gathered himself and led the way. All Theo's injuries ran down the left side of his body, so he favored that side. He moved unsteadily on his crutches because the bandages on his hand prevented him from fully gripping his crutch. He wore knee-length khaki shorts, revealing one leg that was tanned, well defined, and perfect in every way. But I couldn't see any sign of what was left of his other leg.

He clambered up the one step, unlocked the door, and trudged into the house. Theo dropped his backpack inside the door, sat in a ladder-back chair next to the entrance and removed his Nike and sock. He ditched one crutch by the chair and set off with the other, making up for the reduced support by leaning on furniture or bracing against the wall as he bounded around, more agile in his home than out in the world.

With the blinding lights on, the silence was oddly crushing. I studied the vast expanse of dark hardwoods, varnished crown molding, and oriental rugs tossed in every direction of travel. A faded floral sofa sat in the middle of the living room, facing a large flat-screen TV that was too modern for its surroundings. A newspaper lay open on the coffee table next to a stack of magazines and a nearly full cup of tea stained with a half-moon of lipstick. The walls were lined with photos of the brothers — Melinda's handiwork, I guessed — arranged in a timeline. Soccer, baseball, and football pictures alternated with class and holiday photo collages. I meandered along, past Jake's and then Theo's college graduation photos, to a break in the pattern — a missing frame, highlighted by the bright square of wallpaper left exposed, next to a wedding portrait of Jake and Ellie.

"Come on back."

I stopped to touch the lone exposed nail before following the sound of Theo's voice to the kitchen.

Theo limped to the fridge and removed covered dishes, sliding them onto the counter.

"What is all this stuff?" I peeked under a turquoise Fiesta Ware lid, breathing in the aroma of fresh herbs, onions sautéed in butter, cream, and roasted poultry.

"A casserole smorgasbord from the old ladies at Mom's church. They've taken on the project of fattening me up. To them, eating equals healing, and Mom's keeping tabs on me. So the more you eat, the more you help me." Theo winked at me, but he seemed uneasy with the effort they'd undertaken on his behalf. "So this week's special is Mac and Cheese Hotdog Surprise, Tuna Egg Noodle Dream, and what you have there, my favorite: Chicken Pot Pie. I'm willing to share even that." He retrieved plates from the cabinet. "What'll you have?"

"I'll have whatever you're having." I tried to take a plate from his hand, but he held them out of my reach. "Can't I help?"

"Nope. You're my guest. Go sit down." He gestured to

the round, copper-topped table nestled in a cozy nook off to the side of the kitchen. The inky night turned the curtainless, white-trimmed bay windows into a mirror.

I told myself not to ask the question, but then I couldn't help blurting out: "What's the missing photo?"

Theo's slashing, dark brows shot up in question.

"Out there." I pointed slowly to the front room. "There's an empty spot."

His eyes squeezed shut, and he bowed his head.

Why couldn't I hammer my mouth shut? "And there's an empty spot, inside my head, where my brain should be." I scrambled for something better to say, wishing I had a do-over button, because right then I wanted to stab myself with a fork, if that's what it took to distract him from the pain I'd caused him. "I—I'm an idiot. I'm sorry. My tongue moves too fast for me to keep up sometimes. It's like I can't stop myself. I just spit out every little thing that runs through my head, even though there's like these little warning bells. My mouth has a life of its own—"

"Stop." Theo's voice cut in smooth and sharp. "It's all cool." He ran the back of his wrist across his forehead. "Mom frames everything. Something must've got knocked down. There's no need to panic."

I pulled off my hoodie, draped it on the back of a kitchen chair, and sat. "I'm sorry," I said again.

Theo scooped the colorful mush onto plates, glancing at me with unreadable eyes. With deliberate movements, he lifted a plate into the microwave over the oven.

"What are you thinking?" I asked.

"What am I thinking?" He looked beyond me to the dark window, which showed his own refection, and then he smiled. "I'm thinking that for once you're not in black. And I'm thinking I like how you look when you're not wearing black. And you know what else I'm thinking?" He looked at me point-blank. "I'm thinking you look pregnant." He filled stoneware coffee mugs with orange juice. "I don't care about the reasoning. Your secret is stupid."

His words hit me like a spray of cold water. *"What?"*

My throat clenched, and tears burned at my eyes. I refused to cry. I especially wouldn't let Theo see me fall apart. Even as I vowed this, I buried my face in my hands, and sobs ripped through me. Crushing tears with the palms of my hands as fast as they broke free, I gasped to breathe past the ache in my chest.

"Oh no, don't do that. I didn't mean anything. I'm sorry, Meg." He fumbled around the table to the chair next to me, dragged it out, and dropped into it, letting his crutch fall to the floor with a bang. Theo pulled me to him, chair and all. He wrapped his arms completely around me, engulfing me in his warmth. "It's okay... It's okay," he murmured into my hair. I rested my head against his chest and inhaled deeply, detecting the lingering scent of fabric softener mingled with the slightest hint of his salty sweat. The combination soothed me.

"I mean to hell with anyone who can't deal with your situation." I listened to his heart beating and took comfort in the presence of him breathing next to me.

"Thank you," I whispered, and I pulled back from him. "For keeping my secret." I moved to get the juice and plates of food he had prepared and brought them to the table.

We ate in silence, and the food seemed to settle the tension between us. "That was incredible," I said as I finished.

"Yeah, those church ladies are amazing with a little butter and heavy cream." He placed his fork in the center of his empty plate and dropped his folded paper napkin on top. He sighed, and I noted the shadows under his eyes.

"I should probably go."

"You should probably stay," Theo replied. "I promised you TV, and you can't go until you watch some."

"Okay, but Theo... Don't worry about me. I'm battling extreme pregnancy hormones."

I gathered our dishes and put them in the sink. An open door in the corner of the kitchen led to a small laundry room with a trashcan just inside. I stepped in to dispose of my napkin and inhaled the smell of bleach and soap. I caught sight of a large frame propped against the back wall. Sure enough, the glass was broken. A perfect shattered starburst distorted the photograph of Theo in his Class A uniform. Under a black beret, his face was a study in self-confidence. From behind me came a thumping shuffle.

"No worries, girl. Leave that. Let's go chill in front of the tube."

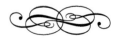

Theo dimmed the lights, and we sat on opposite ends of the sofa. He flipped channels until we agreed to watch *Poltergeist*. The rich meal so late at night sent me on a desperate search through my purse for antacids.

"What do you need?"

"I have heartburn. I don't suppose you have any Tums?"

"Wait here." He struggled to get up.

"I can get them. Tell me where." I perched on the edge of my seat.

"I got it. You stay," he ordered, using his one-crutch method to maneuver his way across the room and out the door.

He returned with a small pillow and a lap quilt tucked under his arm. He tossed them on the sofa, held his fist up to me, and dropped two pink tablets into my hand, his long fingers brushing against my palm.

"Excellent. Thanks." I placed both tablets on my tongue, the chalky, faux-cherry flavor filling my mouth.

"Get comfortable." He collapsed onto his side of the sofa. "You can stretch out." There was something about being on a man's turf that made him relax.

Theo focused on the TV while I snuggled under the blanket and curled up, keeping my bare feet away from him. Hidden under the blanket, I put a hand on my swollen belly. Tomorrow would be my first visit to the doctor, and that made the baby growing inside of me more real, which was the exact reason I'd put off the appointment for so long—way past the acceptable timeline. Once I saw the doctor I'd have to face my reality. At least that was the plan. But I wasn't ready to let go of my secret.

"You don't have to be all balled up. Don't you know how to relax?" He gave me a sideways glance. His hand slipped under the blanket, fingers curling around my ankle.

I yelped, unable to stop myself, but Theo tugged my foot onto his lap. His strong hand warmed my skin. His thumb circled my anklebone, sending pulses of pleasure through me. I sighed and peeked at him. Even as he touched me so tenderly, his focus remained locked on the TV screen, on the demon tree pulling the boy from his bedroom. I allowed my eyes to shut, only half listening to the screams on TV. I lay as still as possible, afraid if I moved he would let go and put up a wall between us. At some point, I must have drifted off because the next thing I knew, Theo was howling and clutching my leg, his fingers digging into my calf.

"Theo, stop!" I scooted back, away from him, and wedged my fingers under his to pull free. He winced and released his hold on my leg. His body curled inward as he doubled over and roared in agony.

My heart pounding in my ears, I hunched down in front of him. "Tell me what to do," I begged, cradling his face in my hands.

"Pills—I need my pain pills," he said through clenched teeth, his eyes wild. "In the bathroom." He flung backwards on the sofa with an agonized roar, his face ashen, glistening with sweat.

I leaped to my feet and darted down the hall. Then I gripped the frame of the bathroom door to check back and make sure he was okay, but the way he'd folded in on himself was anything but okay. The medicine cabinet in the bathroom held no fewer than fifteen prescription bottles of various sizes, all meticulously printed with the name "Theodore Taylor." I scanned the labels of toxic-sounding medications. The beautiful words "as needed for pain" jumped out at me, written on two separate bottles. I snagged the glass on the edge of the sink and filled it to the rim. Water sloshed onto the floor as I raced back to Theo.

"The big bottle." He dragged a hand down his face, his breath fluttering out between low moans.

I popped off the top and poured pills into the lid. He took two and swallowed them dry then chugged the entire glass of water.

I refilled the glass and returned with a cool, wet washcloth. I crouched in front of him. "Here." I pushed the washcloth into Theo's hand.

"Thanks," he mumbled and buried his face, panting ragged gasps into the cloth. Many minutes passed before his breath slowed. His grip on the armrest loosened, and he looked at me again.

"I'm sorry." His brows pulled together. "Are you okay?"

"*Me?*" I asked. "I'm fine. Theo, what happened? Do... do you need help? Should I take you to a doctor or the hospital or something?"

"No, it's not like that." He pressed a fist to his mouth, biting down on his knuckle. Finally, he looked at me. "I'm sorry, Meg. I hurt your leg. The pain hit when I was asleep. I didn't realize I was holding onto you." He scowled at the floor. "I'm really sorry."

"I'm fine," I said again, but my voice wavered. Theo managed so well when I was around him. I'd had no idea up until then the amount of pain he was dealing with.

"You should go home and get some sleep." He heaved himself off the couch.

"Are you kidding? I'm not going anywhere." My mind raced. Not only was I scared to leave him; I was scared to let him walk across the room.

He moved past without a glance my way. "You don't have to stay. I'm going to bed."

"I'll come with you." I stood up. "It's not as though we haven't slept in the same bed before."

While he wasn't inviting, he didn't stop me from following him into his bedroom. Once inside, he watched in silence as I headed to the right side of the bed and slipped under the worn patchwork quilt. I presumed he'd prefer the left side, so the unblemished side of his body would face me when he lay down.

Once I settled under the covers, the bedroom door shut with a soft click and snap of a lock hitting home. The room was blanketed with quiet. Without a word, Theo ambled through the shadows, and then an unexpected burst of light hit my face.

"Sorry." He closed himself in the bathroom, shutting me back in the darkness. The only light was the thin bar blazing from under the door—just like in *Poltergeist*. When the camera panned down the hall to that light, it was a warning that something was very, very wrong.

My eyes adjusted to the dimness of the room, and I looked around for traces of Theo. It had the feeling of a generic guest room, not a place that Theo had left and returned to. I wondered if he felt like a guest in his mother's home.

He came out of the bathroom and got on top of the covers next to me.

He glared at the ceiling in the dark. I breathed in the minty scent of toothpaste. He had removed his shirt, and I lay mesmerized by the rise and fall of his bronze, smooth chest. *Breathe*, I reminded myself.

"Don't do that." He turned his glare to me. "Not you."

"What?" I startled, caught in my inspection of him. Heat rushed to my face with the mortifying thought that he *knew* I was attracted to him. I didn't expect him to have any interest in me, considering I had another man's baby growing in me, but for whatever reason I welcomed his volatile companionship. Our fragile union was something I wanted to keep.

"Don't do what?" I sounded guilty even to my own ears.

"Don't look at me that way. I *am not* pathetic. Don't act all sorry and worried for me."

"No, I didn't mean—"

"I'm sick of the pity." He looked away and crossed his arms

over his chest. "It means more than I can say that you don't treat me that way. Don't start."

"I don't pity you... really, I don't," I insisted. "You know my secret, and when we're together, it's the only time I'm not plagued with guilt. And it's nice not to be so guarded. I wasn't looking at you with pity."

"What was that look for, then?"

"Curiosity."

"Oh?"

"Yeah, I want to know more about you," I said.

"What do you want to know?"

"Are you glad to be home?"

"No," he answered quickly. "I shouldn't be here. It's good to see Mom and Jake and to finally meet Ellie. It's cool to visit friends, I guess, but this is not how I wanted to come home. I let people down."

He didn't need to say whether those people were at home or in Afghanistan. "You didn't let anyone down. This shouldn't have happened to you."

"Don't feel sorry for me." He turned toward me. "Promise you won't."

"I promise," I whispered. "I'm glad I met you. I'm glad you're here." I reached across the blanket, and his hand met mine halfway.

"Sure you are," he agreed. "My problems make yours not look so bad."

"You figured me out." I laughed. "Theo, what happened tonight?"

"I'm cutting back on my pain meds. It caught up with me. Stop worrying. You get some rest, or you'll be miserable tomorrow." He slid my hand back toward me, gave it a squeeze and pulled away. When he shut his eyes, he appeared to find sleep immediately.

The next thing I knew, pale sunlight filled the room, and Theo slept serenely next to me. I looked past him at the alarm clock. If Ellie and I were going to make it to the doctor's on time, I had to move it. I tiptoed out of the room and made a beeline for the front door, collecting my flip-flops, hoodie, and purse along the way. I swung the door open and jumped.

Melinda stood on the other side of the door, keys raised. Her mouth was open, eyes wide, as we both froze for a moment. Then she blinked twice.

My stomach clenched. "It's not what you think." I shifted my stuff to block her view of my bulge.

"Oh Meg, I thought that was your car in the driveway." She smiled in that conspiratorial way as though in on my secret. If only she knew what I was keeping under wraps. Maybe then she wouldn't be so quick to flash me a lopsided grin followed by a giggle.

I scooted past. "I'm late. I'll see you later," I called over my shoulder, picking up my pace.

She watched me pull out of the driveway and waved as I drove off.

Jake and Ellie lived down the road from Melinda's house. I really had no choice but to show up in my sweats. Thank the heavens for looking out for me. Jake had already left by the time I pulled in the driveway.

Unease settled over me. Ellie opened the door before I mashed the bell. Her face shifted to a look of absolute shock. Couldn't pull anything past my girl.

"Meg," she demanded. "How late were you with Theo?"

I couldn't stop myself from smiling. "Busted. We spent the night together."

CHAPTER THREE

W E MANAGED TO SHOW UP on time for our appointment. Not that it mattered; the waiting room was backed up with gestating women. If someone's water had broken, we'd all have been hanging ten. Every so often a door swung open, exposing a hallway leading to the back. The nurse would shout out someone's name, and a pregnant woman would rush back as if she'd been told to "come on down" on *The Price Is Right*.

Looking completely calm, Ellie sat next to me, her golden brown hair fanned out on her shoulders. She loved her appointments — loved to hear the baby's heartbeat, loved getting measured and weighed, loved being told that everything was perfect and to come back in four weeks. I used to love hearing about her appointments, too.

Until I needed one of my own.

"Tell me the real deal between you and Theo." Ellie didn't look up from the baby magazine she was flipping through. She scanned article titles and brought the glossy pages close to her face to check out photos of baby gear, but I was not deceived. She was waiting for full disclosure. On the ride over, I'd filled her in on my night with Theo. I left out nothing except for the longing in my heart to climb onto his lap and kiss his eyelids, his cheeks, the tip of his nose. I left out my desire to put my mouth on his, to hold him and have him hold me.

"What do you mean?" I looked at my feet in order to avoid the glaring baby eyes in the overwhelming collection of brag photos on the wall. "I gave you the facts." I thought that sure, I was attracted to Theo, a situation possibly made more intense by my pregnancy or his injuries. But that was a feeling, not a fact. And besides, wherever my feelings led, it would be a dead-end.

Ellie dropped the magazine against her belly and gave me a knowing look. "Come on. You spent the night with him."

"It's not the way you make it sound." I fidgeted with the hem of my shirt. "Staying seemed like the right thing to do."

She saw right through me. Between her sixth sense and the way she dissected everything, nobody could fool Ellie. She had a flair for taking any situation and seeing every possible outcome, obsessively analyzing the information from all angles until she was certain of the best choice. Once she'd made a decision, she would hold ironclad the belief that no other option was feasible.

But I didn't work that way.

A nurse barged through the door with a file in her hand. "Meg Michaels," she called.

Perfect timing. I jumped to my feet.

"Good luck." Ellie smiled. "They'll call me soon."

My relief at getting out of the interrogation with Ellie was short lived, replaced by queasiness as I followed the nurse through the door. I'd always avoided doctors. No escaping it now.

The nurse, a heavyset, middle-aged woman wearing pink scrub bottoms with a pink-and-blue, baby-bottle-patterned top, trudged through the maze of the office. She stopped at the scale, and I stepped up, still in my flip-flops from the night before. The metal banging and sliding as she weighed me grated against my nerves. She pulled her hand away, and the number I saw burned into my eyes. *Nine pounds?* I'd gained nine pounds... fast!

"Have a seat." She pointed to a white plastic chair as she

fell into a metal swivel stool, skidding to a stop at her desk next to me. "I'm Jen." She held up the ID badge that hung around her neck with her name printed under the photo of a friendlier version of the pinched-face lady in front of me. She gnawed on her lower lip while studying my intake forms.

"Based on what you wrote, the first day of your last cycle puts you at fifteen weeks pregnant." Jen cocked an eyebrow.

"Yes." I took a ragged breath. "That's right."

"And you haven't seen a doctor?"

"No." I knew my answer was wrong by the way she raised her lip.

"We like to see our moms start prenatal care as early as possible." Jen over-enunciated each word, as if I was the dimmest bulb she'd ever encountered. "You should have come in when you first missed your period." She took a slow, labored blink. "*Did* you miss your period?"

"Yes." I nodded like an eager schoolgirl. "And I've been taking my prenatals every day. Even when I was sick." That should earn me at least a few brownie points. I gave her a pleading look and wished she'd drop the condescending tone.

Jen measured my blood pressure, nodding in approval as she wrote the numbers on my chart. Then came the part I dreaded. She shoved her thick hands into a pair of green latex gloves that snapped sound against her wrists. She rolled over to me, boxing me in.

Grabbing my arm, she wrapped a rubber tourniquet above my elbow. "Pump your fist."

I squeezed my eyes closed and did as I was told. The crackling of wrappers filled the air as she opened things I didn't want to know about.

"This won't hurt... this won't hurt... this won't hurt," I chanted.

"Oh, yes it will—"

I opened my eyes just as the needle sank into my flesh, and I cried out.

"Oh, pull yourself together." She scowled, and releasing

the tourniquet, she pressed a tube onto the other end of the needle. My blood rushed into the vial, turning it crimson. She continued to fill up twelve vials in all.

Done torturing me for the moment, she removed the needle and pressed a Band-Aid too firmly on the bloody dot in the crook of my arm. A couple strolled hand in hand in the hallway.

Yay for me! I get to do this alone.

The stench of rubbing alcohol hit my nose as Nurse Jen swiped a saturated cotton ball across the tip of my finger and then slammed down a lancet. *Click.* I inhaled sharply.

"You're cruel." I no longer cared if she liked me or not; we weren't going to be friends. I considered telling her that I'd lied about taking my prenatal vitamins on the days when the sickness knocked me on my ass.

She gave me a sinister smile. "If you're this weak now, wait until that baby wants out."

With a racing heart, I followed her back to the exam room, and she tossed a paper towel the size of a tablecloth on the exam table. "Take it all off," she said on her way out and slammed the door shut.

I undressed under harsh lights in the frigid room and silently cursed my previous ob-gyn, Dr. Lucy Wilson, for retiring at sixty-seven the year before. She'd been my gynecologist since I was fourteen. For over twelve years, whenever I had to undress in a clinical setting, a chirpy little lady with a friendly expression and a soft touch was there to put me at ease. Plus, she had fabric gowns, which, although ugly, were much nicer than the oversized napkin I was presently hanging around in.

I hovered at the edge of the exam table, the protective paper sticking to the back of my thighs and the stupid body drape tucked under my armpits. Focusing on the door, I willed the doctor to come in. After close to a lifetime, a slight tapping came, and the door slowly swung open.

"Hello, Ms. Michaels." A very young, handsome man in a white coat approached me. *A lab technician,* I thought. *Why are they sending in a lab technician?*

His well-manicured hand came at me for a handshake. "I'm Dr. Pruitt. How are you today?"

It was the most basic, widely used question, but I couldn't stop myself from peering around him, hoping the real doctor would walk in. He looked like Mark Wahlberg. Not sophisticated, grown-man-actor Mark Wahlberg, but fresh-faced, Marky Mark of the Funky Bunch Mark Wahlberg. And I was going to give him a prolonged view of my hoo-ha.

"F-fine... I'm fine." I shot my hand out to shake his, and my paper-towel cover slipped.

Nurse Jen banged into the room, but we ignored each other.

"Okay then," Dr. Pruitt said with a measured tone. "Usually, we only listen to the heartbeat, but since this is your first visit we'll take a quick peek so we can make sure everything looks good."

"Why wouldn't it?" My breath caught in my throat as I thought about all the days that had passed since I first peed on a magical stick.

"There's nothing to worry about. This is routine. Lie back for me, please." Dr. Pruitt took a seat between the ultrasound machine and me. He shook a bottle as though he held ketchup then squirted the warm gel low on my belly. I held still, feeling equal parts anticipation and fear. He pressed the probe against my stomach. With eyes fixed on the screen, I waited.

The doctor hummed the theme song from *Star Wars* as he worked the wand across my abdomen. Maybe he was trying to be soothing, or perhaps he wasn't even aware of me. I studied the swirling black-and-white image, waiting for anything familiar to appear.

"There we go." He spoke softly, but his tone was upbeat. "Look right there." He made a little circle on the screen with his index finger.

And then I saw it. I saw what looked like a frail little bird flap its wings. "It's a bird," I said in wonder.

"Here's the head." He pointed. I saw the shadow of little eye sockets and a tiny jaw opening and closing. "And here is the spine." He ran his finger along the curved dotted line. "The flickering spot is the heart beating. Everything looks normal." He pushed a button that caused the screen to go blank.

He handed me a photo of the ultrasound. "Congratulations, Ms. Michaels. I need to do a pap, and then we'll be done." He did his business down there, and I hardly noticed. I didn't care that I'd never had a male gynecologist; I didn't care that he looked as if he was all of twenty-two; I didn't even care that I wasn't on the path I wanted my life to take. I was preoccupied with the most remarkable thing I'd ever seen: An image of the child inside me.

CHAPTER FOUR

S TWINS, STEVE AND I were born into intimacy, but our connection was more than that. While we shared a bond from our first moments of existence, we also had a greater bond that came from desertion by the same woman whose body had given us life. She left when we were barely eighteen months old, too young to remember the lines of her face or the sound of her voice.

And now, I carried a baby of my own. I couldn't keep my secret from Steve any longer. If I didn't tell him soon, he was going to figure it out on his own.

I stood at the front window of the bookstore, looking out at the endless Texas sky. A light wind ruffled the leaves of the Redbud trees that lined the street. The quiet times of the day were the most difficult, spent trying to come to terms with what I had to do.

Jake's truck pulled up, and Ellie stepped out. The door to the extended cab swung open behind her. I placed my hands on the sun-warmed glass of the window. The crutches hit the ground first.

Theo.

After our night together, I'd anticipated hearing from him, but that had been wishful thinking. Finally seeing him again jolted my nerves into high gear. My heart surged. The tint from the bookstore windows prevented Theo from catching me watching him. He looked different. Stronger. His clean-shaven face made him even more striking: a perfect blend of clean-cut and rough-and-tumble.

Wait. Come say hello.

He climbed into the front seat that Ellie had vacated and shut the door. The truck backed out, turned around, and took off down the street.

I suppressed a stab of sorrow. What an idiot I was to think that we shared a connection.

Ellie stopped on her way to the café. "What's wrong with you?" She touched my arm.

"Nothing... Just spacing out." My temples throbbed. "I'm not sleeping well."

"I hate to break it to you, but that will only get worse." Ellie hugged her belly as if to send a message of love to her baby. She waddled to the stone-pillar archway that led from The Book Stack to Café Stay, her share of the company. She'd built out the space adjacent to the bookstore shortly after we graduated from college. It was her long-term investment, funded with the money she'd inherited when her parents were killed in a car wreck. She had walked away from that accident without a scratch.

"Hey, come talk to me while I bake." Ellie insisted on doing all the baking herself. We went back to the kitchen, and I propped myself on a barstool next to the stainless-steel table. Watching Ellie create pastries was strangely therapeutic — especially when she decorated cookies and cakes, spreading frosting smoothly from one side to the other. Ellie cast a sideways glance at me, lowered a white apron over her head, and tied it in the back.

"Meg..." She flashed me a grin. "I'm going to be up-front with you because I know it's what you need."

Uh-oh.

I waited as she reviewed a yellowed recipe card tacked to a corkboard. She wandered from the industrial refrigerator to the chrome open-wire shelving for dry goods, circling back to the stainless steel countertop.

She came to a stop in front of me with her hands on her hips. "People are beginning to comment on your weight gain," she whispered. "I think it's time to consider coming clean on your pregnancy before the gossip gets out of hand."

I winced. "They'll gossip anyway, once they know I'm pregnant."

"Yes, but who cares?" she asked, her voice a little louder.

"I do!" I peered down at my body. "Do I look fat?" I couldn't help it; I didn't want to look fat. My figure was soft where it had once been firm, curved where once angular. Changing. I'd been fooling myself to think I had more time.

"No, not fat, but you keep wearing all those silly baggy outfits. You're starting to get the attention that you've been trying so hard to avoid." She scooped flour into the mixer with too much force, causing a puffy cloud to float up. "It should be your decision to open up." She waved away the smoky plume. "I assumed you would've made that decision by now. Don't you want to tell Steve? He needs to know you're going through this."

I closed my eyes. "Okay, I'll do it. I'll tell him."

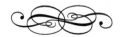

My nearest and dearest had been upset when I called off my wedding to Bradley—except my dad, who didn't care one way or another. He'd given me his token phrase, "You know what's best." Nina, my stepmother, was disappointed because, let's face it, Bradley would have looked good on the family résumé. I knew that some of my friends might tell me to get over my hang-ups or say I had cold feet when word of the breakup got out. However, what shocked me the most was that many of them were straight-up pissed.

Chelsea ran a trendy boutique around the corner from The Book Stack. Chelsea was cute and feisty—about five years older than me, but I swear she looked twenty-one. Chelsea wore her jet-black hair short, similar to Betty Boop—it really suited her—and always looked dazzling in her signature tight dresses. Everyone loved her, but for all the guys she dated, none stuck around, and Chelsea was eager to marry. Convinced that her other half was out there, somewhere, she wouldn't be happy until she had sunk her pearly whites into him.

"You spoiled brat!" she screeched when I stopped by her shop to tell her I moved back to my condo.

"Be nice!" I resisted the urge to be hurt by her words. Chelsea tended to be dramatic.

"You have what we're all looking for, and you walk away?" She rolled her eyes at me. "You don't even know for sure there's someone else."

"But isn't it enough that I don't trust him when he's gone?" I thought my question was reasonable and expected her to admit I had a point.

She turned her back to me and went back to stuffing a mannequin into a black leather dress.

I considered reminding her that there would be other men; I could still end up married one day. But I didn't. She'd think I was only being flippant.

"Come on, give me a break," I pleaded. My friends would have liked a group discussion on whether I should leave Bradley. I wondered whose side they were really on.

Chelsea came over and gave me a hug. With Chelsea, every argument was really about her, so I couldn't take it personally. Her truce came as predicted: She'd find a pair of guys we could double date. She had made her threat almost five months earlier; fortunately, I'd dodged that bullet.

Only two people had known I was planning to leave Bradley. Ellie had returned from her honeymoon a few months before my crisis, and she was still in the throes of newlywed bliss. She was as familiar with my past as her own, and because of that, she knew how sacred trust was for me. She knew I couldn't live with doubts. So she did what Ellie always did—she got out the paper and made two columns. On one side she wrote *Reasons To Marry Bradley* and, on the other, *Reasons To Break Up*. Sure, her method seemed trivial, but filling out the columns reinforced what I was prepared to accept: I was ready to move on.

The other person I confided in was Steve. His first comment after learning I was about to halt my future with Bradley was similar to my father's. "If that's what you want, Meg. Are you sure you're not panicking? You're going to miss him."

"He's never home. And anyway, something's not right."

"So you're not even going to try to work it out?"

"He had a girl in his hotel room in China. I'm not there and I can't sit here and wonder what's going on."

My brother's eyes softened. "I know. You deserve someone you can count on." He wrapped his big arms around me. "I'll miss him on the golf course though." Steve and I both laughed.

Although having the coolest brother in the world and a best friend who always knew what I needed didn't replace romantic love, it certainly eased my desperation for companionship. I knew leaving Bradley was the right choice when I moved back to my condo, because in my own place, I felt less alone.

Later that afternoon, I sat with Ellie while she waited on a bench out front for Jake to pick her up.

"We're clearing out the spare bedroom this weekend, so I can do the baby's room after we find out what it is." Her hands traveled around her belly as if she were peering into a crystal ball.

"I can't believe it's time to do that already."

"Our twenty-week ultrasound is next Wednesday, and we want you and Steve to come over for dinner, so we can announce the baby's gender." The more real her baby became, the more real mine was, too. Ellie was so excited that I forced myself to perk up for her sake.

"I can't wait," I said. "I hope we both have girls, so they can be best friends like we are."

The desire sounded juvenile, but Ellie cheered. "We're going to have so much fun. You've got to tell everyone, so I don't have to keep quiet anymore. You promised—"

"Okay." I held my hand up. "I'll tell Steve this weekend, and then we'll go from there."

Ellie threw her arms around me, and I watched over her shoulder as Jake pulled up. Theo stepped out of the truck, and I was hopeful for a moment. He shot a glance my way, did a half wave, and took off on his crutches across the street to The Tavern. My heart sank as I watched him go.

"Don't worry, it will work out," Ellie said, referring to my talk with Steve.

Jake stepped out of the truck and headed straight for Ellie, his handsome face aglow.

"See ya later." Ellie was lucky she never had to go home alone.

After they drove away, I turned my attention to the door of The Tavern.

I wondered if Theo was hanging out with the carefree brunette. He'd probably take her back to his mom's place and feed her Mac and Cheese Hot Dog Surprise. Then, instead of watching old movies on TV, they'd have hot sex all night and sleep in each other's arms till the sun came up. And since I was torturing myself, I allowed myself to remember how I put my hand in his and he held it for a minute before he pushed it gently, but firmly, away. I thought about how he touched my belly. I had wanted him to kiss me, and I was sure he could tell I wanted him to, but he hadn't. I'd been completely foolish. He'd declared in the beginning that he wasn't about to hit on a pregnant chick.

I went to Steve and told him I was leaving for the day.

"Yeah, you're looking a little rough. You want to hang out later?" He peered at me with concern. For a beat I thought about telling him everything, but then my old friend Fear rushed back in, and I wanted to get away to worry alone.

The baby's father is not who you think...

"No, I only need to catch up on sleep."

He looked as though he would hug me, and I stepped out of reach. I didn't want him to meet my bulging stomach.

For three days, I hid in my condo trying to get the courage to tell my brother what happened. Every time Theo drifted into my thoughts, I pushed him out. Ellie was right; I didn't need the distraction. My life was about to change, and I needed to focus.

On Tuesday, when I called in sick for the fourth day in a row, Steve expressed worry. I told him we should talk and asked him to come by when he got the chance.

I crawled back in bed and tried to lose myself in a Gillian Flynn novel. Ten minutes later, I was still on the same page when someone knocked on the front door.

"That was fast." I stepped aside to let Steve in.

"Tell me what's wrong," he demanded, looking me over. I'd pulled my hair into a sloppy ponytail and was wearing baggy sweats. I slouched against the door with my hands stuffed in the front pocket of my hoodie. I'd grown enough that he should have been able to see my condition without me telling him.

"I'm pregnant," I blurted.

His gaze dropped to my belly and snapped back to my face. To make it easier for him, I pulled off my hoodie. Underneath, I wore my old Dave Matthews shirt that failed to cover my bump.

"Oh shit — you're big!" He swiped his hand over his mouth, his eyes wide.

"Thanks a lot."

"How long have you known?"

I looked away and tugged on the hem of my shirt. "Over two months."

He staggered back, jamming his fists into his pockets. At once, I took in that I had done everything wrong. My sweet brother was devastated I'd left him out of my life. I read the anguish on his face as he turned away and searched the room. I stood there wishing my condo looked more together; the lack of order added to the evidence that my life was a mess.

"Steve, I should've told you sooner. Ellie wanted me to—"

"Ellie knows?" His head jerked up. "What about Jake—does he know too?"

I nodded slowly.

"But you couldn't tell me? Unbelievable." In three long strides, he was at the door.

"Wait, Steve... I didn't want you to be disappointed in me." I followed after him. "Please don't go."

He yanked the front door open and turned to me with troubled eyes. "We had a pact to always be honest with each other." My little brother by minutes stood all grown up, towering over me. His pain from my betrayal left him visibly vulnerable. "I have to digest this."

He turned and walked away.

When Steve and I were kids we rarely fought. Maybe that was abnormal, but the truth was that Dad and Nina worked long hours, and Steve and I needed each other. We couldn't afford to be disconnected because that meant being alone. At times we did get mad. We'd call each other names and shove one another, but soon we'd give in to laughter. And with laughter came forgiveness. But Steve didn't return my calls that night, and he didn't come in to work the next day. No one was laughing.

Ellie could have gotten him to see the light, but she was at her ultrasound appointment. Steve and I were supposed to go to her house for dinner to find out if Jake and Ellie were having a girl or a boy. I worried he might skip the dinner.

Busy with the morning shipment of inventory, I moved about the store, checking on employees who were going through the boxes. When I overheard my name spoken in a hushed tone, I stopped to listen.

"It's break-up weight. She doesn't need to worry about being seen naked, so she's hitting the pizza," one of the college girls on our staff said, twisting her glossy hair around her finger.

She had her back to me, as did Hazel, our oldest staff member. Grandpa had hired her ages ago. She didn't have any family of her own, and even though she couldn't manage to do anything right, Steve and I didn't have the heart to let her go.

"I don't know," Hazel said. "I'm thinking she looks pregnant. When someone's growing a baby they start looking fat, but only in the middle—like Meg."

I stepped behind a bookcase. I still heard them chatting from my new position, but I couldn't make out the words over the pounding of my heart. I was exposed. Ellie was right: they were onto me. I spent the rest of my day hiding in the back storeroom, cowering in my office if anyone came near.

At the end of the day, I slipped out back. I escaped into the rain and climbed into my car. I had to undo my pants. I was trapped with the truth. My body wasn't going to let me be in denial anymore. Had my mother felt trapped when Steve and I took over her body? I pushed the thought away. I didn't want to think of her.

Tonight was Ellie's night. Steve had better be there. He had to forgive me. The grip of regret weighed me down because I knew I'd been wrong for shutting him out. I wanted to take away the pain I had caused. No secrets ever again.

Ellie practically vibrated with anticipation, flinging her door open before I rang the bell.

"Look at your belly. You look great!" Ellie patted my bump. "We had the doctor write the sex of the baby on a piece of paper and put it in an envelope, so we could all find out together, but I can't wait. I wish Steve would hurry up and get here."

"Oh Ellie, he might not come. I told him yesterday I'm pregnant, and I haven't heard from him since."

"Come on." Ellie took my hand, leading me down the hall. "I spoke with Steve, and he's okay. He just feels left out, and he doesn't understand why you didn't want to tell him." She leaned in close, her voice hushed. "You need to talk to him. Get him excited about the baby, and he'll get over it."

The second we stepped across the threshold to the living

room, I saw Theo. He sat in the middle of the sofa with glasses on, reading the e. e. cummings book. I stopped walking so my brain could catch up with the situation.

"Hey there." He peered over the rim of his glasses.

My words dried up in my throat so I gave a little nod.

I should have assumed he would be there, but I'd been wrapped up in my own drama. I recovered and followed Ellie to the kitchen.

"Ellie," I whispered, "you didn't tell me he'd be here."

"I thought you'd know." She tilted her head. "You're a wreck. What is it with you? Are you sure there is nothing going on with you and Theo?"

"Yes, I'm sure. He likes to irritate me."

"Then ignore him. Can you help me with the salad? I want to go check on Jake — I'm afraid he's going to peek in the envelope." Ellie glowed in her emerald-green maternity top, with hair piled atop her head. She slipped out the back door to where Jake was grilling burgers in the drizzle. Unlike the last time I was at Jake and Ellie's house, the pleasant smell of mesquite and cooking cow made my mouth water and my stomach rumble.

I was at the sink washing lettuce when the swinging kitchen door flew open, and Steve and Theo walked in. I dried my hands, and Steve embraced me. My body settled into the comfort of his warmth.

"I'm sorry I didn't tell you." My voice wavered.

He stepped back an arm's length and looked me over. "I can't believe you and Ellie are both having babies." He tentatively touched my bump. "Honestly, I know you two insist on doing everything together, but this is ridiculous."

Theo leaned against the counter on the other side of the kitchen, watching my exchange with Steve.

"Well, there you go, Meg — I told you keeping secrets was stupid," Theo said, and Steve's body tensed as he looked from Theo to me.

"He knew?" Steve asked jerking his thumb in Theo's direction. I didn't move, but Steve read the answer on my face.

"I didn't tell him."

Steve's eyebrows pulled together.

"He figured it out on his own." I pointed at Theo accusingly.

My brother shook his head in disgust and stormed out to the backyard.

"Gee, thanks a lot." I turned from Theo, trying to focus on making the salad, but couldn't resist casting sidelong glances his way.

He picked an apple from the fruit basket and tossed it in the air. "Hey, don't blame me because you excel at being deceptive." His voice was casual, but I sensed undercurrents of hostility. If I were a dog, my hackles would have been raised; I was in no mood for his brand of nonsense.

I turned to face him. "Oh, what difference does it make to you?" I snapped, shaking the paring knife in his direction. "Why don't you mind your own business?"

"Point taken—I'll leave you alone. You don't have to wave that knife at me." He took a bite out of the crunchy apple.

Tired of pretenses, I let my guard down. What did I have to lose? "Why didn't you come see me again... after the other night?" I cringed at how pathetic I sounded.

"You left without saying goodbye. I'm not dense, Meg." His gaze traveled down to look at my belly. "Anyway, you've got enough problems, you don't need me around." His focus returned to the apple. When he took another bite, his lips glistened with the juice. As I watched him chew, my mind went blank.

He looked up at me.

"Don't call my baby a problem." I blinked and stepped back. "I overslept. I had to pick Ellie up for our doctor's appointments, and I was late."

"Nice excuse, but you could've left your number," he shot back.

"You know where I work, you know where I live—you can come by any time you want." My eyebrows shot up. "How was I to know you were waiting for an invitation?"

Jake walked in through the back door with the burgers covered in foil. He shook the rain from his disheveled brown hair. "You guys ready to do this?" He looked from Theo to me.

"Let the fun begin." Theo tossed the half-eaten apple in the trash and pushed away from the counter, returning his weight onto his crutches. He followed Jake to the dining room.

I took my frustration out on an unlucky pepper and a defenseless tomato. Why had I let Theo get under my skin again?

Ellie came in with Steve on her heels and paused to close her umbrella. "I can't take it anymore. I won't be able to eat until I find out what we're having." She rushed to the dining room, leaving me alone with Steve.

I focused on tossing the salad. Out of the corner of my eye, I caught him glaring at me. I sighed, reluctantly turning to him. "Look, let's keep it together for Ellie tonight, and we'll hash it out tomorrow."

"Deal." Steve took the salad from me, and we made our way down the hall to the dining room.

Jake motioned us to our seats. "She's tearing the envelope." Jake hovered near Ellie as if she were a feather floating to the ground, and repositioned himself around her, making sure she stayed adrift. I wanted to know the pleasure of someone holding me up. But maybe some of us were meant to hit the ground. Otherwise we'd never learn to bounce. I could bounce.

Ellie's hands shook as she unfolded the paper. "A boy!"

Jake wrapped Ellie in his arms, stroking the sides of her face, murmuring to her.

"Congratulations, Uncle." Steve gripped Theo's hand. Then he turned to Jake. "It's a boy!" They high-fived.

I hugged Ellie. "Yours better be a girl," she whispered. "I have a closet full of pink."

The festive energy made the time fly by. Jake, at the head of the table with Ellie and me on either side of him, kept the conversation going. Steve sat on the other side of me. The casual observer wouldn't have noticed how much tension hung between Steve and me—except when our elbows would bump, and he'd jerk away as if I'd poisoned him. He cheerfully joined in with ideas and questions about Ellie's plans for the baby's room. I didn't pay any attention to Theo at the other end of the table. Instead, I put all my energy into pretending everything was fine.

After dinner we moved into the living room, and Ellie brought out coffee and a plate of her famous brownies. My anxiety slipped away once she sat with me and we compared our growing bellies. I had tuned out the men, only taking in the soothing melody of their voices mingling. So when the conversation turned abruptly back to me, it took me a moment to catch on.

"Since everyone else here is already clued in, what does Bradley think about all this?" Steve said. The room went quiet. One of my worst fears hit me: Steve assumed Bradley was the baby's father.

"Not now, Steve," I pleaded.

"Come on, Meg, don't tell me that even Bradley doesn't know you're pregnant?"

He waited for me to speak.

"No, he doesn't know."

Steve's jaw clenched. "Crap, Meg—if I was going to be a dad, I'd want to know. This isn't only about you."

"Leave her alone, man." Theo's tone was low, but firm. All eyes turn to him.

"Stay out of this!" Steve snapped back, and Ellie gave me a pained look.

"Let's all calm down," Jake said.

I got up because I knew I had to leave once I revealed the truth. Turning back to the room with my arms crossed in front of me, I took a deep breath.

"Wait a minute," Steve said, the hard look on his face made it clear he'd had enough of my vagueness. "I'm calling Bradley, tonight. He has a right to know."

I blinked, still trying to work out how to explain *that* part of the truth.

Theo crossed the room to Steve. "Back off, man," he barked, getting right in Steve's face. "It's not your place."

"Dude, I'm not going to fight a man on crutches — move out of my way."

"Steve..." I looked around the room, trying to mask my embarrassment. "Bradley did not get me pregnant."

His eyes narrowed. "Who, then?"

"After Bradley and I broke up, Jason and I reconnected... on Facebook."

"Are you *kidding* me?" Steve's hands were knotted into tight fists at his sides. "Why haven't I seen him around? Did he get a divorce? Did you tell him?"

"Don't worry about it."

"Meg." Steve closed his eyes. "How many times are you going to let that dirtbag hurt you?"

"Yes, he knows." I nodded. "He's back with his wife."

CHAPTER FIVE

THUNDER BOOMED AS I RACED, splashing through puddles, across Ellie's rain-soaked lawn. Rain pummeled me and seeped through my layers of clothes. I fumbled with my keys. Shivering, I bit down on my lip. I flung the car door open and collapsed onto my seat, choking out sobs. I jammed my keys into the ignition, managed to start my car, but couldn't calm myself, trembling as rain and tears dripped from my face.

The car door flew open.

My gaze shot to Theo. "Have you not had enough of the train wreck of my life? Go away!" I yelled over the downpour drumming against the car.

Lightning flashed, illuminating Theo. "Scoot over to the other side. I'll drive." At first I didn't move. "Listen, I got my driving leg, and that's all I need to get you out of here. I'll take you home." His calm manner and words were exactly what I needed. I wanted home.

When I climbed across to the passenger's side, he tossed his backpack and crutches into the back and situated himself in the driver's seat.

At first we drove in silence. I sat with my back angled toward him, dragging fingers through my wet hair. Theo deftly maneuvered through the downpour. His driving kept me preoccupied. It hadn't occurred to me that he could still drive.

He glanced my way. "I keep my old chopper in Mom's garage. A Harley-Davidson." He spoke as if he were talking about a lover. "I miss her. It's only a matter of time before I ride her again."

I looked at his profile in the darkened car and tried to imagine him racing down the highway on a bike. I figured he needed more than time to get back on a bike, but I could imagine his long, hard body straddling a motorcycle, his face set in an unapproachable, cool-guy expression. Theo was hot enough to pull off any variation of the American bad boy.

"Why can't you get a car, like everyone else?" I asked.

"Because I'm not everyone else." He rubbed his hand over the top of his head. "Who's Jason?"

"My best friend growing up. *Our* best friend. Twins share everything, you know?" Leaning my head against the cool glass of the car window, I sighed. "He lived down the street from us. The three of us did everything together."

Theo nodded, keeping his eyes on the road.

"Well, until high school when Jason and I started dating. He was my first love."

Remembering that time still made me sad, not for the loss, but for how easy and simple falling in love was back then, full of naive dreams that things were meant to be. I shuddered to think about all those years I had wasted, heartbroken over him.

"Steve didn't take it well?"

"No, he had it out with Jason. Steve's always been extremely protective of me. My relationship with Jason had destroyed his friendship with Steve. But I couldn't stop seeing Jason. First love is powerful. It consumed me. It also put a huge strain on my relationship with Steve."

Theo gave me a knowing look.

"We were all going to go to University of Texas, but out of nowhere, Jason decided to move over an hour away and go to

Baylor. He promised me nothing would change between us, but once he left, I didn't hear from him again."

The corners of Theo's mouth turned down as he drove through the dark streets. *"What?"*

"I know. I couldn't understand it either. I went to confront him. We'd only been apart for a month. I thought maybe he needed to see me to remember what we had. A girl answered his door. She was alone. I told her I was his girlfriend, and she said Jason told her he'd dumped me. So I turned around and went home."

Theo shook his head in disbelief. "He didn't call you?"

"No. But I waited anyway. For a long time I believed he'd come back. But he never did. I learned later that Jason married the girl after she got pregnant. For a while I wanted to be Jason's pregnant wife more than I wanted anything else." I was fully aware of the irony of what I was saying. "But Jason moved on without even telling me goodbye."

"That story is a pretty close match to your one with Bradley," Theo said.

"Yes, my history repeats itself," I agreed warily.

"Did you sleep with Jason to get back at his wife?"

"No, I would never do that."

"So when the chance came, you hooked up with him?" Theo turned into my parking lot.

"It's not that simple."

"It can't be that complicated." Theo circled the parking lot, looking for a vacant spot.

"I was on Facebook one night after Bradley and I broke up. Jason contacted me, and I gave him my phone number. The timing seemed perfect to reconnect. We talked for hours that night. He'd been married for seven years, and they had four kids. He left his wife after finding out she was having an affair." I wanted to justify my actions, but I still felt the bitter aftertaste of shame after I swallowed the explanation.

"He said counseling didn't help and they were preparing to divorce. I told Jason all about how I had called off my wedding.

After a while, we stopped talking about our exes and moved on to reminiscing about our past. He called me again the next night. And then every night for a week. He was an escape. I saw my chance for closure." We were sitting in the dark corner of the parking lot. The rain had eased to a light sprinkle. Theo turned off the car but made no move to get out; he reclined in the driver's seat. Even with his injuries, he looked powerful, his hand behind his head, eyes locked on me.

"That Friday morning, Jason called and told me to pack my bags. He insisted we should be bold and jet off to Cancun for the weekend, celebrate being single again. The idea was outrageous, but I went with him. We reunited for the first time in eight years at the airport in Houston. We had a toast to our freedom, and then we jumped on a plane to disappear for forty-eight hours. I emailed Steve that I was visiting an old college friend who was struggling with an impending divorce and told him I'd be back on Monday. He emailed back to ask who I was with, but by then I was already in Cancun. I never replied." I didn't want to tell Theo about the drinking and dancing Jason and I did on the beach. "It started out pretty cool, being with him again after all those years. But something was off, and Jason knew it, too. We used each other to fill the missing spot in our hearts. Being with Jason was familiar and safe, but we didn't have a real connection. By the next morning, I wanted to come home."

"And that's it?"

"Yes. We both knew our night together was a mistake. Even though he was separated from his wife, even though she had had an affair, Jason believed he'd betrayed her. He was determined to go home and do whatever he had to do to mend his marriage. So we came back and went our separate ways. And that's it."

Theo's gaze penetrated me. "How come you didn't make him use protection?"

The question was almost too personal, but I couldn't blame anyone for asking.

"I did." My face heated. "We bought condoms on the way

back to the room that night. I thought he used one." I looked away. "But in the morning I realized he had never opened the box. We both drank so much. He claimed he forgot, using the excuse that he wasn't used to needing them."

Theo punched the dashboard, and I jumped.

"I know..." My stomach churning with the memory of how reckless I'd been. "The whole weekend was a mistake."

"I'm not pissed at you. I'm pissed at him."

"I found out I was pregnant, and I called Jason. Before I shared the news, he cut me off. He didn't want to meet or even talk. He said things with his wife were better than they'd been in years, and he was grateful to me for helping him see the light, but he insisted his wife could never find out about our trip to Cancun. So I said it. I said: I'm pregnant."

Theo's eyes smoldered with concern and interest. I was grateful to have someone to talk to, someone who didn't seem to judge me for messing around with an ex.

"Jason stopped short of asking me for an abortion, but his relief was obvious when I told him I would do it all on my own, that I didn't need his help."

Theo's eyes scanned my face for several moments. "He doesn't want the baby? He doesn't care?"

"He has four kids already, and he knows I have support."

"Support?" Theo coughed as if he was choking on disbelief and his eyebrow arched. "From who? I haven't seen anyone around here taking care of you."

"Well, I have my brother —"

Theo interrupted me. "You mean that guy back there?" he asked with a jerk of his thumb.

I waved away his concern. "He'll get over it. Plus I have Ellie and Jake and my other friends and family."

He shook his head slowly. "Other than Ellie and Jake, does anyone know?"

"No, but the point is," I said, placing my hand on my belly, "we don't need him."

"You are a stubborn woman." Theo opened his door and

pulled his crutches from the backseat. He came around to my side before I had both feet on the ground, and he reached for my hand. "I should go kick that guy's ass."

Startled by his words, I couldn't stop myself—I grinned foolishly at Theo.

Returning to my condo with Theo was not what I had anticipated for the night. I found it cathartic to dump the events with Jason that had led to my present state. Being candid with someone who was completely removed from all parties was about as close to therapy as I was going to get. It would be a lie if I claimed I didn't care what Theo thought of me. But if Theo passed judgment on me, it didn't show.

"You cool if I crash here tonight?" he asked on the way to my door. "I mean since we're turning into sleepover buddies and all, I think it's my turn to be your guest."

"I suppose so, but don't have high expectations in the accommodation department. I don't have a guest bed for you."

"I'll take the sofa."

"I don't have a sofa." I slid my key into the lock, Theo standing close behind me.

"What do you mean you don't have a sofa?" I walked in, switched the light on, and he followed me. "You're still moving in," Theo said.

"No, I moved back months ago. All my stuff is here, or at least what I decided to keep. But I'm still unpacking." I looked around the room and tried to see it from his eyes. My condo was empty, with the exception of the boxes scattered around the room. Worse still, the boxes were covered with a thin layer of dust. "Actually, I gave up on unpacking. I'm in no hurry." I dropped my keys in the bowl on the kitchen island.

Theo looked in one direction and then the other, his eyes growing bigger. "Why don't you have a sofa?" He walked through the empty dining area and to the kitchen. "What do you have against furniture?"

I kicked off my shoes, picked them up, and dangled them from my fingertips. "We gave away everything in the condo when we moved. Bradley wanted a fresh start for our house. When our new beginning tanked, I took only what was mine from before I met Bradley. So this is my new, new beginning." I smiled. The spare bedroom had previously held my library, but I'd need that room for the baby. The majority of my boxes were filled with books. I needed to find a place to put them, because parting with them was out of the question. They were a part of me, a part of my past. From Kurt Vonnegut to Nora Roberts, I had many traveling companions. Their stories had taken me away when I'd needed an out. They filled me with hope when I needed to know love could last. For me, a book held the potential to change my life, at least for the moments lost between the pages.

I padded barefoot along the path of boxes to my bedroom in the back corner of the condo. "I have big plans to renovate, but so far I've only finished my bedroom. It's more comfortable back here."

The truth was, my place looked pretty deserted. Before putting it on the market, I had painted everything neutral, making the place a clean slate for any potential buyers. The nice thing was, I didn't have to try to erase any lingering traces of Bradley. I knew my initial asking price was much too high, but since the condo was the first place that was all mine, I hesitated to walk away from it. In retrospect, I wondered how much faith I had really had in my new life with Bradley. Maybe I had known I was going to need an escape hatch.

Funny how life can double back on itself.

"Come on in." I led the way to my bedroom.

"Have you done anything to get ready for the little guy?" Theo asked. "How much time do you have?" He went to the corner of the room, dropped his backpack on the floor, and took a seat on the ottoman of my reading chair.

"Oh, seventeen weeks down—twenty-three weeks to go." I stepped into the closet to find pajamas. "I've got plenty of time." I grabbed deep purple cotton shorts with tiny dots and a soft lavender cotton tee. I headed to the bathroom and quickly changed. I pulled my hair into a high ponytail and washed my face, scrubbing away the dried tears. I brushed my teeth and noticed my beaming reflection. Aside from the current state of drama in my life, I was hit with a sudden rush of happiness to be sharing another night with Theo.

I returned to my room to find he'd explored my reading table and was flipping through the copy of *A Girlfriend's Guide to the First Nine Months* that Ellie had lent me. He looked a little out of place.

"Discover anything shocking?" I lowered myself into the chair, facing him. I tugged my shirt down to hide my tummy.

He slammed the book shut. "Nope. This stuff is sugar coated." He raised the book for emphasis and tossed it on the reading table. "AIT is shocking."

"And what's AIT?"

"The army school where I learned to be a medic," he said.

"I can't even imagine."

He adjusted his one leg and I thought about the medicine cabinet loaded with pill bottles.

"How are you doing?" I asked. "How have you been?"

He slid his hand over the angry scar on his neck. "I'm fine," he replied. "Getting better every day." His words rang true: He looked better, no gauze on his neck, more of his arm exposed, only a few bandages. The unveiled skin showed more than a hint of the violence he endured. Raised, red flesh that had been knitted back together snaked out from under the covered wounds, running up to his elbow and under his shirtsleeve.

"And what about you, girl? You went into your own battle tonight. Are you all right?" There it was again, the look of genuine, unadulterated concern. Theo's core of kindness sparked out in contrast to his cocky self-assurance. The combination was truly alluring.

"Tonight was tough," I said. "Let's not get into it again. But I have something I want to show you." When I pulled myself out of the chair, I bumped against Theo's knee and stumbled.

He caught me, his hands firm on my hips. "Steady now."

"Sorry, sorry," I mumbled and moved toward my dresser. Steady? Not even close. *Calm down*, I thought, and pulled in a slow deep breath. I picked up the ultrasound and walked back to Theo on shaky legs. I handed him the image of my unborn child and sat in the chair again.

A huge grin shot across his face. He had a gorgeous dimple on his left cheek that I hadn't noticed before. Something stirred inside me, a desire much deeper than attraction. When he looked at me like that, my insides trembled, and every cell longed to reach out to him.

"Ah, Meg, this is amazing. Look at your little baby." His eyes sparkled as he gazed at me and then back at the photo. I became acutely aware of his proximity to me. My knees rested next to his one knee. We were eye to eye, and my mouth went dry. "Thank you for sharing this with me." He took my hand and placed the photo in my palm. I twisted back to leave it on the table next to my books. At the same time, he reached down, cupped my foot in his hand, and pulled it to his lap.

"You look so uptight. Everything will work out. Relax." He squeezed my foot, applying glorious pressure in all the right places. I dropped my hands to my sides and sank into the chair. I'd been alone for so long, for too long, and his touch was incredible. A moan slipped out of my mouth. "Good girl... Just give in," he murmured.

He grasped my ankle firmly with the hand from his injured arm, and with his other hand he squeezed, pulled, and stroked my foot; he worked his way up to my ankle and calf muscles. By the time he reached the back of my knee I was writhing, groaning lasciviously with my eyes clamped shut.

I failed to contain myself as he seamlessly switched to my other foot, starting all over again. My breath was coming out in short, ragged gasps by the time he stopped. I opened my eyes and was devoured by a full-body flush.

"Did you like that?" Theo asked, his eyes glassy, his voice thick and husky. Damn him for being so sexy.

"Thanks." It came out as a croak, followed by a shaky laugh.

"Sure thing." He cleared his throat. "Can I have a glass of water?" Immensely grateful for the diversion, I bolted for the kitchen and took the opportunity to gather myself.

He was in the bathroom when I returned. I placed the glass on the bedside table and went to the other side to slip under the covers. I pulled my hair free of the ponytail and let it fan out behind me. I faced the wall, so my back would be toward Theo when he came out.

The bathroom door popped open. Several seconds ticked by in silence. I turned back to look.

He stood in the doorway with the light behind him. "Um, I take it you're okay if I sleep with you?"

My pulse galloped, my imagination getting the best of me. "Yeah, sure, of course." Our sleepovers were unexpectedly gratifying.

Resting my head back on the pillow, I pulled the covers to my chin. I listened as he approached the bed, felt the pull of his weight as he sat on the edge. I could hear the sound of him unzipping his backpack and the rattle of his bottle of pills, followed by the sound of drinking and the thunk of the glass being placed back on the table. The light went off, and then something different happened: Theo crawled into bed with me. Every other time we'd ended up in bed together, Theo had stayed on top of the blankets. Sharing the space under the covers, our bodies were closer than ever before. Theo's breath heated the back of my neck, and I squirmed.

Maybe I was single and pregnant, but that didn't mean I was used to being between the sheets with a strange man.

Theo was quiet, and I held still, waiting. About the time I calmed down and my breathing became even, I was kicked. Not by Theo.

"Oh my gosh—it kicked me. The baby kicked me." I wasn't sure if Theo reached for me or I reached for him, but the next thing I knew, his hand was between my belly and my hand. I knew it should have seemed too intimate, but at the time, everything felt perfect, natural.

"Oh, there it is." His tone was animated; the rush of his breath ruffled my hair. In the cocoon of darkness, he carefully pushed my hair away from his face and slipped his hand back down around me. I felt tapping from the inside again, and Theo pressed against the same spot. "Wow, that's your baby. I really feel it. Tell me you're not excited." He held onto me under the covers.

"Yes. Yes, I am. I'm afraid to show it. How can I be proud of a situation that's so far from perfect?" Theo's warmth and closeness welcomed me. His arms, locked around me, offered shelter, security.

"You're absurd," he said, making his words seem a compliment. "Don't miss this while you're waiting for a moment more perfect than right now." His voice was gentle, but uncompromising. "Miserable couples reproduce all over the world, and you are better than that. You can offer your baby better than that. Don't idealize a fantasy."

And he was right. Because I was hung up on approval, I hadn't forgiven myself. Focused on my indiscretions, I was denying myself the chance to rejoice in the wonderment of what was happening to me. I was going to become a mother.

"Okay, from now on this is a celebration," I said, and he held me a little tighter.

"That's my girl." He placed his hand on top of mine, and at some point we drifted off to sleep in each other's arms. I was certain if I had turned, he would have kissed me. Who knows what could have happened? I chickened out on all thoughts of putting the moves on Theo that night.

The one thing I was sure of, even though he wasn't my husband or my boyfriend, even though he wasn't the father of my baby: I was overjoyed to share the baby's first kick with Theo. He allowed me to experience delight in the milestone, without fear of the unknown. I could almost pretend I wasn't alone.

CHAPTER SIX

I WOKE EARLIER THAN USUAL. THEO nestled against me, one arm snug under my head, the other draped over my torso, cradling my belly. There was an unmistakable something pressed against me, but I wasn't about to acknowledge that. I wiggled a little, but pretended to sleep. That worked, and he rolled onto his back with a slight groan. The memory of the night before felt too intimate in the morning light.

I tumbled out of bed, rubbed sand from my eyes, and made my way to the shower. Once I got the water near scalding, I stepped in and lathered up, worries about the day ahead and the night before keeping my attention until the hot water ran cold. I blew my hair dry and covered my body with coconut butter. Wrapped in a terrycloth towel, I tiptoed back to my room. Theo sat in the reading chair appraising me; his gaze raked over my round midriff and down my legs. His blazing eyes stopped at my bare feet and retraced their journey back up to meet my mine. "Hey there."

"Good morning." I glanced at the alarm clock and realized I had to get on the road in less than twenty minutes, so I hurried to the closet. "I have to get moving. I have staff meetings today."

I turned on the closet light and stepped in, pulling the door shut behind me. Nothing fit. After trying on three different outfits, I found a pair of black leggings and paired them with a black tunic and my Donna Karan sleeveless sweater coat, also black. I slipped ballet flats on swollen feet and rejoined Theo.

"Is there a funeral, or are you going to a poetry reading downtown?" He smirked.

"Real funny, you're a regular wiseass." But I laughed with him.

"I'm just saying, you don't look as if your life is a celebration."

"I know, I know."

I excused myself and headed to the bathroom, where I did a speedy make-up job and considered what he'd said. After a final swipe of mascara, I went back to Theo.

"You're right. I don't fit into anything I own. I'll hit the stores... soon." I struggled to suppress a rising giddiness at the doubtful look he gave me. "Hey, why don't you drop me off at work and come by later for lunch?"

"Sounds good." He caught the keys I tossed him, but he didn't get up when I moved to the door.

"What's wrong?" I asked.

"I got a proposition for you."

I studied his face and decided that what I saw was hopefulness. "Proposition? What do you have in mind?"

"When you were in the shower, I looked around your place. You got a lot to do before you have that baby."

"Cut me some slack," I said with a dismissive wave. "I'll step up at crunch time." I crossed my arms and ignored the fluttering in my chest.

"How about I move in and help you out?" He shrugged. "Whether you do anything or not, time is passing by, and it's going to get harder for you to paint and unpack boxes."

"You want to live with me?" I swallowed, and my brain switched to Analyze and Evaluate mode. Did he like me? Feel sorry for me? Maybe he really wanted to help? Or was he trying to get into my maternity pants? Some men have a fetish for that. Uh-oh. I was pretty sure I wanted him to want to get into my pants. My head was spinning.

The corner of his mouth kicked. "No, I want to rent a room from you in exchange for work. At the rate you're going, that baby's going to end up sleeping in a drawer with a cardboard box for a playpen."

"Gee, you sure have a lot of faith in my ability to provide for a child."

"The truth is, I got to get out from under my mom. She's driving me nuts, wants to coddle me all the time. The stress is taking its toll on her. If I move out, if she's not worried about me being alone, maybe she'll chill before she puts herself in the grave." He maneuvered his crutches and heaved himself up, pulling his backpack on as he headed out of the room. "So really you'd be doing me a favor, but that's cool if you're not into it."

"Hey, wait."

He stopped, but didn't turn around.

"You're not worried?" I asked.

He spun back to me, his eyes wild. "Worried about what?" His mouth formed a tight line. "I might not move as fast and freely as I used to, but you have no idea what I'm capable of." His words rippled with anger.

"Stop it, I'm not talking about you."

"Then what?"

"I'm pregnant. What will people think if you move in with me?"

"Hell if I care." He took a deep breath.

"Okay, then." I failed to control my trembling voice. "You're right, I need help. Your idea is fantastic. A little unconventional, I don't even have a bed for you..."

"Don't sweat it, I'll take care of that. Don't worry about anything, I'll help you get this place ready and be gone by the time the baby gets here. You can count on me."

Maybe he needed a distraction in his life, too. I was willing to be that for him. With my hand on my hip, I feigned confidence. "So when do we start?"

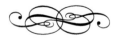

Theo dropped me off at the bookstore just after eight. That gave me a little less than an hour before everyone rolled in for our meeting. The lights were on, which meant that Steve had made it to work before me. I dropped off my purse in my office, and on my desk I found a huge bouquet of sunflowers.

"I'm sorry I gave you a hard time." I turned to see Steve braced against the doorjamb with a brown grocery sack in his arms. "I'm the last person who has any business judging you for who you sleep with."

"That's what I was going to say!" I couldn't resist giving Steve a jab, relieved he'd moved past the need for details.

He held up the bag and then crossed the room to my mini-fridge. "I got you a stash of yogurt and cheese sticks, some crackers and juice. You're not allowed to skip meals anymore."

As if on cue, my stomach growled. "You didn't have to do that," I said, smiling at my brother's back.

"So we're putting the secrets behind us. Did you tell Mom and Dad?" Steve still called our stepmother "Mom," but I had started calling her "Nina" by the time I was in high school. By then she was fine with it, because she hoped people would assume we were sisters. As long as I didn't have to call her "Mom," I didn't really care what people thought.

"No, I'll give them a call. Or shoot them an email..."

"Meg..." he said.

"Okay, okay, I'll call them." I wasn't looking forward to hearing Nina's response. She had a way of cutting me down when Dad and Steve weren't around.

As if hearing my thoughts, Steve said, "Maybe this will help you and Nina get closer."

"I don't see why. All aspects of a baby will probably gross her out. She's not exactly warm or fuzzy... or all that human."

"Ha! Give the woman a break. It's not her fault you never wanted to play Barbies. At least she tried."

I gave him a pained look. "Dragging a seven-year-old along on spa days does not equal trying."

"Just call them. Nina might surprise you." Steve gave me a pat on the back. "You know, it's about time somebody called me Uncle Steve." He smiled, his eyes lighting up. "Do you want to make an announcement in today's meeting? The sooner everyone knows, the faster the whispers will fade."

I clutched the front of his sweater. "Not yet. I can't tell everyone."

"Hey, Meg..." Steve took my hands and held them. "Stop making this harder for yourself than it has to be." His words reminded me of the promise I had made to Theo the night before. The promise I had made to my baby. "Besides, look at yourself. If I'd paid closer attention, you wouldn't have gotten away with this for so long. If you want, I'll make the announcement for you." Then he uttered those stupid, ominous words that always left me waiting for the other shoe to drop. "What's the worst that could happen?"

"Okay, let me think about it," I said warily.

After Steve left, I returned to my desk. I took a deep breath and tried to believe the truth would set me free.

The staff filed into Café Stay, chatting and helping themselves to coffee and juice, fresh-baked banana-nut and blueberry muffins. Sunlight sprinkled through the front windowpanes, casting dreamlike warmth where everyone gathered. I looked over our extended family. We employed a few older men, who had been hired by Grandfather, and then there was Hazel, but the staff primarily was made up of college students. We had twelve full-time employees, and Ellie had another half-dozen working for her. Steve, Ellie and I gathered on the little stage that was normally used for poetry readings and open mike nights.

"Before we begin the meeting... Everyone!" Steve whistled, a high-pitched, demanding sound. "May I have your attention?"

My heart stopped. I never agreed to the announcement, but Steve was going ahead without my permission.

"This is an exciting time at The Book Stack," he said. The room went still, and the remainder of the conversation trailed off, but my head was spinning. He was about to reveal my pregnancy, and once everyone knew, there would be no going back. But Steve plowed forward. "Meg has news."

The room seemed to shift as everyone turned to me. I didn't want to make the announcement.

Ellie took my hand and whispered, "*Do it.*"

"I... I'm... I'm pregnant."

I swear all air was sucked out of the room, and the building lifted off the ground and then slammed back down. Cheers erupted. Everyone looked joyful, and the café filled with chatter. For a moment I believed everything would be okay.

"Is the wedding back on?" shouted Hazel, putting her nose where it didn't belong.

One of the men shushed her. Then Jessica, a girl from Ellie's staff, called out, "That's so old-school, Hazel!" I shot her a mental high five.

"All right, quiet down!" Steve commanded the attention again, while Ellie stayed by my side. My cheeks burned from the smile frozen on my face, and I fought the urge to bolt. Steve redirected the meeting, and amazingly, I performed okay when my turn to speak came. I counted down the minutes till Theo would swoop in and take me away.

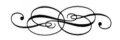

Okay, so maybe I was a little sensitive about how everyone reacted, but wasn't that a side effect of pregnancy? The volume of my mood was cranked to eleven, and someone kept mashing the buttons to change the stations. But when Theo pulled up and made the simple decision to get out of the car, hobbling around to the passenger side to open the door for me, I was moved. I liked having someone do something nice for me. And what would be a kind gesture from any man became even more touching from a one-legged man.

"How's your day?" He propped himself against the car, drumming his fingers on the roof. I took a seat, and the scent of cheeseburgers and fries embraced me.

"Well, you'll be pleased to know that the secret is out."

"Good for you." He shut the door and went around the back of the car. I eyed the Sonic shake in the cup holder.

Theo lowered himself into the driver's side, turned, and pulled his leg in. He finished by yanking his crutches in and slammed the door shut. We looked out the windshield. Staffers standing around the registers looked back.

"Don't worry," I said. "They're not staring because you have one leg. They're gawking because they're wondering if you knocked me up."

"That's fascinating stuff. Hmm..." He smiled broadly. "So everyone thinks we're doing the deed?"

Heat flooded my cheeks.

Theo's laugh filled the car. "Don't look at me like that—you were pretty enthusiastic about the foot massage. Maybe you'll get lucky, and I'll show you my other skills." He was so brazen I joined in with his laughter.

"Maybe I'll get lucky?"

He got quiet then, but his eyes held a spark of mischief as he gunned the engine.

"Dig in." He reached in the back seat and pushed a Sonic bag at me. "There's a chocolate shake too." He nodded to the cup holder and eased into traffic. "You need to fuel up."

I stuffed my hand into the grease-speckled bag, and I breathed in the delicious aroma. My stomach growled in approval. "This isn't what I had in mind when I suggested we have lunch together." But I eyed the shake as I started eating the fries. "Where are you taking me?" I didn't really care; I was just glad to be away from work, hanging with my soon-to-be roommate.

"You'll see when we get there." Theo drove with ease, steering the car with one hand, his injured arm resting in his lap.

I bit into my cheeseburger and suppressed a moan, my mouth full of tart pickles, sweet ketchup, and juicy, hot meat. In the midst of my food orgasm, I glanced at Theo, and he flashed me a bright smile. I was again taken aback by his magnetic pull. I swallowed and reached for the milkshake.

"So what have you been up to since your return?" I wanted to know what made Theo tick. From the corner of my eye, I thought I saw him stiffen at my question. He wore tan shorts with a hunter green, short-sleeved, collared shirt that clung to his muscular chest. His brown hair was growing longer, softening the military look.

"You know, hanging out and stuff. I have doctor's appointments and physical therapy. Seeing old friends." He watched the road while he talked.

"I bet it's good to reconnect with old friends."

Theo's brow furrowed as he spoke. "Yeah, it's kind of strange, though. I saw a few of my college buddies, and they acted really cautious around me. One guy's wife actually cried when she saw me."

"Geez, that sounds awkward."

"Sure. The worst is when people treat me as if I'm a nut job because I've seen action." His smile seemed forced. "I'm not damaged goods."

He had good reasons to turn the conversations away from himself. I wanted to take his darkness and make him feel light. "Suuuuure you're not," I teased him, trying to brighten his mood. "I can see how people might assume that about you."

Theo chuckled. "You better watch yourself, girl." He poked me with his elbow and pulled to a stop in front of A Pea in a Pod Maternity Store.

My eyes widened with realization, and a jolt of alarm shot through me. "Oh, come on. You can't stuff a woman full of cheeseburgers and fries, force a milkshake down her throat, and then expect her to try on clothes. You should have given me a warning."

"And take the risk that you'd ditch me? I don't think so." He slid out of the car. I tried to figure out a way out of shopping, while he came around and held the door open for me. "Get out, Meg. We'll have fun. Everyone knows now. You might as well dress the part."

He had a point, but I'd never shopped for clothes with a man before. Not even with Steve. Theo reached out, and when I looked up into his sparkling hazel eyes, I couldn't say no. I took his hand. We were greeted by a bubbly saleslady, who promised she would give us a chance to look and then followed hot on our heels.

"When are you guys due?" she asked, looking from me to Theo. I opened and closed my mouth, but Theo didn't miss a beat.

"What've we got, babe? Twenty-three weeks to go—plenty of time." He repeated the words I said from the night before. His response caused something inside me to swell. *We.*

"Oh, the time will fly by," she said. "Before you know it, you two will be arguing about whose turn it is to change the baby's diaper."

"I doubt that," I muttered, as I sorted through a rack of dresses.

"We've already worked out those details. I get full-time diaper duty." Theo beamed at me, clearly enjoying every minute of pretending.

"Honey, you got yourself a good one," the saleslady said. "Let me start you a room." She took the dresses I had selected and walked off to the fitting rooms.

"Why are you doing this?"

"Because it's entertaining. Lighten up. I thought girls were supposed to love shopping." He held up a short red dress with a plunging neckline. The kind of thing I'd never wear. "How about this one?" He grinned. I rolled my eyes but took it from him.

By the time we circled the store, the saleslady had moved a mountain of clothes into the fitting room for me to try on. "I left you loads of space on the bench in the dressing room, so you can make yourself comfortable," she said to Theo. "You can watch while she tries on her outfits." Her eyes kept darting to his missing leg, and I resisted the urge to tell her not to stare. I wasn't used to the territorial protectiveness I harbored for Theo.

"Thank you." Theo nodded and then went in and had a seat. "I promise not to peek."

I followed him in and threw him a dirty look before locking the flimsy door. Although I wasn't sure I believed him, he looked worn out from walking around the store, and I wasn't about to make him stand outside.

I proceeded to try on dresses and jeans, suits and shorts, and a billion different maternity tops.

Beyoncé pumped through the speakers as I modeled the clothes for Theo. "Okay, check it out." I sashayed around the fitting room with the red dress I had saved for last. The dress managed to showcase my full breasts in a fertility-goddess sort of way.

Theo clapped his hands and whistled. "It's a keeper. Put it in the 'yes' pile!" He'd been laughing nonstop since I'd started trying on clothes.

I checked myself out in the mirror. "I don't know. It's a little snug."

"It's excellent."

The saleslady tapped on the door. "How are those working for you?"

"Does this look tight to you?" I pulled the door open as I asked.

The saleslady's eyes bugged out. "Oh, yes. You need a bigger size—"

Theo interrupted her. "It appears your clothes are cut small." He turned his head, but I saw him wink at the woman. "We'll take the dress and everything in this pile in the next size up. Does that sound good to you, Meg?"

"Sounds like a plan," I agreed. I didn't want to stock up on clothes that would be too tight in a few weeks.

The woman giggled at Theo and gathered my "yes" pile.

"Will do. You two are a lovely couple." She backed out of the room, leaving us alone again.

Theo's eyes locked onto mine across the ten-foot-long room. "You have no idea how beautiful you are." His smile was gone.

"You're warped." My mouth went dry as he stood and closed the space between us.

He pointed to the full-length mirror. "Look at you," he demanded, and I obeyed.

"I see a bloated, puffier version of my formerly attractive self."

"Shut up, girl." His tone was soft, and he shook his head as if trying to erase my words. "What I see is a beautiful woman with seductive hips." His hand slipped down my side. "A luscious belly, voluptuous, knock-your-socks-off breasts." He turned me slightly, and we both watched my profile as he ran his hand down the back of the red dress, stopping at the small of my back. "And the finest ass in town."

Flattered and flustered at once, I opened my mouth to speak, but no sound came out.

Time slowed as Theo continued. "Add that to your angelic face, unbelievably sexy hair and swollen, kiss-me-now lips, and I'm amazed The Book Stack doesn't get mobbed every day." His words soothed me, and I turned to him. His hand cupped the back of my neck, and he eased me closer, bringing our faces only inches apart. I lowered my eyelids. The heat of his breath fanned against my cheek before he caught my mouth with his. His tongue separated my lips, coaxing gently, and I opened to him. The kiss deepened. I clutched his shirt as his hand delved into my hair, holding me firmly. I trembled. He nipped along my jaw, and a moan spilled from my open mouth.

Theo lowered, pulling long, slow kisses from me, hot and slippery; my mind evaporated as my thoughts scattered. A pulsating throb pumped through my body. The sweet warmth of his mouth consumed me. As he pulled away, my chest heaved.

He grabbed his other crutch and jiggled the latch on the door. "You look amazing in that dress." He opened the fitting room door. "I'll wait outside while you change." The door slammed shut, and I was alone.

CHAPTER SEVEN

THEO WAITED OUTSIDE THE STOREFRONT with his face raised to the sun. A woman with a little boy passed him. The boy stared at Theo. As they went by, the child spoke to the women and pointed at Theo. I could guess what the kid was asking.

The saleslady looked me over while she folded slacks. "He already took care of everything, honey. We even got your bags out in the car for you."

I hadn't anticipated that, but then again, everything with Theo conflicted with my expectations. "He wasn't supposed to pay," I said, unable to hide my confusion.

"Oh yes, he was. Once they put a baby there, you have to get what you can. Let that man take care of you, child. He was better with you than all the able-bodied men who come in here." She nodded her head as if agreeing with herself.

I thanked her for her help and went outside to join Theo.

I'd spent countless hours hiding the changes my body was going through, yet at the same time, I'd aligned myself with someone who couldn't conceal his injuries. Theo stood out, and people stared. They didn't notice that he was charming and kind, a true hero who had sacrificed for his country. People looked at Theo because he was different. He was a young man with a badly damaged body. He couldn't hide that.

I pushed my way out of the store, into the afternoon. Theo turned to me. "Are you ready?"

"You shouldn't have done that." I went to him, but he pulled back, and it troubled me that he might've thought I meant the kiss. "Tell me how much I owe you," I clarified. Theo buying clothes for me wasn't appropriate. I could take care of myself. Even with Bradley, I did the books to keep everything a controlled fifty-fifty between us.

"Don't worry. You don't owe me anything." He headed for my car, leaving me behind. The breeze twisted around me, lifting my hair off my shoulders. Even with the sun warming my skin, I shivered. I didn't know what to do, so I followed him. He waited by the open car door for me.

"Theo, I can't let you buy me clothes. You're being very generous, but..." I dug through my purse and pulled out my wallet. "Tell me how much?"

"Too bad. I don't want your money. Has nobody taught you how to be gracious? Are you not used to people doing nice things for you? Say thanks, and get in the car." His mouth was a tight line, his cantankerous side seeping to the surface.

I climbed into my seat and stared straight ahead, my hands resting on my belly. Theo gently shut my door and got in without saying anything.

I considered arguing with him, but I didn't want to ruin our day any more than I already had. We drove back to the bookstore in silence, Theo's face impassive. My lips still tingled from his kiss.

"I can't take your money," I finally said. "You don't even have—" I stopped myself. I didn't know his status in the Army, but how rude of me to point out his lack of employment.

"What?" Theo hit the brakes a little too hard at a four-way stop. He stared at me. Behind us, a horn blared.

"Thank you."

"You are welcome." His face smoothed out, and the corners of his mouth lifted. "Now, was that so hard? I've been stashing my money for years. What's it good for if I never spend it?" He pressed down on the gas pedal, and we proceeded to the next intersection. We flew through a yellow light. "I only wanted to do something nice for you."

When we were almost at the bookstore, I pulled out a business card, adding my cell and home-phone numbers. I didn't want there to be friction between us; I could accept his extravagances, if only to raise his spirits. But it made me painfully uncomfortable. He had brought me lunch, taken me shopping, and paid the tab for maternity clothes. It was every woman's fantasy, only better. My dark and brooding Theo. He was unfailingly kind and thoughtful. And I didn't know how to take it.

After he parked, we met on the sidewalk in front of the car. He handed me the keys, our fingers brushing. I wanted another kiss, but the moment had slipped away. I was tempted to toss composure aside and go for it; however, being pregnant, that didn't appear to be the appropriate tactic.

"Here's my card. Call or text me when you figure out your plans. I'll get a key made for you." I ignored the creeping uncertainty about our decision to move in together. The arrangement might not be the best choice for either of us. I should be cautious, especially considering the kiss... the kiss that might mean nothing, but could mean everything.

"Sure. See ya later, Meg." He stuffed my card into his pocket and ambled across the street to The Tavern.

Back at the store, my employees floated through the charged air around me. That afternoon, conversations faded to whispers whenever I approached. Steve and I had managed to keep the family atmosphere that my grandfather had created. But for the first time, I felt as if I were the outsider looking in.

Hazel — the only one with the nerve to ask what everyone wanted to know — cornered me. "Does this mean you are going to reunite with our Bradley?" She spoke in a sticky sweet tone, her hands clasped under her chin. Hazel's unwanted attention reminded me that having an extended family at work cuts both ways.

"No, Hazel, there will be no reuniting." I stepped around her.

"You'll make a lovely family together," she called after me. "The kind of family anyone would dream of having."

I snuck back to my office, intent on avoiding everyone, but Ellie surprised me with a plate of cookies at the end of her shift.

I bit into one as she lowered herself as close as she could to the loveseat, and collapsed the rest of the way down with a grunt and a sigh.

"Have one with me." I offered her the plate and Ellie shook her head.

"The ob's office called this afternoon," she said. "I failed the blood glucose test. I have gestational diabetes."

"Oh, no," I said around a mouthful of cookie. "Don't they let you take the test again?"

"No, this *was* the second test. I didn't mention it when I failed the first one. "

I put the cookie plate on my desk and brushed crumbs off my belly. "You could've told me. So, what happens now? What does this mean?"

"No more cookies. They're going to watch the baby a little closer and put me on a special diet. It's not that bad. I don't feel any different. I just can't eat for two anymore. I don't want to dwell on it, though. Now, tell me about your day. How does it feel to be footloose and secret-free?"

I wanted to ask more, but seeing the stress around Ellie's eyes I realized she wanted to drop it. "Ask me later. I still have a few more people to clue in." I leaned back in my office chair with my hands on my bump. "Look at us! We look like we're smuggling a couple of beach balls."

"Whatever, you're still small, but you're definitely showing now. And your growth rate is accelerating."

To take Ellie's mind off her worries, I told her all about shopping with Theo, but I left out the kiss. Even though the memory was foremost in my thoughts, I was slowly convincing myself I had blown it out of proportion. Otherwise, Theo would have acknowledged it upon returning to the car. At least, he would've given me a goodbye peck. Instead, he hobbled fast as if he were trying to get away from me. He all but ran me down on his way to The Tavern.

"Shopping for clothes with a man sounds pretty intimate to me." Ellie knew I wanted her opinion, although I had not asked. "Was it a date?"

"Not a date. Not at all, I'm sure." I focused on a spot above Ellie's head, and didn't mention the kiss. If she knew, it would certainly create the illusion that the day meant something more. "He wants to help me. It's not that strange an idea, really. He needs a place, and I have a spare room, for now." I busied myself organizing my desk, avoiding eye contact as I dropped the bombshell. "He offered to move in and help me get the condo unpacked and set up for the baby."

Ellie gasped, and when I turned, she was frowning, shaking her head. "Oh, no… no, that's a horrible idea. You can't let him move in, Meg." She shifted on the loveseat, kicked her shoes off, and pulled her feet under her, leaning forward. "He's injured. He's weak. He needs to take care of himself. How can he help you?"

"Don't let him hear you talk that way." I fanned my face, Ellie's fixed stare making me feel as if the office walls were closing in on me. "It's not like he's building a home from scratch. He wants something to do. This will be good for him. I'm not asking him for anything. He offered. He needs focus."

"And you're the focus," she huffed, jabbing her finger at me. "Oh my gosh—you're really into him."

"No, I'm not." My words came out in a rush.

"Yes you are."

"Honestly, I'm not," I said, but I thought about him cradling my belly the night before and the compassion he showed me. My stomach did a little flip, and I threw my arms out. "Okay, I am! But so what? He's lonely—what's the harm if we hang out? I have nothing going on."

Her gaze drifted to my belly. "Yeah, other than a baby on the way, and what's Theo going to do then?"

"He's only going to stay a few months, and then he'll be gone."

"This is a bad idea on so many levels. Jake is not going to be happy about this."

When did I agree to run my life past Jake? I took a deep, shuddery breath. "Jake can mind his own business. I mean really, we're all adults here."

"What do you want from Theo? Do you think he'll stick around? Are you hoping he'll play the father role? Is that even fair to ask of him?"

"No, you're blowing this way out of proportion." I struggled to keep my voice even. "Can't I get to know him better, without having to make a lifetime commitment to him? I don't expect anything. I just enjoy him."

"Exactly, and once you've gotten used to him, attached to him, and then you have this baby," she wagged her finger at me and then pointed to my midriff as if I needed a reminder, "and if he's not ready to man up and he backs off, where will that leave you, Meg?"

"I'll be fine. The baby's not his responsibility. I'm clear on that." However, Ellie had made her point. Was I trapped in a cycle of men who were destined to abandon me, or was it a pitfall that I subconsciously sought out on my own? Still, I had no doubt that I would not—no, could not—walk away from Theo. Like a gazelle, fully aware of the risk of crocodiles, but driven by thirst to the river's edge, I could not turn back.

After Ellie left, I slipped out the back door and wandered around the corner to Chelsea's Boutique. I might as well take on whatever abuse I had coming from my friends and get it over with.

"So it's true! You little hussy!" Chelsea rushed around the

counter and put both hands directly on my middle. I was going to have to get used to people groping me. We were good friends, but I don't think Chelsea had ever had occasion to touch my stomach before.

"How did you know? Who told you?" I was glad I didn't have to go into announcement mode, but caught off guard by the realization that Chelsea knew everything.

"I had lunch with Steve today," she said, in her singsong tone. "But I couldn't get any other details from him. Pay up." She snapped her fingers rapidly, rushing me to get on with it already. "Who's the daddy?"

"Jason."

"Ah, so he knocked you up on your little tryst." Chelsea was the friend I didn't hold back with. She appreciated people behaving badly. "Being a single mother is so in vogue these days. So Sandra Bullock." Chelsea tucked a glossy lock of hair behind her ear, the unedited commentary racing from her mouth. "I bet Bradley would take you back. You don't have to do it alone."

Chelsea had that way of going too far, too fast. Coming from anyone else, those words would make me want to scream, but I cut Chelsea a lot of slack. She had a good heart. She did not have a good verbal filter.

I went through the routine with Chelsea. I answered all her pregnancy questions, nodded my head in agreement when she gave me the single-mom pep talk, and promised to let her babysit. Once she was satisfied, I steered the conversation in a different direction.

"Why were you having lunch with Steve?" I couldn't imagine the two of them together, but that wasn't the point. Steve and I had rules about where he was and was not allowed to dip his hand in the cookie jar. Because he was the charming chick magnet, I had to keep him on the no-friends, no-neighbors plan.

"Oh, it was nothing. I sprung by The Tavern for a bite, and he was at the bar. Your life provided the amusement. Now tell me about this army guy. Really, Meg, you don't quit, do you?" Chelsea's smoldering eyes were about ready to pop. Her polished black fingernails tapped on the glass display case while she waited for me to spill.

I couldn't believe the way Steve was putting the word out for me. I know I asked for it, but he went too far.

"Steve is quite the gossip." I leaned closer to a mirror, trying on a pair of large, red-framed sunglasses. I peeked over the top of the frames at her. "But I'd tell you anyway. I met a cantankerous army medic. He was badly injured, and I think I like him. How does that sound?" I pulled the glasses off. "Actually, I *know* I like him."

Chelsea squealed. The wonderful thing about Chelsea was she'd say, "Go for it," even if everyone else knew that it was a bad choice. Chelsea considered being moderately self-destructive a small price to pay if it meant good times ahead. She bought into a "have fun now, deal with the fallout later" philosophy that worked well for her. It made her the best person to chat with when everyone else was looking down on my decisions.

"Oh, you need to nurse him back to good health." She shot me a wicked grin and rubbed the palms of her hands together. "You lucky girl. Have fun and stay out of trouble or get in trouble as long as you're having fun. I don't care, as long as you tell me all about it." She laughed a loud "ha ha ha."

"You don't think it's bad if I date someone while I'm pregnant?"

"Hey, motherhood does not end your life. Maybe makes it a tad more complicated, but at least you know that if a guy likes you, he really likes you. Anyways, how are you going to score a baby daddy if you don't get out there?"

I had to laugh with her.

Two women came in to browse the store, and I snuck away with a wave. Before I stepped out into the fading afternoon light, Chelsea called out to me, "He'd better be good to you, or he'll have to answer to me. I show no mercy." I had no doubt she meant every word.

Once home, I had to make two trips back to my car to bring

in all the bags from A Pea in a Pod. I put the five heavy bags on my bed, but I wouldn't allow myself to dig in until I finished my duties, so I called Dad and Nina. Their machine answered on the third ring. I left a message, surprised at feeling disappointed that I was going to have to wait to tell them the news.

I took a quick shower and slipped on my Gap elastic-waist, smoky-gray pajama pants and a white cotton top that left a full two inches of my belly exposed. Dinner was a peanut butter and honey sandwich with banana slices wedged in. As I poured a tall glass of milk to go with my dinner, I noticed the light on my answering machine flashing. Assuming my parents had returned my call, I mashed down the play button.

Instead, Theo's maple syrup voice filled my kitchen. I sat there with my glass halfway to my mouth as I listened to him.

"Hi Meg. I wanted to say goodnight. I hope you have fun with your new clothes. Enjoyed spending time with you. See you around."

The click of him hanging up the phone was loud, definitive. I hit the play button again and again. I analyzed the nuance he placed on each word. I certainly enjoyed spending time with him, too. I cursed myself for being in the shower when he called. Stupid personal hygiene! His number was on my caller ID—I could call him back, but if he had wanted me to, wouldn't he have asked? Was he still planning on moving in with me? Or was I such a thankless oaf after shopping that he had second thoughts? Couldn't blame him. If he talked about our arrangement with anyone and got the same reaction I got, then he was sure to change his mind.

Finally, I focused on his parting words: "See you around." As in, I'll see you when I see you, but don't seek me out.

CHAPTER EIGHT

I WAS REARRANGING A CONTEMPORARY YA display and momentarily lost myself in the first pages of John Green's latest release, when Hazel came out of nowhere.

"I knew you were pregnant." Her eyes gleamed.

I slammed the book shut, sliding my fingers across the glossy cover. "Oh?"

"Sure did. You always eat Ellie's chocolate layer cake when it's that time of the month. I could set my clock by it. Haven't seen you eat any cake in some time."

My shoulders sagged, and I returned the hardback to the shelf.

"Meg, tell me you're not one of those women who decided to make a baby without a man. Like one of those girls on reality TV? Just because it can be done, doesn't mean it's a good idea, you know."

"This is not appropriate work conversation. But a man *was* involved." Once the words were out, I realized how they sounded. I was on the verge of talking sex with a woman more than twice my age. Uh-oh. We were rapidly approaching a door that, once opened, would be hard to shut.

"It's okay to have fun with the boys. We all have needs." Her words made me want to poke myself in the eye with a pencil. "There's this fellow I've been seeing—"

"Hazel, stop!" I held up both hands, as if to hold her back. I wasn't going to cower about my condition. Something caught Hazel's attention over my shoulder, and I latched on to my escape. "Let's return our focus to work—there is plenty to do around here." I spun on my heels and abruptly smacked into Theo's chest.

"Hey, Kitten, where are you scurrying off to in such a hurry?" To my horror, he winked at me right in front of Hazel.

Talk about being dazzled. His massive hands gripped my upper arms to steady me; all the while he leaned on his crutches. My palms were flat on his firm chest. I could feel the heat of him against me, the heat of his hands on my arms and the heat of something else pooling inside me. I sucked in a breath and swallowed. In a moment of self-preservation, I took an unsteady step back, my knees weak.

"What are you doing here?" I winced. *Why couldn't I be more graceful? Graceful at all, for that matter.* "I mean I'm glad you're here, I—"

"I'll leave you two lovebirds alone." Hazel waltzed off, probably ready to fire up the rumor mill.

"I've tied up all my loose ends." He squeezed the grips on his crutches, his forearms flexing. "I've got transportation. I bought an old F-150, since I'm not ready to get back on my Harley. All ready to move in, if we're still on." He smiled. "By the way, you look nice."

My stomach flipped. "Thank you. I have a key for you." Ever since his offer, I'd kept the spare ready in my purse. Days and days had passed since he'd first suggested moving in, and I'd wondered if it would happen. He'd finally shown up, and I wasn't the only one to notice.

Everyone in the bookstore seemed to stop and stare as we headed back to my office. Walking past an antique bookshelf, I spied Theo's reflection in the glass. His eyes were trained on my ass. I threw a little more sway into my hips, but then I caught Hazel smirking at me from the Greeting Cards department, and my face warmed. I told myself that by having Theo in my home, around all the time, I could build up a tolerance, and having him near me would no longer set my body on fire. But still, the idea of Theo under my roof made me foolishly excited.

If Theo noticed the attention, he didn't seem to care. "I'll move in today. And as soon as you're ready, we'll figure out what all needs to be done. That work for you?"

From a drawer in my desk, I retrieved my purse and rummaged through it for the spare key. "Okay, sure. Make yourself at home. *Mi casa es su casa.* I learned that in the Language section." I held the key out to Theo and smiled.

Steve walked in, a cup of coffee in hand. "Oh, hey man, what's up?" His tone was friendly and in no way matched his confused frown. I waited for him to head to his office, but he stood frozen, glaring intently at the key I held out to Theo.

Theo nodded at Steve. "Just picking up the key." He took it from me, our fingers brushing, then twirled the key ring on his finger casually before shoving it in his pocket.

Steve stiffened, pinning me with his steely blue glare. "What key?"

"You didn't tell him?" Theo chuckled at me and then clapped his hand on Steve's shoulder as he went past. The jolt to Steve's arm sent a stream of steaming coffee over the edge of his mug. "I'm moving in with your sister." Theo hesitated at the door, his expression playful. "See you at home, Meg."

Steve waited until Theo cleared the doorway then kicked the door with enough force to make it slam shut. He set his coffee on my desk and swiped his damp hand on his jeans. "What the hell is that about?"

I dropped into my chair and leaned back to look up at Steve. "It's not the way it sounds." I smiled like the Madonna and rested my hands on the ledge of my belly.

"Then what way is it? What is it between you and that guy?" Steve gripped the back of his head. "He's not putting the moves on you, is he?"

"Oh, please!" I kicked Steve's shin. "Like I'm a great catch these days! I'm a niche fetish, at best."

Steve snickered and sat on the arm of the loveseat. "Yeah, but he hasn't been around too many girls for a while. His standards are probably on the lower end of the scale right now."

I smacked his knee. "You pig! Shut up!" And because we were joking around and Steve had lost the chip on his shoulder, I threw in, "But since you asked, we're shacking up."

Steve's shoulders slumped momentarily, and then he laughed, wagging his finger at me. "You had me for a minute there. There's no way you're doing this."

I crossed my arms and kept a straight face. "I'm serious. I'm renting him the empty bedroom in exchange for help getting my condo ready."

"I'll help you get ready, Meg. Don't get close to that guy." His hand went to the top of his forehead as if he was bracing a sudden headache. "Who knows what kind of problems he's got festering inside him?"

"Wow, are you serious? Give the guy a break, why don't you? He didn't escape from a mental hospital—he was in the army! You know, protecting his—our—country."

Steve flushed red. "Look, I get it. You pity him, and you want to take care of him, but that isn't going to make your problems go away. You're only going to find new problems with a guy like him." His fists clenched.

"Did it ever occur to you that he's doing me a favor? That he's helping me?"

"No," Steve barked back. "He's helping himself, Meg. You don't need his help. Whatever you need, I can do. If you don't want to be in your condo alone, move in with me. I have room. I'll be there for you and the baby—you know that. Trust me, this guy is up to no good."

"You don't know what you're talking about." Even as I said the words, I knew he sounded more sure than I did.

"Fine, you do what you want, but I'm going to keep my eye on him." Steve got up to leave and looked back at me. "You think you've got it all figured out, but don't forget who's always been there for you." He pulled the door open.

"Steve, wait! I can take care of myself. Don't worry about me."

"I'm not going to worry, but I *am* going to watch you closer." He disappeared into his office, slamming the door shut behind him.

Tired of all the fuss, I went back out front to finish stocking the new releases. My eyes wandered to the clock every few minutes, my mind unable to fully immerse in my task because I was beset with the idea that Theo was in my home—in my space—settling in to stay for a while.

The baby turned and kicked, and I put my hands to my belly. I looked up in time to catch Hazel tracking my every move.

By the time I left work and made it back to the condo, it was after eight. I'd turned the lights off when I'd left that morning, but the windows were lit up once again. Maybe he wasn't technically waiting for me, but I didn't care. He was in my home, and soon I'd be in there with him.

I searched the place with increasing disappointment before figuring out that he must have left. Why had he left the place lit up? The door to the spare bedroom was open wide, but those lights were off. Temptation pulled at me to check if he'd brought his things over. I wasn't sure of the proper etiquette on how to treat a new roommate who'd bought me sexy clothes and kissed me without warning, but I stayed clear of his door and went about my business as usual.

Trying to ignore the drop in my mood, I warmed up a can of instant tomato soup and chose a cookbook to browse, like I did every night with dinner. I turned the glossy pages of The Barefoot Contessa with one hand, while my mind wandered. For once in my life I couldn't lose myself in a book. The screwed-up pregnancy hormones made focusing nearly impossible. But when my thoughts returned to Theo, I had no trouble concentrating.

I finished dinner and then paced the condo while waiting

for Theo, taking looping trips back to the bathroom to put up my hair and brush my teeth, only to decide to let my hair down again. Just before I climbed into bed, curiosity got the best of me, and I crossed the condo to his door.

The long and narrow room that would one day belong to the baby was on the opposite side of the condo from the master bedroom. It had gone through many occupants. Steve had claimed it during our years at UT. Once he'd moved out during senior year, the room had served as my library. When Bradley moved in, he'd settled in with the books and used the space as his office. He'd hung heavy faux-wood blinds over the double-hung windows to block the sunlight. He couldn't stand a glare on his computer screen. I had not removed the blinds, but for the first time, they were pulled up as far as they could go. Under the window, Theo lay on a twin-sized air mattress I'd never seen before. His eyes were shut, arms resting at his sides, a backpack and a large duffel bag the only other additions to the room. I couldn't walk away from him like that, laid out bare and alone without even a blanket to snuggle. Finally, something I could fix. I snatched a lap quilt from my room and went back to him. I unfolded the soft fabric and settled the blanket over him. When I looked at his face, his eyes were open. I jumped back.

"Um… Sorry to intrude." I took another step back. "I brought you a blanket."

"Hi. Come over here," he murmured, his smile sleepy. "It's okay. Sit with me." He stretched and tucked his uninjured arm behind his head. "Did I get you in trouble with Steve today?"

"No. Well, maybe a little." I sat on the floor cross-legged, facing the head of the bed. The moonlight cast an almost magical glow over Theo. If I reached out to touch him, I couldn't be sure he wouldn't disappear altogether. He looked like a guardian angel who'd been through battle. Maybe those were the best kind.

"He's right to be worried," Theo said. "If I had a sister, I wouldn't let some chump move in with her."

"So you admit to being a chump?"

"Nah, I'm harmless." He stared at me. "We're friends, right?"

I searched his eyes and felt a connection between us. Had he changed since we first met, or had the change been in me?

"Yes, friends. Are you sure you're going to be okay here? This setup looks a little not-so-comfy." I considered my next question and decided Theo appreciated my directness. "Does your leg hurt?"

"Yeah, it does." He rolled onto his good side, his hand going to the hem of his shorts. "Do you want to see it?" He looked me in the eye as if daring me to say "no."

I shrugged. "Sure." Of course I wanted to, especially if he felt confident enough around me to show me what seemed so personal.

He pulled up the edge of his shorts, exposing what was left of his thigh. It was half the length of his other one. He smoothed his hand over the long scar at the end of his stump.

"See these little marks?" He pointed to evenly spaced dots along the pink line. "That's where they put in staples to hold my skin together."

My heart ached for the devastation that he'd gone through, although the wound didn't look as bad as I thought it might — it looked surprisingly healed.

"Usually I wear a special sock to keep the swelling down, but I take it off at night." The way he handled his leg was intimate, as if he were familiarizing himself with the change.

"You seem to be getting better."

He straightened his shorts and fell back on the pillow. "I am. Better every day."

"You know you're welcome to come sleep in my bed, right?" I raised my shoulders. "As friends of course."

"No, I'm good. I'm watching the sky." His eyes were still locked on me.

"Okay, suit yourself. We can go over everything tomorrow." Once I stood, his hand wrapped around my bare ankle, squeezed, and ran up the back of my leg, palming my calf muscles.

"Goodnight." I stepped away from him and made a quick

path to my bed, where I tossed and turned and twisted in my sheets for hours, thinking about Theo.

"What do you think?"

Theo and I stared at the bare wall, and I tried to imagine the built-in bookshelves he wanted to install. A girl like me could never have too much shelf space.

But Theo's question sent my brain in the wrong direction. What did I think? I thought he was hot. I thought of how my body tingled and everything seemed to sparkle when he was near me. I thought I was falling hard... fast.

"Meg?" He leaned forward, his smile fading.

"We could buy shelves. That was my plan originally. I love the idea of built-ins, but that's a lot of work for one person to take on."

"Whatever you want." He rubbed the back of his hand across his forehead. "But I'll have help, so that shouldn't be the reason you turn me down. We can build the shelves in no time."

He had a friend, someone to keep him company. That was good; I wouldn't have to worry about him getting hurt. He was a grown man; he'd made it that far in life without me. "Okay." I smiled. "Build me some serious shelves. Transform this place. Let it rival the Library of Alexandria."

I left for ten hours and came home to find his truck backed up to the sidewalk loaded with wood, a lanky guy sitting on the tailgate. Excited to meet Theo's friend, I went to introduce myself.

"Hello?" I came around the truck. He had thick, dark curls and coffee-colored eyes.

"You must be Meg," he said, and when his hand came up to shake mine, I would've expected more from myself—my reaction should've been graceful, but as my palm grazed his prosthetic fingers, I yelped and pulled my hand away.

I pressed my knuckles to my mouth, and my cheeks burned. "Oh, I'm so sorry—I didn't know."

"It's okay." His hand, a stiff-fingered device and almond colored to match his skin tone, almost passed for real. That's why I had been startled to feel it. I felt embarrassed. "Happens all the time," he said with a friendly laugh. "Don't worry about it." He raised the prosthetic device, which hummed as it spun in a rotation that no real hand could mimic, and touched the brim of his cap with a slight nod. "I'm Cortez. I've heard all about you."

"Well, you're ahead of me. Theo's told me nothing about you. Did you serve together?"

"No, no. We met at physical therapy. I was a medic too." He held up his fake arm again. "Back when I had a real one of these."

How do I respond? "I'm so sorry."

"Me too. It didn't work out so well." Cortez bellowed with laughter and then stilled. "Hey, could you go see what's taking Theo so long? We got to unload this wood soon, or we'll be late for poker."

I found Theo at the breakfast bar, drinking a glass of water with his backpack on his lap.

"You okay?" I asked.

"Did you meet Cortez?" He swiped three pills off the counter, popped them in his mouth, and chugged down the remaining water. The backpack slid from his lap and onto the floor with a thump.

I refilled his water "Yes. So he's your help?" I hauled his backpack onto the bar, wondering what he stored in there besides his pill collection.

He buried his face in his hands, sighed, and finally looked at me. "Yeah, he's my help. No worries."

"No worries," I reassured him, but I lied. I was plenty worried, and not only about Cortez. How could I not be concerned with the wary, pained look on Theo's face? Was I kidding myself that I could be something good for Theo?

I cut out of the bookstore early the next day and detoured to stock up on groceries. I also scored a pair of T-bones, potatoes, and salad fixings: dinner for my new roomie. Dressed in a light-blue and white maternity sundress, I practically danced through the store. I looked forward to having someone to go home to. But I wasn't the only one with a plan. The smell of baking garlic bread hit me before I crossed the threshold.

"Back here," Theo called from the kitchen.

My mouth watered, and the baby kicked as if to hurry me along.

"Hi." I placed the groceries on the counter. Theo stood at the oven, stirring a pot of bubbling red sauce that smelled so good my toes curled. "You cook," I said, surprised.

"I'm not a one-trick pony." He winked at me. "I have many skills."

A vase of black-eyed Susans sat in the center of the already set table. That might as well count as him giving me flowers. Yes, I could definitely get used to coming home to him every night. I moved to unload the bags.

"I picked up a few things. I don't want you and Cortez to go hungry while you work." Theo didn't respond. My back was to him as I stocked the shelves of the pantry. "Tomorrow I'll make dinner." I half turned to see if he was even listening.

He stood leaning against the counter, one crutch at his side, staring at me. The hungry look in his eye wouldn't be satisfied with the meal he was making.

"That dress suits you." His low voice rumbled, his gaze skimming over me. "The truth suits you, too."

He was right. Somewhere in the process of acknowledging my condition and finally switching to appropriate clothing, I had become proud of my bump. My womanly, fertile figure felt sexy. And I was actually going to be somebody's mom, which made me love my new shape even more. "Thanks," I replied. "For everything. You've already done so much for me." I looked out into the living room full of boxes. "I'm ready to make this place a home again. Somewhere I can raise a baby." We'd only known each other a short time, but already I could open up to him. After being guarded for so long, I was relieved to let go.

"I should be thanking you for letting me move in." Theo leaned back against the counter and held out a basket to me. "Bread?"

I almost drooled down the front of my dress, and not only because of the fragrant garlic bread. Theo's broad shoulders, sculptured arms, and chiseled chest were what I really wanted to taste. All that, combined with his relaxed confidence, and I couldn't suppress the shiver of desire that ran through me. I grabbed for the bread. "Mmm..." I took a bite, and my body relaxed. I kicked off my shoes and hopped up on a kitchen stool. "Having you here is going to work out for the both of us."

He gave me a big smile, one that lit up his eyes and hit me with a surprising jolt of accomplishment. He turned back to the stove, fished out a strand of spaghetti, and tested its doneness.

I swallowed my last bite of bread and dabbed at my mouth with a napkin.

"Shit!" Theo dropped the pot onto the stove with a scraping bang. Steaming water sloshed over the edge, but he steadied the pot before all the contents spilled. He reeled backwards, flinging off oven mitts and slamming against the cabinets. He braced himself, as his crutch slid out from under him, clattering to the tile.

I leapt up and scurried around the bar. "Here." I snatched his crutch off the floor and pushed it at him. "Are you okay? Did you get burned?" I reached for his hands, but he flinched.

"I'm fine." He cleared his throat. "Can you drain the pasta?"

"Sure." I thought about what the misstep cost him, and my stomach clenched. I picked up the oven mitts and moved the pot of boiling water to the sink to drain. We moved around the kitchen together, careful not to get too close, each lost in thought. By the time we sat down to eat, I had no appetite. I wanted to make everything right, but instead, we ate in silence.

"Dinner was good. Thank you," I said.

He nodded and placed his napkin to the side of his plate.

"Are you okay?" I asked.

"Are you?" he replied.

"I'm fine."

"Me too," he said, but that hard edge faltered, and his eyes glazed over with unshed tears. I went to him, swiftly moving around the table. Theo's tense body didn't budge when I put my arms around him and cradled his head to my chest. I began to fear that I had crossed a line—that I might have been too forward—but then he sighed and pulled me tight to him, one arm locked around my waist. His other hand deftly seized the back of my thigh, hauling me into a straddle on his lap. I was as much aroused as taken aback by his strength. His head came down on my shoulder, and I stroked the back of his neck, kneading his tight muscles while I hugged him. Minutes passed, and then he lifted his head slowly, still nestled to me, the heat of his breath on my neck. I shifted against him, my legs falling open and folding around him. His lips grazed the side of my mouth. My breath caught as he pulled back from me. Theo caressed my cheek with his thumb, his eyes on my mouth.

"Meg, do you want me to kiss you?"

I angled toward him, but he tilted his head.

"Ask me to kiss you. Tell me to."

"Kiss me," I whispered. "Please."

Theo's lips brushed mine softly at first, and then, with urgency, his mouth took mine. With wet, hot pressure, his tongue parted my lips, sliding sweetly against mine. I moaned into his mouth as our bodies eased together. As his hands gripped my hips, a burning need seared through me. My hips, hitching on his lap, found purchase on his rock-hard erection. *Oh, hell yeah!*

"Meg..." Theo let out a low groan. Our bodies aligned perfectly, even with my baby bump nestled against him. His lips were wet, his breath warm on my ear, the drag of his shaven jaw tantalizing as he nuzzled my neck. "This feels good."

"I'm pregnant," I whispered.

He smiled playfully, a dangerous look in his eyes. "I know."

His thumb brushed over my shoulder, stopping at the strap of my dress.

"It's okay." My breath came quickly. I tugged free of the thin straps on my dress. Theo unhooked the front clasp on my bra, exposing my swollen breasts. His palms rose; he barely touched the rosy peaks of my nipples with his fingertips, and I arched into him, urging him on. He responded by lowering his mouth to a hardened nipple. Everything in me turned liquid and hot. Theo tenderly kissed one breast, suckling it into his mouth while he exquisitely tugged and stroked the other.

I rocked against him as the draw of his mouth on my breast ignited a pulling inside me. Molten heat soared through me from the sensation of Theo's hands and mouth, lips and tongue, working their pleasure on me. His tongue flickered against my nipple. He lifted his gaze to mine and tucked a strand of my hair behind my ear. "Should I stop?" he asked.

I couldn't speak.

I entangled his head in my arms, and he kissed me again, his mouth covering mine, his tongue pressing inside, with a hunger that exhilarated me. I closed my lips around his tongue, sucking, pulling him in and tasting his sweet breath. I quivered at the feel of Theo so hard and thick beneath me, only a few layers of fabric separating our most private and aroused body parts. Every time I thought the kiss would end, his embrace held firm, his touch tender yet unrelenting.

His hands ran down my back, came around my hips and slid up my bare thighs, slipping beneath the thin material of my sundress. A moan escaped from deep in my throat as he caressed the tender skin of my inner thighs.

He hooked one arm around my neck, pulling my ear to his mouth, and whispered again, "Do you want me to stop?"

Oh... heavens... NO!

My arms were braced on his shoulders, my head bent down. I shook my head for an answer, hair tumbling down over my shoulder.

Theo's breath fanned against the side of my face. "Say it." His fingers pressed into my hips, pulling me firmly against him.

"Don't stop... *please*," I whispered, my throat closing up, tight with need. My eyelids fluttered shut as his fingers traced the edge of my panties, and I strained against him. He rubbed me harder, his fingers stroking me through my wet panties. My body burned; the pleasure peaked to madness. Theo's other hand fell low on my back, encouraging me to rock into him, my hips against him, pressure and hot friction merging with an urgency that pushed for release. "Wait," I cried out.

"Don't wait," Theo whispered. "Let go." He pulled me tight, kissing my shoulder. "Let go," he murmured, stroking me again and again. "That's my girl." My insides tightened and flexed as I bucked helplessly in his lap. In tumbling spasms, I cried out my release.

CHAPTER NINE

"A M I CRUSHING YOU?" I wasn't sure how much time had passed since the most fantastic orgasm of my entire life, but huddled on Theo's lap, my bare breast pressed into his chest, I wanted to stay put. I snuggled against him while he stroked my back.

"Maybe a little." He smiled broadly, and his whole face lit up. "But I'm not complaining."

I pulled back, and Theo's eyes went to my boobs. I tried to straighten my bra, but I had trouble shoving all the flesh back into the lacy contraption. Theo kept chuckling, so I finally shucked the torturous device, draped it over his shoulder, and popped my arms back in my dress sleeves. Standing up, I wobbled, and Theo reached out to steady me.

I had hoped something special would happen that night. We'd finally crossed a line, a sort of first date, except the part about him fingering my panties—not exactly the way I'd traditionally done a first date. But then again, we'd already slept in the same bed. Somehow, I never imagined he would be giving me orgasms right at the kitchen table. Theo's touch was like nothing I'd ever experienced. I wanted more.

"You want to go to my room?" I bit my lip, my body still humming with unequivocal desire.

Theo gave me a lopsided smile. "I *do* want to go to your room, but first can you find my bag for me?"

"Sure." I went to his room, grabbed the backpack that he took everywhere, and brought it back.

Theo sat frozen in the same spot, gripping the edge of the table. He reached for the bag and dug out his pills. I cleared the table, worried that I might have caused him pain. The phone rang, and I ignored it, allowing the machine to pick up. The caller hung up without leaving a message.

I stood across the table from Theo, my hands resting on my belly. "Did I hurt you?" I asked softly. I hated to ask, but the thought tugged away at me.

"Hush, girl—I'm fine. You made me feel... well, you definitely didn't hurt me." Theo waved his hand at me, clearly wanting me to drop it.

The phone rang again.

I moved to the bar and glanced at the caller ID. "It's Nina," I said. To Theo's questioning look, "My dad's wife. I'll call back later." I crossed my arms, hugging myself as I went back to the sink to rinse off the dishes. With the water running, I didn't realize what was happening. I had forgotten that I had the volume on high from listening to Theo's message the other day. After the final beep, Nina's voice filled the room.

"Meg? I just found out on Facebook that my daughter is pregnant, pick up, I know you're there." My hand flew over my mouth as all the air left my lungs. My eyes darted to Theo, and he mouthed, "Uh-oh."

I snatched the phone. "Nina—"

"What is going on? Tell me Steve is playing some kind of thoughtless prank," she demanded. "He won't return my calls. People are posting congratulation messages on my timeline, making grandma comments. This is creating a lot of negative attention on my page."

Shit. A full week had passed since Steve had made the announcement. I'd waited too long. I should've known something like that would happen. But how could he do that to me? Things must have been so simple back before online social networking. These days it didn't matter if people didn't see you, speak to you, or hear from you. Everyone knew someone, who was connected to someone else, who had dirt to post, tweet, or blog about you. Even if it started as honest and heartfelt congrats from a good buddy, inevitably some third party would shoot your news to your stepmother in a "WTF" email.

"Didn't you get my message yesterday?" I asked. "It's okay, Nina—please don't worry."

I turned my back to Theo and walked through the dark, almost empty living room and sat on a box of books. I embraced my belly as if to protect my baby from the hurtful words Nina would surely say.

"So, it's not true. Fabulous, dear, you had me concerned for a second. I don't appreciate this. You know the value of a good image. We are businesswomen. We need to hold ourselves to a higher standard." Ugh. I hated when she ranted about her image. She'd get herself all worked up about the double standards between men and women. In her eyes, everything came naturally for Dad, but she had to fight to maintain respect in the eyes of clientele and associates. And in the real estate business, everyone was a potential client.

I pulled in a deep breath. "Nina, it's true... I am pregnant." Silence.

My pulse raced while I imagined all the things she might say. Her lack of response propelled me to babble. "Listen, don't worry about it. Everything is under control." I compensated for my distress by getting diarrhea of the mouth. "I'm eighteen weeks now. Bradley is not the father, and the actual father is out of the picture, so that's not even an issue. Steve and Ellie and Jake are all here for me, and so is Chelsea, so no need to worry about that." I paced the room as I talked, marching between the rows of boxes. "Everyone at work knows—it's no biggie. The doctor said everything is fine, and in two weeks we'll find out if it's a boy or a girl. It'll be okay, Nina. I even found someone who'll help me with the condo—you know, get everything ready for the baby."

I paused.

"The baby." She said the words slowly, as if trying them on. "How sweet... *everyone knows?* Even my colleagues and friends. They all knew before me? You know, your choices do have bearing on other people. Eighteen weeks? When were you planning on telling *us*?"

"I don't know. I knew you'd be upset."

"Yes, you're right. I am very upset."

"I'm sorry. It never felt like the right time."

"Oh, so it's my fault I'm the last to know? Stop it with the sob story. Your father and I gave you everything, and you pout around as though you're Cinderella. You need to get your act together." Her coldness fell over me, her words drenched with disappointment. As much as I might hope for more—hope she could possibly be excited about her grandchild—I knew better than to have expectations that the woman who played the role of a mother to me would have a motherly reaction. "I need to do damage control," she said. "And it looks like you're going to be needing a nanny. I hope you're happy."

Tears ran down my face, but I kept my voice composed, knowing Nina would be irked with my display of emotion. I had nothing else to say, so I worked my way out of the conversation and hung up.

Theo came up behind me. "You okay?"

"Yes. It's what I expected from her. That's the way it goes." I sniffled and wiped off my face off, turning to him.

The residual raw feelings from the conversation with my stepmother blended with my fear that Theo's appearance in my life was going to be short-lived. I stood on my tiptoes and slid my arms around his neck. "I don't want you to go."

He leaned in, encircling me with his arms, and kissed the top of my head. "I'll stay in your room tonight," he said, and even though we meant different things, I was glad to have him for the moment.

"Nice," Theo said from under my plush cotton duvet, when I emerged from the bathroom wearing the knee-length pink nightgown. The short sleeves delicately capped my shoulders, and a thin satin ribbon decorated the empire waist. The soft cotton hugged every curve in a way that was flattering even for the knocked up.

"Thank you." I did a pirouette, followed by a small leap in the air. "My professional shopper selected it for me."

"Get in here, silly girl." Theo lifted up the covers and patted the mattress. "Pregnancy ballet—now, I'd buy a ticket to that."

I burrowed under the covers and moved closer to him, his arms scooping me up, gripping my back, as we wiggled in toward each other. He kissed me deeply. Without a shirt on, delicious heat swirled off his skin. In the dark, I ran my hands down the smooth planes of his chest. The muscles of his knotted abs flexed beneath my palm when I skimmed over the waistband of his shorts. He gripped my wrists, pinning them to my sides as he pressed against me.

"We need to slow this down, or I'm not going to be able to put on the brakes." He pulled back far enough that he was no longer touching me. In the dark, I was unable to make out the expression on his face, but his body seemed to say he didn't want to stop.

I didn't want to stop either. Not ready to give up, I reached for him, but he flinched and scooted back again. "What is it?" I tucked my hands under my chin. "You're half naked in my bed—I think the signs point to all systems go." A thought I hadn't considered popped in my head. "Oh, wait... Can you?"

"Of course I can—"

"How do you know?"

Theo groaned. "Trust me, I know. Meg, I won't have sex with you. This is not a good idea." He reached out and stroked the side of my face. "I barely moved in, and I want to help you with your home. This is dangerous. Let's back it up a notch."

"Oh." I pushed his hand away from my face, the pangs of rejection mingling with a flood of embarrassment. "I get it." I flipped over, turning my back to him.

"Whatever you're thinking, you're wrong," he said from his side of the bed. "I want to. I want you bad, but you're pregnant, and I can't look past that."

I inhaled sharply, feeling a rush of fresh anger. "I'm right. That's exactly what I was thinking." I sat up and swung my legs off the side of the bed. "Why'd you do all that?" I gestured toward the kitchen. "Why'd you touch me like that if you're not attracted to me?"

"Whoa, slow down. Don't get yourself all worked up. I *am* attracted to you. Get back under the covers."

"No," I snapped, turning away. The bed shifted under me; I could hear the rustle of the sheets moving. He gripped my hips in the dark and hauled me back to the center of the mattress. "Stop it," I squealed as he braced against my wiggling and molded his body to mine.

He locked his arms around me, one curved under my head and the other splayed against my belly to hold me spooned against him. "Do you feel this?" he whispered hoarsely over my shoulder as he pressed his hips against my backside, his rock-hard shaft nestling against me.

His arousal was undeniable. "So what?" I said, afraid to hope that Theo might want me. "Just because you have an involuntary response doesn't mean anything. You said yourself, my pregnancy is a turn-off."

"Honey, I said no such thing. This" — he nudged his pelvis into me — "is me being involuntarily turned on by you, all of you, exactly the way you are." He slid his hand down to my hip. "I'm not sure having sex with me is the best thing for you."

"What, are you worried I'll get attached to you? Expect things from you?"

"No, I'm not worried." His tone was gentle and sincere, but the words were not what I wanted to hear. "I can't make any promises right now. I don't know where I'm going to be in three or six months from now. I like you, but I don't want to complicate things for either of us."

"Who says sex has to make things complicated?"

"I don't want to add confusion to your situation, because I care about you." The steady rise and fall of his chest against my back soothed me, along with his palm, which was making a lazy orbit on my belly.

"What if I said I don't care?" We were breathing in unison. I wasn't going to beg for sex, but I was willing to negotiate. I'd already exposed my desire, and in the veil of the night, I forged on. "We enjoy hanging together. We sleep well together. Can't we throw a little therapeutic sex into the mix? What if I promised no expectations, no attachments, no drama?"

My questions hung between us.

"I'd say that's a proposition that is nearly impossible to resist. But I want you to be sure. Go to sleep. I'm a gentleman, and I don't have a condom, but don't push me, because I'm no saint."

I thought about his words, what he was willing to offer, his concerns and his warnings.

"Theo..."

"What?"

"I'm sure."

"Goodnight, Meg." I could hear the smile in his voice.

CHAPTER TEN

ORTEZ ARRIVED THE NEXT MORNING before I left for work. Saturday was the busiest day of the week at the bookstore. I spent most of my day circling the store, assisting customers, and directing staff.

One of our biggest weekly events was the Saturday morning Then and Now Story Time. Hazel and I shared the hosting duties. I read *Blueberries for Sal,* and she followed with *Skippyjon Jones.*

My love of books had developed at an early age, so I was thrilled to watch kids light up over stories. With gusto, I read each scene with an animated voice, hoping to captivate the hearts and attention of our little readers. I had to admit that Hazel, too, was a natural at putting the kids under the spell of a story.

Tracy, one of my college friends, showed up with her son, Max, and I joined them at the end of Story Time. I was chatting with her when a mother I recognized as a regular approached, dragging a tot behind her. "Look at you, congratulations on your pregnancy! How did I miss the announcement?" She grabbed my hand, pointedly checked out my ring finger and asked, "Where's that beautiful ring of yours?"

I stared at her, with my smile frozen in place.

Tracy leaped into mix. "You remember how fingers swell

during pregnancy?" she asked the woman and draped her arm over my shoulder. "Poor Meg's swelling so bad, she even gave up her trademark heels." Both women looked down at my feet, not swollen and totally glam in Marc Fisher peep-toe flats. I had ditched the heels, but that didn't mean I was going to slum on the footwear.

A woman in red, holding the hand of a chubby-cheeked little boy, jumped in. "Hang in there, girl. Things are going to happen to your body that you never dreamed possible, not in your worst flippin' nightmare. Swelling is the tip of the iceberg."

The crowd shifted, and next thing I knew, a swarm of six women dished candidly about shocking changes their bodies had gone through in the process of being pregnant and giving birth. In the last few months, I'd discovered that the beauty of pregnancy and childbirth was ninety percent pretense. As if to reinforce my discovery, the moms assaulted me with stories of cracked nipples, bleeding hemorrhoids, vaginal tears, and pooping on the table during labor.

By becoming pregnant, I'd unsuspectingly signed up for a club that I couldn't cancel the membership to. The rules of the club were that one must smile and nod politely while being force-fed graphic information about a billion little nasty things that would most definitely happen in the near future. Politely backing away from those conversations would've been nice, but I discovered no exit. Attempts to flee led to strangers following me, clutching at my arms. "No wait, no wait, let me tell you the worst part about what happened next..." they'd plead, with horrified joy in their eyes. So I learned to wait it out and take in the stories with a smile plastered across my face.

Later in the afternoon, we had a book signing with a notoriously cranky sci-fi author, followed by open mike poetry reading in Café Stay. The steady flow made the day whiz by, to my relief, because I couldn't focus for more than five seconds on the roller coaster of thoughts from my night with Theo.

I tried to catch up with Steve throughout the day, but we kept missing each other, and then he disappeared for a few hours around midday. As the day wore on, I grew paranoid that he was avoiding me again. By six o'clock, I was beat and ready to call it a day. My feet were throbbing, and my lower back ached. I dreamed of slipping into the tub filled to the brim with hot water and perfumed bubbles.

I took a quick peek in Steve's office. "Hi, there," I said, pleased to have finally cornered him.

"Hey Meg." He swiveled in his chair to face me and gave me a once-over. "I've been watching you all day, and I swear you're getting bigger each time I look away." He propped his feet up in the chair next to the one I'd already dropped into, a goofy grin splashed across his face.

"Stop! No, I'm not." I smacked his leg, laughing. "You are!"

He reached out and rubbed my belly affectionately, as though he were sizing up a puppy. "I'm messing with you. You look good. Doing alright?" I caught the weight in his question, and my heart lurched.

"Yeah, I'm cool. Have you heard from Nina and Dad?"

Steve ran his hand through his hair and looked away. "Dad called last night." He shrugged. "At least they know now, right?"

"Was it bad?" My lungs constricted, as I waited for the full impact of my parents' disapproval.

"You know how they are. If it's not work-related, they don't know how to deal with anything. They'll get over it."

After all the time that'd passed I still—stupidly—wanted Dad and Nina's approval. Why couldn't they simply be there for me? And they had no apparent interest in the light at the end of the tunnel: my baby. Their grandchild. I hadn't even heard back from Dad.

Steve sat forward and gripped my hands. "Hey, don't look so dejected. You've always got me."

"Thanks, Steve. Did I ever tell you, you're the best brother in the world?" I hugged him tight, so grateful for the unconditional, unwavering love.

"You don't need to tell me what I already know. Now get out of here—you work too much." He shooed me off, and I slipped through the Saturday-night-date crowd, weaving my way out of the store.

As soon as I settled into my car, the first moment I had to myself all day, thoughts of Theo flooded my mind. I replayed all the highlights of our evening together. Remembering my naughty offer for no-strings-attached sex left me blushing, yet hopeful. I had no awareness of the drive home, but I pulled into my parking lot hoping to find him waiting for me. All hopes were dashed when I popped the door open to find the lights off.

I slammed the door shut behind me, smacking the light switch on and making my usual route to the bar to drop off my purse and keys. Halfway there, I stopped cold in my tracks, and my keys skittered from my fingertips, crashing onto the floor. My mouth hung wide as I did a slow circle. The boxes that declared my state of transition were no longer the focal point of my home. They were all pushed into tight rows in my dining room. My cold and sparse living space, though furniture-free, held endless potential. The hardwood floor gleamed, unencumbered — a clean slate.

My heart swelled, and I laughed. The smell of fresh-cut wood filled the room, a testament to my new beginning. Even with our talk about what Theo would do to the condo, it was still a surprise to come home and see progress.

Then I had an idea. Digging through my undies drawer, I scored a matching red satin demi-cup bra and thong set. Clad in the lingerie, I did my make-up and swept my hair into a seductive up-do. I went to my closet and shimmied into the red dress Theo loved so much. Finally, I stepped into my lucky Pedro Garcia stilettos. Once my work was done, I checked myself from all angles in the bathroom mirror, and I was pretty satisfied that I'd get Theo's attention.

Then I ran out to Walgreens to buy a box of condoms. With my prominent baby belly, dressed to the nines in naughty hottie gear, lugging a super-sized box of rubbers to the counter, the looks I got were priceless. The young guy at the register raised his eyes at me, and I winked and tossed a pack of peppermint gum on the counter, to go with my Trojans.

When I returned home, I was seized with a wave of panic. Theo's truck was back; he was home. I almost shifted the car into reverse and abandoned my mission. But then I thought of Theo's smile, the comfort of his voice, and the rush from his caress. I couldn't leave. Like a herd of wild horses galloping toward the edge of a cliff, I was going to see my plan through. The risk of rejection loomed like an outcrop of boulders at the end of a free fall.

The cool night air whispered against my bare legs, fluttering the hem of my dress against my thighs. The click of my heels on the sidewalk gave me a bump of confidence, so that by the time I'd made it to the door, I was strutting. I closed the door behind me and waited.

"Meg?" he called out from his side of the condo.

My breath froze in my chest, and my heart tried to jackhammer its way through my ribcage, but it was the passing thought that he might say "no" again that sent me over the edge.

I listened to the mismatched thumping of Theo's approach. He stopped once he turned the corner, and his eyes landed on me. Water dripped from his hair; a towel was draped over one shoulder. Theo's running shorts hugged his hips, revealing his thickly muscled, tanned thighs. The view of Theo's almost naked, powerful body was breathtaking. Even though one of his legs ended in a stump, he was the most virile and striking man I'd ever laid eyes on.

A wicked smile sprang to his lips. "Come here." He held out a hand, and I was no longer apprehensive. The look on his face told me we wanted the same thing. I moseyed over to him, watching his gaze travel the length of my body. The corners of his mouth notched up with each step I took, a flame aglow in his eyes.

I halted before we touched, the inch of space between us charged. "I wanted to show you my gratitude for all you're doing." I peered up at him from under my eyelashes.

"Just part of our deal." His eyes bore into me, his chest

heaved with each breath, his nostrils flared. Theo was ready to pounce.

"And for our other deal..."

"Yes?" he asked.

"I brought you these, because you are a gentleman." I cracked open my purse, the giant box of condoms instantly evident.

Theo's hands abruptly came up and captured my face, his head lowered. His mouth landed on mine, his kisses untamed, possessing me with a feral need. He pinned me against the wall, muscular hardness pressing against me, his skin hot and damp. I ran my hands down his sides, clutching him to me, feeling his mouth hungry on mine, the pressure of lips, his tongue penetrating my mouth. His sweet taste filled me; desire blazed through my body, and I melted against him.

Theo tore his mouth from mine, his hand braced on the wall above me. I swayed, drunk with passion. "Go," he insisted. I did not hesitate — I knew where he wanted me.

I tucked my purse under my arm, striding purposefully to my room, where he followed me to bed.

CHAPTER ELEVEN

I TOSSED THE CONDOMS ON THE pillow and turned as Theo entered the room. He sat on the edge of the bed, his eyes never leaving me. Needing his skin against mine, I grasped the hem of my dress and peeled it up and off. The only light glowed from the bathroom, falling across the bed.

Love was something I couldn't afford to wish for. That option was never put on the table. I engaged in a game of Russian roulette with my emotions, but the way Theo looked at me, I never felt safer. And I never felt more visible in all my life. When he reached for me, I went to him.

His hands feathered across my naked body, and his lips rained down perfectly delicate kisses. "You're so beautiful, the most beautiful thing I've ever seen," he murmured.

I threaded my fingers though his hair, lowering my mouth to his. His kisses were soft, exploring, his tongue tracing my lips. A warm hum spread through me as the intensity of his kisses increased. Wrapped in his arms, a tingling heat coiled low in my belly.

He reached behind me and unclasped my bra, sliding the straps off my shoulders. He cradled my breasts in his hands, brushing his thumbs across my nipples, teasing them to tight, aching buds. His mouth covered my left nipple, sucking hard and hungrily, and my knees weakened with desire. I clung to his shoulders, my nails digging in as I groaned.

"Get up here and play with me, wild girl," he growled.

I crawled on all fours to the middle of the bed. Theo hooked my panties on one finger, tugging them ever so slowly down my legs and over my shoes. Clad in only my stilettos, I rolled onto my back and thrilled as Theo came to me. His sheer masculinity stopped my heart, and when he shucked off his shorts, I wanted to sing. I writhed in anticipation as he hovered over me and in delight as he slid his body against mine. Theo covered me in tender kisses; he buried his face in my neck, giving hot nips along my throat, which caused me to quiver. His teeth grazed my nipple, and I cried out. Wet heat pooled between my thighs. I throbbed with an urgent need to be touched, a hunger to be filled by that man.

But Theo had a different plan. His tongue circled my navel and then traveled south. I realized where he was headed, and I tensed. Against my will, my mind's eye flooded with Bradley's it's-just-not-sanitary explanation for never going downtown.

"Wait, not that." I attempted to wiggle away, but he gripped my hips, kissing and licking the curve of my hipbone. "It's okay, you don't have to do that." I squirmed beneath his strong fingers.

"I want to," he murmured, his voice thick and smooth. He planted one kiss after another, warm and velvety, low on my stomach. "Trust me... You'll like this."

He parted my knees, and I gasped as he pinned my legs wide. He playfully bit my inner thigh, and I whimpered, arching my spine. His mouth pressed against me *there,* and I cried out, blind with pleasure. Steady, strong flicks, slippery strokes, rhythmically licking me, his skillful mouth devoured me; my legs shook as the throbbing ache swelled and resonated through me.

Each thrust and pull of his tongue reached deeper, lapping over me. My hands fisted the sheets, my hips rocking into him with legs splayed. I writhed against him, against the pressure building inside me, winding me tighter. And still his tongue lashed at me, licking and licking, until I thought I'd lose my mind. My muscles clenched and flexed, and when he plunged his fingers into my tight wetness, my whole spine arched.

"Oh, Theo..."

Pushed over the edge, I shattered, and cried out as orgasms burst through me.

With eyes shut, wracked with spasms, I panted, out of breath. Theo pressed kisses along the side of my face. I heard the tear of a condom wrapper, and then he was between my legs, ready.

Theo nibbled my ear. "This is what you want." His words were raspy in my ear. I shivered.

I thought I couldn't take any more. I needed a moment to catch my breath, but when he thrust into me, I sobbed, overwhelmed at the sheer pleasure of Theo, thick inside me. He pulled back and then shoved deeper, a long groan escaping his mouth. "Oh, Meg."

Theo hovered over me, watching me, cautiously impaling me, slow and firm. My body yielded to him. A shudder swept through me. I needed more, so much more. Hips hitching into him, I cried out. My skin hummed from the top of my head to the tips of my curled toes; tiny spasms swirled into waves of rocking liquid heat, my body quaking from the inside where Theo plunged on. I gripped his strong, broad shoulders, holding on as the sweet building pressure wound tighter and tighter, until the tension shattered me.

Seconds later Theo's body went rigid over me. He called out my name at his release. The sound of his voice, the emotion behind the one syllable, swept through me. He buried his face in my hair, collapsing next to me in bed.

I held him in my arms while we lay there, catching our breath. He ran his fingers over the side of my face, brushed my hair back, placed his hand on my belly, and kissed my shoulder.

As it turned out, playing Russian roulette with my emotions was more dangerous than I thought. I knew, with every part of me, I was deeply and irrevocably in love with Theo.

CHAPTER TWELVE

TIME WAS MEANINGLESS IN THEO'S arms. Ignoring all responsibility and accountability with the rest of the world was fine, as long as I could remain limbs entangled, skin on skin with Theo.

But my body had different plans.

"Are you hungry?" Theo lifted his head, kissed my forehead, cradled my nape and kissed me again. My body stirred, and I kissed him back, only interrupted again by my stomach's insistent growl.

"I'm going to feed you." Theo pulled away, and found his shorts.

While he ventured off to the kitchen, I slipped into the bathroom. Snapping on the light, I was stunned by my reflection. I looked different. It wasn't the way my body was still taut, dusted with a heated flush, or that my kiss-swollen mouth bore a startling color match to my sensually abused nipples, or that my wild hair told the tale of earth-moving sex. The change was found when I made eye contact with myself. Sure, we'd made a pact. But even so, I couldn't deny my attachment to Theo.

I returned to the bedroom to find Theo propped on the pillows with a pie and two spoons. He smiled as he watched me. "Chocolate pie?"

My hunger overpowered any shyness I had about walking naked across a lit room.

"You know how to feed a girl." I settled in next to him, accepting the spoon he offered. "Oh, this is homemade. Did you make it?"

"I don't make pie. The church ladies are sending food this way now. Mom brought it by this afternoon. She says 'Hi.'"

"What do you think the church ladies would say if they knew you were using this as sex fuel?" I asked. Theo held the pie plate between us, and our spoons clinked together as we ate.

"They'd be pleased I'm not eating alone." He swiped his spoon across my nipple, leaving a trail of whipped cream that he promptly devoured. I continued to eat. I had to; I was starving. My nipple puckered at his attention, and soon enough the pie plate was tossed aside, and we played together again and again into the night.

The sun was high when I woke up, naked and alone. My body vibrated with elation and soreness from the most inspiring sex of my life—all-encompassing joy, found in the arms of the man I loved.

The aroma of bacon and coffee called my name. I pulled on a robe, tying it below my breasts, and made my way to the kitchen.

Theo orchestrated the stove, an assembly of pots and pans in front of him. "Good morning," I sang as I headed for the coffee maker to cash in on my allotted one cup a day.

Theo grabbed my arm and tugged me to him. He clasped me in a full-body embrace. Pulling back to kiss me tenderly, his hands moved down my sides, cupping my bottom through the robe.

He groaned and pulled back. "Good morning yourself, Sleeping Beauty." He returned his attention to the stove and flipped the pancakes.

"You taste good." I poured my coffee, squeezing in every drop I could to still make it count as one cup, and then topped off his mug.

"Ah, the princess likes bacon breath in the morning." He beamed at me, and I moved both our plates to the table.

We ate in silence at first. Every time I looked up, Theo's gaze was on me. While we ate, he randomly reached under the table and squeezed my knee, or he'd slide his hand over mine, finding some way to touch me as if to make sure I was really there.

"Hey, I love the wood you picked out." I sprinkled salt on my eggs.

"Yeah, Cortez will be over later. I'm ready to get at it."

There came a knock at the door, and Theo looked up. "That can't be him. He's never up this early."

I probably should have considered how it appeared, me lounging in my robe and slippers, late-morning dining with Theo. But when I saw Jake through the peephole I didn't hesitate; I pulled the door open.

"Good morning." Jake came in and strolled across the room to Theo. I shut the door and leaned against it, considering whether I could make it to my room without Jake noticing. He wasn't there to visit with me. But as his disapproving eyes wandered from Theo to me in my robe his expression changed.

"What's going on?" Theo asked him.

"Ellie's in the hospital—"

"Uh-oh, what happened?" I asked.

Jake only looked at Theo as he talked. "The baby is fine. Ellie's blood sugar numbers went through the roof. She's not well. They're pumping her with insulin and fluids. She's pushed herself too hard." He leaned against the kitchen counter, cramming his hands in his pockets. "They're putting her on full bed rest."

"Oh no," I said.

He turned to me. "She can't have anything to do with work."

"Of course not," I said, my brain racing. "Let me get dressed, and I'll go to the hospital with you."

"No, she's coming home in a little while. I'm heading to the house to get her clothes—she was in her pajamas when we went in last night. Come over later and help me keep her spirits up. She's worried, and that's no good for her or the baby."

"Okay, I'll get ready."

While I changed, I listened to the low rumble of the men talking. I couldn't make out what was said, but I wasn't fooled. Hushed voices passed hard judgments.

Jake did not approve.

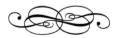

"Looks like you have the golden pass from the bookstore," I said, climbing into Ellie's bed. Ellie huddled under the covers. With no makeup on, she looked fifteen.

"I'm sorry. I'll get my staff together, and we'll figure it out." She sniffled and dabbed her eyes with a tissue.

I reached across the bed and took her hand. "Look, you're going to have to forget about work for a while. I'll handle everything. You need to rest and let this little guy grow."

Ellie's lip trembled and tears slid down her face.

"It's going to be okay," I promised.

We exchanged a look as the sound of the men coming down the hall got louder and louder until Steve, flanked by Theo and Jake, entered. Steve walked to the foot of the bed while the other guys hung back at the door. "Hey, you two." He pulled off his size twelve shoes, dropping them on the floor with two loud thunks, and wedged his way onto the bed between us. His arrival was met with a deep exhale. He flopped onto his back, arms spread wide, Ellie and I each cuddled into him on our own side. "Ah, now this is the way I really wanted to spend the day—in bed with my two favorite girls."

"Don't forget whose bed you're in," Jake grumbled, going to the far corner and plopping down in front of the vanity. I worried his powerhouse body would demolish the tiny chair. His focus was on watching Ellie like a hawk.

Theo looked equally uptight perched on the edge of a chaise lounge on the other side of the room. I noted the tightness around his eyes as he massaged his thigh. A muscle twitched in his jaw, but when he caught me staring, he smiled.

"Oh, I know it's your bed, man, but I can't help feeling like a king sandwiched between these bountiful beauties. Remind me not to bring any of my ladies around you two. Is it the water?" he went on, making us all laugh.

"But it's your turn now," Ellie told Steve. "You need that special someone."

Steve beamed. "I have someone special."

"Yeah, right," I said. His someone special changed as often as the supermarket sales.

"Hey, I'm not dumb enough to bring her around for your interrogation."

I looked over his chest at Ellie. "If Steve is calling a girl special, he's already on the downward swing of losing interest."

He shot me a dirty look. "Cut me some slack. You know, you haven't exactly mastered the whole relationship thing yourself." He poked me in the belly, and I pushed his hand away.

Although I knew Steve's comments were made with a light heart, I was busted. I looked to Theo before I could stop myself, and he gave me a wink. I flushed and cut my eyes to Jake, who scowled at both Theo and me. Steve was right; I had no clue what I was getting myself into.

"All right, the bookstore is calling my name. You say the word, and I'm back here for you, Ellie, for anything." He kissed the top of her head. "Meg and I will cover work. Don't sweat it." Steve put his shoes back on and strolled to the door, turning back to Jake and Theo. "Take care of my girls, men." He bowed and backed out of the room.

I rolled off the bed. "Steve, wait." I raced down the hall and caught him at the front door. "I'm glad you came. I know it matters to Ellie, and it matters to me too."

"No big deal. I've always been on your side. Why do you expect it to be different now?"

"We have a different way of dealing with things," I said and noticed Theo's backpack propped against the wall next to the door. "Your way of being on my side can be stifling at times." I reached past Steve and hauled the bag onto my shoulder.

"What do you expect? You fall too fast, too hard, every time. What kind of brother would I be if I didn't try to look out for you? What's up with the way Theo's looking at you?" Steve eyed Theo's bag. "It's getting serious, isn't it?"

Not as serious as I want it to be, I thought, but I wasn't about to say that, so I gave Steve the short answer. "I like him."

Steve's face darkened. "Don't keep doing this. It's time you stop getting messed up over guys who aren't going to stick around."

"How do I keep someone from leaving?"

Steve gave me a look that was too close to pity.

"Go. It's okay. Besides, I'm a big girl now. I can take care of myself." The statement sounded lame, even to me.

"Okay, then, big girl." He pulled me to him and hugged me too hard. "I'll be here when you need me." I waved him off and went back to join Ellie.

They were talking about the baby's room when I returned. I placed Theo's bag next to him and took my spot in bed again.

"You have to let me do the nursery, Jake. It's a rite of passage," Ellie said.

"No, you have to rest. Tell me what you want, and I'll do it."

"That's no fun," Ellie said.

"I can help." They both turned to me. "I need to go to all the baby stores anyway. We'll plan your room together. I'll buy stuff and return what doesn't work. Then Jake can put the room together."

"Are you sure?" Ellie asked.

"Are you kidding? We'll have a blast. It'll be almost like you're there with me."

From the corner of my eye, I noticed Theo discreetly taking his medication.

"It might work," Jake said, and for the first time all day, he dropped the scowl and his face relaxed.

"Okay, I guess, as long as you don't mind," Ellie said.

"I'll help, too," Theo said. "Why not? It's a boy's room and you need a man's vision."

"Good point," Jake said, warming to the idea. "Theo's help will keep you girls in line."

"We'll do your baby's room at the same time." Theo watched me closely. "Since we're doing your place up anyway, might as well do the baby's room."

Ellie perked up, "That's perfect!"

"Okay, if you really want to," I said softly. I looked forward to any and all time with him after our night together, but shopping for a baby's room with Theo was a big step. I wondered if what we felt in the dark still existed in the light of day. We were friends, we were preparing for my baby together, and we'd entered into a special sleeping arrangement. Could I keep my end of the no-strings-attached agreement?

The boys finally left, and I thought Ellie and I would take a nap, but the minute they were out the door, Ellie was on me.

"Okay, tell me everything."

"What are you talking about?" I was being coy, and she knew it. We were both grinning like kids about to dive into the cookie jar.

"Spill it, girl. I heard you and Theo have a pretty cozy setup at your place. Did you have *sex* with him?" Her fingers curled around the edge of the comforter, and when she said "sex," her eyes got really big. "You did!"

"Sshhh..." I put my finger to my mouth. Ellie held her breath, waiting. I nodded yes, and we both busted out giggling.

Life's greatest moments were only made better by sharing them with a true friend.

CHAPTER THIRTEEN

MY LIFE CHANGED CONSIDERABLY AFTER the weekend I began sleeping with Theo, and Ellie was put on bed rest. Those events pulled me in two directions, accelerating the pace of my life in ways that were at times fantastic but also bewildering.

Theo encouraged me to buy a sofa, chairs, and tables for the living room. The bookshelves were finished; a wall the entire length of the condo housed my library. Row after beautiful row of books lined up. When I bought a television, he bought a gaming system, and Cortez came over more often. Whenever I was around, the guys would talk about the baby. They argued over whom I should name it after if I had a boy.

"She's naming it after me," Cortez said. "Right, Meg?"

"Hmmm... Cortez Michaels. I like that."

"She's not naming it after you." Theo came up behind me, putting his hands on my belly. "It's a girl." He was sure of it.

Theo went with me to my twenty-week ultrasound. He couldn't wait to find out the gender, but the baby kept it hidden during the ultrasound. The technician told us she'd look again at my twenty-four-week checkup. Somehow, not knowing the sex of the baby made it easier for me to remain distant from the radical changes my life was about to take. I had no doubt I wanted the baby, but the thought of becoming a parent was so big, I couldn't manage to grasp it. Secretly, I wondered if my motherly instincts were ever going to kick in.

Sleep was bracketed by intimate moments with Theo naked in my bed. To my delight, acquiring time with him had become effortless, and I never had to beg for his touch again. Our relationship, although undefined, was the most passionate connection I'd ever had with anyone.

But no matter how hard I held onto that happiness, I was always aware of the cracks in our alliance.

One thing that seemed to cheer Theo up was shopping for the babies. A few days a week, he'd pick me up for lunch, and we'd go to all the baby shops and furniture stores. Theo followed me around with paint chips. He had big plans for painting the baby's room. I learned he had once aspired to be an artist. He saw colors differently from me—where I saw yellow, he saw butter cream, cadmium, daffodil, or gold. While we shopped, I would pick out things for Ellie, and Theo would pick out things for me, but he'd always make me look away. The room was a gift in progress, he told me, and I couldn't see it until he was finished.

The arrangement was fine with me. The nursery frightened me. For once, I found it easier to give up the control than to hold on tight, but that only added to my guilt. Shouldn't a mother be able to plan her baby's nursery? I wanted to create a magical place, but no matter how hard I tried to envision it, I came up with nothing. So I welcomed Theo's enthusiasm.

Because of his boundless energy and his growing strength, I wanted to assume he was healing, but pain dogged him. With the added time we spent together, I noticed he relied more on pills than I'd originally thought. On his bad days, his eyes would be glassy and feverish, his words slurred. On his worst days, he would be sullen, haunted, and withdrawn. He was given a starter prosthetic to train with, but it only brought him frustration.

Theo took his leg in for adjustments, but when he tried to

master it, pain raged with each step. His doctor and prosthetist informed him it shouldn't be that way, but after multiple refittings, he stopped going back. Preferring his crutches, he abandoned the prosthetic leg in his closet. His rehab was a subject he wouldn't talk to me about. I tried to find my way in, but Theo shut me out.

Cortez, who had a whole array of arms to wear, but most often used his hook, assured me that what Theo was going through would eventually pass.

"When will it get easier for him?" I asked one afternoon when he'd stopped by while Theo was out.

"No amputation is the same," Cortez said. "The doctors can't even answer that. Phantom pain is a bitch that screams so loud you can't think about anything else. Theo's trying to control it on his own, and that doesn't usually turn out good."

"So what do we do?"

"Wait," he said frowning. "There's nothing else we can do."

But waiting for Theo to get worse or to ask for help was not a plan I could follow.

"Hey, I have an idea," I said one rainy afternoon when we were lounging on the sofa, watching old Seinfeld episodes, each eating Ben and Jerry's out of the pint.

Theo looked as if he couldn't wait to hear what I had to say. "What's your idea?" He spooned a bite of his Cake Batter ice cream into my mouth and then helped himself to a scoop of my Cherry Garcia.

"Since you go to my doctor appointments, I could go with you to your physical therapy."

His face became unreadable, but he stiffened. "Nope."

"Why not? I want to."

"I'm done with physical therapy. I know what I need to do." He turned up the volume on an argument between Jerry and Newman. "Don't worry about it. Here comes the good part." He pointed at the TV.

So I ate my ice cream and watched Seinfeld and worried about Theo. He kept me at arm's length, never talking about the future, never talking about the present, and in the small stretches of stillness, his eyes illustrated the truth that he was not really there with me. I held on to that truth, telling myself that knowledge could be armor for the heart. But no matter how dark Theo was within, his touch was always tender. His body language whispered of the connection we had in a way his silence withheld. I couldn't reconcile my desires with our reality, so instead, I put on a happy face, determined to enjoy what was in front of me.

CHAPTER FOURTEEN

I STOOD ELBOW-DEEP IN FLOUR AND sugar when Bradley walked into Café Stay. I'd convinced myself that baking would be a fun respite, but it wasn't as relaxing as observing Ellie do her magic in the kitchen. I wanted back with the pretty books.

He wore a suit and a blue tie that brought out his eyes. Bradley looked as if he had stepped out of a Hugo Boss ad. "Lord have mercy, it's true!" His arms spread wide, his mouth open, eyes bright as if I had performed the most amazing magic trick. His gaze went from my face to my belly and back again. "Wow! It is good to see you!" And then before I could recover from the unexpected arrival of my formerly declared life mate, now ex, he wrestled me into a hug. I felt myself naturally redistribute, as if my body had muscle memory of being next to Bradley, and I settled into him in a familiar way, like coming home.

He sniffed my hair. "I've missed you. I got back this week, and a little birdie came by and told me about this." Bradley gestured at my belly, as though he couldn't come up with the words to describe my condition. "I had to come see for myself."

I pulled back, conscious of Theo sitting beyond the kitchen doorway. I glanced over Bradley's shoulder and saw Theo sketching in his notebook. He seemed absorbed in what he was doing, but the tightness in his jaw and the calculated impassiveness of his face gave a hint that he was aware of my company.

"Yes, it's true. I'm having a baby." I wasn't prepared to have the pregnancy conversation with Bradley. "How was your trip? You've been gone forever." I went back to spooning cookie dough onto a sheet.

"It's all good. You exaggerate. I came back to put the house on the market, tie up loose ends. They want me in China full-time, but I miss you." He stayed close to me, but he carefully avoided getting too close to the table. Couldn't risk getting flour on his fancy suit.

"Bradley, that's great about China. That's what you wanted." The timer went off, and I welcomed the chance to move away from him. Grabbing the oven mitts, I called over my shoulder, "I'm happy for you."

He stepped close to me again. "Meg..." He waited until I looked him in the eye, then pointed at my belly and then at his chest, "That's not—" He looked almost hopeful.

"No, no." I shook my head for emphasis.

Bradley's face dropped. "You're sure?"

"Yes, without a doubt." I held my breath, waiting for him to ask for more details, but he didn't.

"Have dinner with me tonight, Meg. We can catch up."

"I don't know. There's not much else to say." I looked to Theo, but the reality was, we weren't even dating. We hung out, ran errands together, watched TV and ate together, plus we were smack in the middle of a mind-blowing sex routine with each other, but to say we had formed any real union was premature.

"Come on, one last dinner. I wish I'd come back for you before now. I get it. I wrecked everything we had. I'm sorry. Give me one last dinner, a final farewell."

Against my better judgment, I gave in. "Okay, one dinner." Maybe Theo would tell me not to go. Or perhaps the dinner would be the nudge he needed to realize he was madly in love with me. Sometimes a push was good. A girl could hope.

Bradley embraced me again, planting a warm wet kiss on

my cheek. I suppressed a shudder and nodded as he told me he'd pick me up at my place at seven. I watched him go out the door and caught Theo sizing him up.

Theo shut his notebook, stuffed it in his backpack, and shuffled back into the kitchen.

I snatched a cookie from the cooling rack and took a bite, not sure how to juggle between dealing with a man from my past and the man here and now. "These aren't too bad," I said with false cheer. "Want one?"

Theo stared at me.

"That's Bradley." I sighed, throwing my cookie in the trash. "We're having dinner tonight."

"Have fun," Theo mumbled, turning away. "I'll be at The Tavern."

"Wait..."

He gave me an impatient glance over his shoulder.

"It's for closure. The dinner doesn't mean anything." I went to him and looped my arms around his neck, lifting up on my tiptoes to give him a kiss.

At first his lips were still against mine, but when I traced his mouth with my tongue, his resistance crumbled, and he kissed me back hard. His arms came around me, and he held me tight. He ended the kiss first, tucking my head under his chin, still holding on. "You don't owe me any explanations," Theo whispered.

When I'd first left Bradley, I was gripped with a guilty fear, worried I might have quit too soon. He was sweet and comfortable, but a void stretched between us. I could ignore it when he came home every night, but when he traveled, everything missing became larger. Whoever said absence makes the heart grow fonder was delusional. When your man is gone all the time, sure, you miss him at first. Until you realize you hardly notice he's gone, except when he calls to tell you all the fun he's having in a new place. You laugh and say nice things, but you look around at the sameness that surrounds you. Over time, you begin to wonder why you're waiting while he's out there living. And then one day you realize being alone is better than waiting on someone to remember you're there.

Our breakup took place over the phone only because he was staying in China for another month, and I couldn't put my life on hold any longer. Bradley asked me to wait until he got back. But being abandoned in the four-bedroom house we had built depressed me. I grew up with parents always gone, always at work. Bradley pleaded with me to join him in China. He promised I'd be happy there, but if he really knew me, how could he ask me to leave my brother and my bookstore? Bradley loved his job, and I couldn't ask him to leave. And I couldn't deny the changes in him after he left for China. We couldn't connect over the distance. And then, of course, I'd wondered about the girl who'd answered his phone.

I perched on the steps out front, waiting for his arrival. I didn't want to bring him into the condo. We had too much of a past there. Plus, although I hadn't seen Theo since I'd told him my dinner plans, I still didn't want to invite Bradley in and risk Theo showing up. No point in dealing with that awkwardness.

Bradley pulled up fifteen minutes late and waved when he saw me. I lowered myself onto the passenger seat and thought about Theo making his way around the car to open my door. Bradley wasn't rude — he was a modern guy who spent his days around computers and computer parts, engineers and programmers, drinking large amounts of coffee under fluorescent lights. Conversations with him usually involved him looking at his Blackberry instead of looking me in the eye.

"I can't get over how much you've changed," Bradley said while I pulled the seatbelt under my bulge. He gripped my belly with one hand, like he was checking on the ripeness of a melon. I smacked him away in a faux-friendly, "don't touch me" kind of way.

"Tell me about China." With that request, Bradley was happy to talk about himself, and while he rambled on, I listened to his soothing baritone and marveled at how the past six months seemed to slip away. Riding next to Bradley in his Beemer was so ordinary that the fact that I hadn't done it in so long was the only thing that seemed off.

He pulled up to Mesa Rosa, our favorite Mexican restaurant, where the hostess sat us at the table we'd called ours, and then over the course of the next hour and a half, every waiter stopped by to congratulate us on our baby. I panicked at first, unsure how to reply, but Bradley was gracious, thanking each person who stopped to talk to us. My worries about the evening faded, and I relaxed into the familiarity of being with Bradley. But I shouldn't have let my guard down, because once I did, the questions began.

Bradley eyed me warily. "I have to ask..." He crossed his arms, his body folding in. "Were you seeing someone when you broke up with me?"

"No, I promise I wasn't."

"Who's the father?" He studied my belly, waiting.

I felt my cheeks heat. "It doesn't matter."

"How can you say that?" he asked.

"Because this isn't about you."

"You had to have gotten pregnant the minute you called us off."

I put my head in my hands, exhausted. "I'm sorry." I sighed. "I know how it looks. But it's not about you."

"I should have made you go to China." He quickly reached across the table for my hand. I pulled away, but he grabbed my wrist. "I shouldn't have left you behind."

He couldn't be serious. "I would've never gone."

"We can fix this. Go back to the way we were. I'll help you make this right. You can't do this alone. We'll raise the baby together."

"No, Bradley. We can't go back. Our relationship is over."

"I already inquired at the office. There's a position available with less travel. We could make it work. Everyone thinks that's my baby. Why won't you be reasonable and take me back?"

"But it's not your baby."

"You're being ridiculous." He leaned into the table. "Nobody has to know. It'll be our secret."

I groaned. *"No!"* My resolve fresh, I searched his face for understanding, but instead he reached in his pocket and pulled out the small, fuzzy black box that I used to call my own.

"This belongs to you. I want you to take it back. Sell it, and get something for the baby. Or throw it off a bridge if you want. It's yours. You get to decide." He took my hand in his and placed the box in my palm, curling my fingers around it. I was speechless.

Not so long ago, the ring had felt as much a part of me as my own finger. I opened the box, touching the diamond. The ring once stood for so many things. Like the banners that trail airplanes in the sky, I wore it as if to say, "Somebody loves me enough to keep me forever." By the time I had called off our engagement, and removed the ring, its weight was too heavy. It symbolized the cage I needed to get free of. In spite of that, looking in the box, all I saw was a beautiful ring.

"I can't take it," I said.

"You have to—that's all I ask."

He wasn't going to back down, so I closed the box to slip it in my purse, but then I had that old fear I'd lose it. The ring had always been a little loose, ready to slide off and disappear. I popped the box open again, plucked the ring free and slipped it on. For the first time, it fit perfectly. I couldn't resist the urge to hold out my hand, fingers outstretched to admire the magnificent ring.

Bradley took my hand, keeping eye contact with me as he kissed it. "Thank you."

We stood and hugged; my eyes filled with tears. My heart ached for all the things we'd never be, but I also knew I had done the right thing. We drove in silence on the ride home, and for the first time, I understood what it meant to have closure at the end of a relationship. There were no more what-ifs or possibilities. The finality of the end freed me to focus on what was real and worthwhile. For me that was Theo, and I couldn't wait to be with him again.

Theo never came home that night. He didn't answer his cell, and I didn't risk pushing him further away by checking in with Jake or Cortez. My worry turned to frustration. The next day I dragged myself through the hours at the bookstore, followed by an evening of hanging out with Ellie. Finally I went home and found him in my bed. He lay in the dark, arms crossed behind his head, his chest rising with each breath.

I marched over to the bed. "Where have you been?"

Theo, though still, looked tense and wound tight. He wasn't asleep. The moonlight streaming through the windows lit up his eyes. I recognized the medically induced glaze in them.

"I hope I didn't wake you," I whispered, going to his side. I'd hurt Theo by going out with Bradley; I could see that now. That was why he'd pulled away, but that didn't excuse his leaving me worried. "Why do you do this to me? Do you have any idea what it's like to sit here and wonder where you are?"

"You're right." He reached for my hand. "I'm sorry. I'm no good for you. I try and help, and all I do is screw up everything. You deserve better." His voice cracked.

"I couldn't sleep last night without you," I confessed. "I deserve a phone call if you need time away. I deserve the Theo that is here when you are *present*. I can't take it when you disappear. When you disappear it hurts me. But that doesn't mean I don't want you."

He didn't speak when I climbed into bed; he didn't even move. I placed my hand on his cheek and kissed him, and though he looked me in the eye, he was still and silent. Longing to connect with him again, I kissed his chest and trailed my hands down his sides. I worked for any reaction, but he remained immobile while I kissed the tight rippled muscles of his abdomen. His breath caught when I licked the warm skin below his navel, dragging my tongue wetly from hip to hip, dipping below his waistband. I put my hand on the bulge in his pants. He was ready for what I had to give.

He lay impassive as I curled my fingers around the waistband of his shorts, tugging them all the way down. I kneeled on the bed between his legs. But as I stroked his thighs and kissed his lower belly, he lost his fight to resist the pleasure I offered. He let out an anguished groan, and I gripped his shaft, lowering my mouth onto him. My hair cascaded over him, and I watched his reaction as I licked him. I swirled his salty moisture with my tongue, finally taking Theo deep in my mouth, working my tongue as I sucked. I wanted all of him, and as I pulled with my mouth, his reserve shattered. He gasped and moaned, his fingers weaving through my hair. Pressing gently into my scalp, he held on, and I matched the rhythm he set.

He grasped me. "Stop!" The word startled me. Theo sat up and reached for me, tugging at my clothes. Climbing on top of him, in a hot slide of bodies melding, I cried out as he thrust inside me. I tightened and clenched around his girth; his hands bit into my hips as he plunged up into me. My head rolled back, bliss tightening every muscle, and I cried out.

His hands moved over me, brushing against my breasts in soft circles. Liquid fire flowed through me. I was sure Theo loved me when I looked into his eyes, full of desire and need. He continued to pump into me, steady and deep; my heart fluttered, pleasure thrummed through my veins, my skin hot all over from his touch. I couldn't hold back. I moaned and thrashed upon him as heat and wetness surged through me. I came quivering in his lap, and he continued thrusting into me. He went rigid as his whole body shook with release.

He rolled me carefully next to him. Smoothing my hair back from my face, he kissed my forehead, my eyelids, the tip of my nose and my cheeks. He hugged me to him and stroked my back in the dark, dropping kisses along my shoulders and neck. Theo was attentive and affectionate, and I reveled in the moment with him, waiting for him to speak. And in the process of waiting, I fell asleep.

When I woke up, he was sitting on the bed next to me, holding my hand. I smiled at him, confused by the angry glare in his eyes.

"What's this about?" His tone edged toward irate, and when he held up my hand, the light caught and sparkled on my diamond ring, still perched on my finger for the entire world to see.

"It's nothing." And then I added more bashfully, "Bradley wanted me to take my engagement ring back, use it to get something for the baby. It's no big deal."

Theo sat on the edge of the bed, holding my hand, staring at my ring. All the comfort from our night together slowly evaporated like little bubbles popping in the air.

"It doesn't mean anything," I said.

He winced and dropped my hand. "It means *nothing*? He picked this ring out for you. He wanted you to wear it forever, didn't he? And now you're with me, but you have on *his* ring."

I took the sheet with me when I moved off of the bed. My clothes were strewn about the room during the throes of passion last night.

I snatched my shirt off the floor. "It's not his ring. It's my ring. That's why he insisted on giving it back to me." How could a stupid ring mean more than the night we'd had? "I only put it on so I wouldn't lose it." I'd located my pants, but still searched for my panties. I needed my panties; going commando was not an option when walking through an emotional hailstorm. Exposed, I longed for the security and comfort that comes from being snug in my underwear.

"Well, that makes perfect sense," Theo grumbled and walked out of the bedroom, leaving me alone to hunt for whatever security I could find.

CHAPTER FIFTEEN

THEO SPENT THE MORNING HOLED up in the nursery. The room was off-limits to me, so I paced in front of the closed door. "Can't we talk about this?" I hollered.

"I have nothing to say," he called back.

I gave up and went to get ready for work. On my way out, I tried again. "See ya later."

I faintly heard him mutter through door.

"Can't I have a goodbye hug?" I pleaded. I was about to give up when the door opened, and he shuffled out on one crutch. He looked at my hand, on which I still wore the ring.

"I'm going to see about selling it today. I don't want to carry it in my purse and risk losing it." On one hand, I knew I was giving him excuses, but on the other hand, the ring didn't mean anything to me anymore. He was making a big deal out of nothing.

His lips twitched and then curled into the smile I loved. Theo took me into his arms. The warmth of his body against mine eased my tension. He held me tight, and if I could believe in the message of his body language, I would know that he wanted me as much as I wanted him and that what we had would last through anything. But Theo didn't speak. His breath was hot in my hair, and when I pulled back his mouth came to mine. His kisses, tender at first, became possessive.

The front door swung open and Cortez glared at us.

"Aw, come on, guys! You knew I was coming—tone it down." He kicked the door shut and marched to the baby's room, swinging a gallon of paint.

Satisfied that everything was okay in the world again, I left the boys to work.

I spent most of the day in my office, trying to catch up on piles of paperwork. Between juggling Ellie's workload, shopping for two, afternoons in bed with Ellie, and evenings in bed with Theo, I was falling behind on everything. If I only pushed myself harder, I could get it all done.

Midday, I went to Café Stay to help with the lunch rush. More than once, I caught women glancing from my ring to my belly. I knew the fixed stare of the single woman. We've all been trained by the princess fantasy, the hope of one day being swept off our feet by a handsome prince. The apex of the dream is the ring in place of a glass slipper, and the happily ever after is a baby on the way.

I probably shouldn't have been so comfortable being a fraud, wearing a ring that no longer proclaimed engagement. But I reveled in the approval of strangers, transformed by their acceptance. The whispers and looks stopped. Let's face it; being pregnant alongside a devoted man was way more acceptable than just being pregnant. That reality was a truth I carried every day.

Even Hazel agreed. I was lugging a stack of magazines to bring to Ellie's house, trying to make my way to the front door, when she blocked my path. "There's that gorgeous diamond again," she gushed, clapping her hands together rapidly. "We were all so happy to see Bradley, yesterday."

Was that only yesterday?

Perhaps I should have stopped right there and explained the situation. However, it really wasn't her business, and Ellie was waiting for me. Ellie spent hours alone in bed, and she counted on my time with her. So I breezed past Hazel with a smile on my face. "Goodnight, goodnight," I sang cheerfully.

My approval rating plummeted at Ellie's house. After filling her in on all the highlights of my dinner with Bradley, she fastened onto one detail. "I can't believe you have that ring on your finger." Ellie finished the grilled chicken salad I had picked up for her at The Tavern. Because Ellie's diabetes diet was so restrictive, I didn't want her to have to watch me eat. I'd scarfed down a burger in the car and brought in an apple to nibble on.

"What's the big deal? It's nothing more than costume jewelry." I shrugged, flipping through a baby magazine. "I'm creating the illusion of a woman following a traditional path." That sounded like good reasoning to me, but Ellie, with her mouth full of lettuce, rolled her eyes. "Besides, I'm not keeping it forever. I'm going to hock it. Bradley doesn't care."

"What does Theo think?" Ellie, being Ellie, brought it back to the real issue.

"That's the million-dollar question. What does Theo think?" I sighed. "Initially, he was pissed. But when I explained why I had it on, he understood."

Ellie set her empty salad bowl on the bedside table and sifted through the pile of pregnancy and baby magazines. She shot me a skeptical look. "He understood why you're trying to look married?"

"No, originally I was wearing the ring so I wouldn't lose it, and he seemed to get that. Today at work, I realized people were less in my business, so I'm thinking I'll keep the ring on for a while."

Ellie gave me a skeptical look. "I don't know. That sounds sketchy, Meg." She propped her expectant-mom mag on her baby bulge, mirroring me. The belly shelf—another pregnancy perk to add to the list.

"Whatever. It's a façade." With the ring, I had stumbled onto an invisibility cloak and could disappear from everyone's radar. Who could resist that?

"Theo cares for you," Ellie said. I knew he spent a lot of time with Ellie since she landed on bed rest. "I'd hate to see you hurt him."

"*Please*, I'm with him almost every day. We laugh, we have fun together, but he's going to leave me. I can sense it. Once he's done helping me, he'll move on." It occurred to me that I wasn't doing a good enough job looking out for myself. The pain hit me all over when I thought about Theo going away. I knew better than to let myself get too close, but I had done it anyway. "Honestly, if the ring bothers him, I'll take it off."

"Hey, check this out." Ellie leaned toward me, and I realized she was ready to reroute the conversation. "This was printed in the UK and the title of the article is: 'What Kind of Mum Will You Be?'" Ellie giggled. "What kind of mum will you be?" She repeated, embellishing the words with an English accent.

The question frightened me. My mother had thrown in the towel before we'd hit two. Then Nina came along and treated Steve and me like her favorite emerald earrings, something she carefully put aside until the right occasion when she needed to impress someone. But when she could get away with it, she wore her dissatisfaction at being a stepmother like a medal she had earned along the way. I wanted to do better than the women who came before me.

I should have gotten a dog to practice with, or at least a fish. I needed mom training. Was I genetically predestined to fail as a mother? What if I created another human being that was going to go through life knowing she was not whole, because how could she be if her mother couldn't love her? Crap. Wasn't it a little late in the game for me to fall apart in complete panic over a simple question, with a British twist?

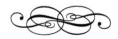

By the time I returned home later that night, my condo was dark. Theo and Cortez had cleared out, leaving no evidence they had spent the day working. The closed door to the nursery loomed in front of a room full of secrets and surprises. I wondered what was going on in there. But I promised Theo I would wait.

I went to bed alone and unsettled, missing Theo by my side. I wanted to get back to the place where we connected, but I also considered mirroring his withdrawal and putting up walls to protect myself before he pulled out on me. Self-preservation. I sensed his departure coming; I could feel it in my heart and in my bones. My thoughts kept me awake for so long that I was convinced I wouldn't sleep at all, but after enough tossing and turning, I gave in to a fitful slumber. The rattling of pills in a bottle pulled me back to the surface. I listened to the sounds that were all too familiar: pills in bottle, a pause as he popped pills into his mouth, swish of water, gulp, pill bottle being tossed into bag, bag zipped shut. Then he landed clumsily onto my bed, wrestled himself out of his clothes, and worked his way under the covers until he found me. His hands moved across my body and I rolled into the warmth of Theo.

"Mmmm... I thought about you all night," he whispered, his breath hot on my neck.

"Me too." I was flooded with relief, which washed away when I smelled alcohol seconds before he kissed me, and then I tasted it on his lips.

He pulled back and brushed his thumb across my cheek. "I worry about you."

I laughed. "You worry about me? I worry about you."

"But you shouldn't." He flopped onto his back next to me. I could barely see the outline of his profile. He sighed, sounding impatient. "You should worry about yourself. You see everything all wrong." His words slurred.

"What does that mean?" I asked, my chest tightening.

"Well for one, you don't see that I'm messed up."

"Oh, on the contrary, anyone can see that you're a train wreck waiting to happen." I slipped my hand under his shirt. "Have no illusions about that." The truth was, I wanted to fix Theo, but if I couldn't, if there was nothing that would make him well again, I still wanted him. If he was going to be in pain and medicated for the rest of his life, I still wanted him. But I couldn't humor myself with the idea that he might stay with me. If there was one thing my life had taught me, it was that people leave no matter how much you want to hold onto them. Or maybe there was something about me that wasn't worth sticking around for.

"Well, that should be a warning sign." He sighed. "The baby is going to be here soon. I shouldn't be wasting your time. You don't need my problems." He took my hand and moved it from his waist to his chest. His heartbeat thumped against my palm.

"Stop talking that way." My voice broke. "I want you here." I wrapped my arms around his shoulders, my breasts and belly pressing against him as I clung to him. "Theo, have you thought at all about going back to physical therapy? There has to be a way to help you get better."

"Sshhh..." He took my hand and pressed kisses along the inside of my wrist; his other hand stroked my thigh. "I'm not done with my list."

"I don't care for your list. I'm serious." I turned his face to mine, trying to get him to focus, but he closed his eyes. "Listen to me. You've only been getting worse since you stopped going. Maybe we can find you someone new to see. I'll do whatever it takes, whatever you want."

"Then listen to me." He took a deep breath. "You need to hear this. You still got that damn ring on?"

"I don't want to get into it again about that." I removed the ring and reached across Theo to put it on the bedside table. He gripped my hips, holding onto me.

"Do *not* put that back on your finger." He laced his fingers through my hair, making me look him in the eyes. "I want you... I *need* you to be mine," he said.

I leaned my forehead against his. "I'll never put it on again," I promised. "I'm sorry, Theo."

He kissed me then. Sliding his hand up my thigh and reaching under my nightshirt, he tugged at my panties. I wanted him to keep talking. I longed for his words. I would have held my breath for a promise. Any promise of a life with Theo. Instead, I helped him remove my underwear. He eased inside me with a deep sigh and I let go of my thoughts and responded to his touch. Our bodies moved together. After we cried out to each other, he curled around me and said, "I love you, Meg." He covered my mouth with his palm. "Sshhh... Don't speak." He whispered into my hair, kissing me below my ear. "Just know I love you." He held me tight against him, his eyes shut, and he murmured, "I love you."

I watched as he fell asleep, his chest rising and falling. I traced his scars, kissed his fingertips, and worried. I worried that he'd leave me soon. I worried that he would never truly be better, and I worried that with each pill he swallowed, I was losing a little more of him. The pills were taking his pain, and they were taking him with it.

And when I woke the next morning, he was gone.

CHAPTER SIXTEEN

"How do you know if you're in love?"

Steve was lying next to Ellie, and I was sitting cross-legged at the foot of her bed. Sunday mornings were one of the few times that Steve and I spent together that wasn't at work. He usually hosted brunch at his house, but with Ellie's required bed rest, we'd taken our routine to brunch in bed. The looks on their faces suggested I had informed them I had dynamite strapped to my chest.

"You can't trust your feelings when you're pregnant," Steve said, and he failed to pull away before Ellie smacked him on the shoulder. "Ouch. Why'd you hit me?"

"What do you know about pregnancy? Or feelings for that matter?" she asked. "You've managed to stay emotionally removed from every woman you have ever gotten involved with." Then to me she said, "What makes you think you're in love?"

I opened my mouth and then shut it, unsure how much of the night before I should share. Steve cut me off.

"See, that's just it: If you have to think about it, it's not love."

Ellie looked at him with skepticism. "When have you ever been in love?"

"Besides with you... never."

Ellie groaned. "Well, loving me doesn't count!"

Steve shook his head, looking more serious than usual. "I'll tell you exactly why it does count. Every time I think I love someone, I talk myself out of it."

"Well, that's romantic," Ellie said. "No wonder you can't keep a lady."

"Wait—indulge me for a moment here. I know I'm not in love with a girl if I can talk myself out of it. When I was in love with you, Ellie, no matter what I did, the feelings were still there. I couldn't escape it."

Ellie put a hand on Steve's shoulder. "Don't do this. You're breaking my heart."

Steve took her hand. His eyes danced with humor. "Give me your heart, Ellie, and I promise you'll never regret it." He tried to kiss Ellie's hand, but she pulled back, squealing. He told her, "We can be gone before Jake gets back. I'll raise your child as my own."

"My husband will hunt you down and kill you. Quit with the flirting! Knock it off so Meg can tell us what's going on."

While they went through their routine, I thought about what Steve had said, and I decided he was onto something. "So how did you get over Ellie?"

He shrugged and crossed his arms behind his head. "When I accepted that my feelings for her would never be reciprocated, I moved on."

Ellie giggled. "You mean you moved on to the next girl."

"Whatever works, my friends, this man will do. There are many women in this world, and I don't want to sleep alone."

"So who is she?" I still didn't know anything about his mysterious special someone. "Are you in love again?"

"Tell us about your new lady," Ellie said.

"Like I said, I'm not big on falling in love, and you two don't need to know who's been sleeping in my bed."

The little one did a somersault on my bladder, and I got up to pee, although fifteen minutes hadn't even passed since the last time I relieved myself. As I shut the bathroom door,

Steve called out: "So, Meg, are you and Theo taking it to the next level?"

"Nope," I said sharply and slapped the door shut, stunned by how quickly I knew the answer. Even though I'd craved Theo's declaration of love ever since the first night we were intimate, I couldn't acknowledge what had happened the night before unless he told me he loved me again. While sober. Maybe I was being unfair, but I couldn't hold onto words spoken by a man hopped up on alcohol and pills.

When I came out of the bathroom, Steve was standing. "Hug me," he said. "I'm going to the store for a bit. I better not see you in today."

As he left, Ellie called out to him, "Hey, Steve..."

"Yes, dear?"

"I will always, always love you!"

"Yeah, yeah, like a brother, I know. Moving on." He blew her a kiss and left.

Ellie motioned me to the bed. "Spill it, Meg. What's going on with Theo?"

I pulled back the covers to climb in, rearranging the pillows to support my belly and lower back. "Last night he said he loved me." Ellie gave me a wide grin, showing all her teeth. I snuggled under the blanket, dragging it up to my chin. "But he was drunk, and on pain medicine... and we'd had sex. It was late."

"How did he act this morning?"

"I didn't see him. He was gone before I got up. He disappears a lot, actually."

"Well, don't decide anything yet. Wait and see what he says later. If he loves you it won't matter what time it is, or what's going on with his body, or around him. If it's love, then it's in spite of everything else. That's how you know it's love. You feel the way you feel despite the circumstances."

"Is that how you knew what you and Jake had was real?"

"Yes. My love was louder than anything else in my life. I loved him when I brushed my teeth, I loved him when I was sitting in traffic, I loved him while I paid my bills, ate lunch, and went grocery shopping. Before every breath I took, my mind pulsated with the thought: *I love Jake.* And when he told me he loved me, my whole life fell in place." Ellie spread her arms wide, her eyes shining with the memory. "Everything lined up for me with a divine perfection, like the planets in our solar system."

"But I remember you being so afraid to love him."

"Yes, I was afraid, but love trumps fear. Your love has to be greater than the fear that goes with it. It's okay to be afraid. You have to keep moving forward." Ellie leaned in closer. "Plus, with Theo you must take into account what he's going through."

"I do. I always do."

"I know, but he's *still* struggling... adjusting. His darkest days may be ahead of him."

She was right. Who was I to expect so much from him? He said he loved me, and one thing Theo never did was lie. I didn't know what was going on with him. He had people he could relate to. Guys that understood him in a way I never would. Adding alcohol to his meds couldn't be a good thing; nevertheless, I didn't know how to confront him. Yes, I wanted to help him. I wanted him to lean on me. But that wasn't my decision.

And I had no idea where he'd gone, where he was, or when I'd see him again. Again.

Jake returned from work early in the afternoon, so I left. Holding on to hopes Theo might be around, I called his cell, but as usual, he didn't answer. Not in the mood to be home alone, I decided to shop for Ellie's baby shower. At the Super Baby Depot I checked out invitations, thinking about a theme for the party. More exhausted than I'd realized, I mourned that I was no longer an energetic person full of spark. Just under twenty-five weeks, I was a bloated load of tiredness at a time I was told was supposed to be the best of pregnancy. The strain of everything was taking its toll. I was big, and tired, and hungry all the time. I'd finally given in and bought a pair of shoes a half size larger and wore clothes only with a waist made of the kindest elastic for a generous give. My days of buttons and zippers were over for a while. Even the sexy little black number I bought was cut like a tent that could comfortably sleep a family of four or one pregnant woman deep in her second trimester.

Walking past the gliders, I went to the one Theo and I had purchased a few weeks ago and took a seat, propping my feet in the matching rocking ottoman. The one we bought was hidden away in the baby's room with everything else we'd purchased. If the motion soothed the baby the same way it soothed my nerves, it would end up being the best purchase I made. I cradled my belly and rocked away to the singing of The Bangles, telling me to Walk Like an Egyptian.

A couple checking out baby carriers caught my attention. The man strapped on a Baby Björn, chuckling with his wife, who looked as though she was either past due or carrying twins. My poor legs already ached in constant protest. If I grew to that size, I would have to hire someone to cart me around in a wheelbarrow. She held a cherub-like baby doll with a smooth, round head. Her husband took the pseudo infant and tried to slip it into the carrier. The woman's patience dwindled, and she snatched the pink, vinyl feet, yanking them into the leg holes, which made my skin prickle in a response that was an absurdly protective, considering no child was harmed. She waved her iPhone around, ordering her husband to smile for a photo.

I rocked to the rhythm of Katy Perry on Muzak.

Turning my focus to a woman about my age strolling along with an older version of herself—clearly her mother—the companionship void in my life widened. Their shopping cart was full of baby bedding, a matching lamp, and an excess of bottle paraphernalia. At the diaper display, they debated brands.

"Mom, the one that costs the most isn't necessarily the best," the younger woman said. Her hands pressed into the small of her back. She exhaled, sticking out her lower lip, and blew wispy bangs off her forehead.

Busy inspecting the boxes, her mother didn't look up as she spoke. "I know, but you don't want to get the cheapest ones, either. Let's buy a couple different kinds and let the baby decide which one he prefers."

"But I don't want him to like the most expensive ones," she protested as her mother stacked at first two boxes of diapers on the cart and, after hesitating for a moment, added a third.

"Now let's pick out a wipe warmer." The mother steered the cart, and her daughter shuffled along. A twinge of regret hit me that Nina couldn't be like one of those moms.

I eyed a group of four pregnant women. One held a tiny outfit over her belly as if she could check the fit on her baby in utero. I missed Ellie. I couldn't imagine having a husband to anticipate my child's birth with, or a mom who would know what I needed better than I did. However, I had a friend who stayed by my side no matter what. I needed my BFF. Her bed rest wouldn't go on forever, and before too long Ellie and I'd be shopping with our babies in tow. I focused on that happy thought.

I closed my eyes, lulled by the gliding rocker.

Sun warm on my upturned face... The glow of light penetrating my eyelids is riveting. I'm swinging fast, laughing hard.

"Higher, Momma, higher!" Steve squeals next to me. His stocky little-boy legs flail as he goes backward and forward, opposite of my forward and backward.

A firm push on my rump and I sail up, up, up. My feet reach for the sky; the pink Mary Janes I'd begged Daddy to buy me for the first day of kindergarten float above me. The white lace on my socks flutters around my ankles.

Then I fall back toward the earth. She laughs behind me, lilting waves of joy. I must see her, but when I try to turn in my swing she pushes me harder. I should say something.

"Watch me, Meg, watch me." Steve leans back, dangerously far — he is flying. And then she moves between us, glides by. A glimpse of her profile, and I am watching her walk away. Her hair, so similar to ours; a veil of silky blond curls flows down her back. She waves without turning. I can't slow the swing; I can't get off. She's at the end of the street and glances back as she turns the corner, but she is too far away. I can't see her face. I twist back to Steve; his

*swing is empty. I am alone, anchored to my swing, fluctuating like a
pendulum, moving but not going anywhere.*

Alone. I am all alone.

The displacement of air startled me. I opened my eyes, the
dream fading.

Theo rocked in the glider next to me, and for a flash I thought
I had moved back in time to the day we shopped for the glider.

"When are you going to take better care of yourself?" Theo
took my hand in his and squeezed. "I need to pick up one last
thing for the baby's room, and I find you back here sleeping."
He gave me a long, amused look, with wary eyes. Up front,
Cortez flirted with the cashiers.

"You're done?" We hadn't talked about what we'd do
when he finished the baby's room. "Does this mean I get to see
it now?"

"Not yet. I still have a few things to do." Excitement radiated
off of his body, and I savored the moment of normalcy. But
disoriented from my nap, I was missing something.

The realization hit me, and I spoke in a mindless rush.
"You're leaving."

"No," he said, but his face fell. "I will guard everything
within the limits of my post and quit my post only when
properly relieved."

"Theo..." I started to rise, but even with his crutches, he was
faster, offering a hand.

"Meg, you've got to quit worrying about things before they
happen." He helped me to my feet and draped his arm across
my shoulder. "We have an agreement."

"I know. I want to talk about that." After last night, I should
take the gamble. I couldn't let Theo leave without knowing
my heart.

"There's nothing to talk about. Hey, anyway, we got two
days until your future becomes clearer."

"You're still going to join me?" I was surprised he
remembered the ultrasound appointment and was counting
down the days.

"I wouldn't miss it for anything." He placed his other hand on my belly. "I want to find out exactly who's in there."

Comfort. Theo always brought me comfort.

"Me, too," I said. "I'm finally ready for this."

"That's my girl."

"Are you coming home now?"

"No, we have things to do." Theo pulled away from me. "Do you need something? You craving anything?"

My every craving began and ended with Theo. "No, I'm good."

Theo leaned in and kissed me. "Do me a favor?"

"Sure." He never asked me for anything.

"Try not to fall asleep when you're out by yourself." He tucked a lock of hair behind my ear. "You're too trusting."

"I trust you."

"Yeah, and how's that working for you?" Again with the sad eyes. "Come on, I'll walk you to your car."

On the way out the door, Theo called to Cortez. "Hey man, let's hit it."

"Yeah, yeah, I'll be right out." Cortez shot him a meaningful wink.

We crossed the parking lot to my car, and he took my keys and opened the door.

I didn't want to leave without him. We had a distance between us I had yet to bridge. "I have to tell you I'm sorry," I said, trying to close the gap. "I'm sorry I wore the ring."

Theo shook his head, put his hand up to stop me. But I continued.

"I was thoughtless. I care about you, and I shouldn't have used the engagement ring for security."

"Don't." He took my hand, brought it to his mouth. "No worries." He kissed my wrist.

I sat in the car waiting for him to say more.

"We'll catch up later." He shut the door, and again I found myself alone. In the silence of my car I realized we'd never acknowledged what had happened the night before. I wasn't sure he remembered what he'd said.

CHAPTER SEVENTEEN

I ROLLED UP MY SWEATS, TIPTOED across the wet kitchen floor, and filled a bowl with corn flakes. I sliced an overripe banana on top and snatched the near-empty quart of milk from the fridge, draining the carton, which only contained enough milk to half cover my cereal. Tears came with a rush. In the kitchen, with a bowl cradled in my hand, I ate my cereal and cried.

The front door opened. I choked back a sob and forced another bite.

Theo came into view.

"Watch out, the floor is wet." I pointed with my spoon, eyes not meeting his. I continued with my corn flakes.

"You're crying in your cereal."

What could I say? He didn't remember.

"We're out of milk." I swiped at my cheeks with the back of my hand between bites, but the tears kept coming.

"I'll get more tomorrow." He reached out and pulled a few tissues from the box, and walked over to me.

I turned my back to him and rinsed my bowl, put it in the dishwasher.

When I faced him, he dabbed my cheeks. "The house looks great. You're nesting."

I sniffed, went up on my toes for a kiss. He met me with forceful need. Wrapping me in his arms, his mouth took mine. Beer lingered on his breath, with a trace of something stronger. He swayed against me. I tried to pull back, but his hand moved up my spine, his strong fingers cupped the back of my neck, holding the kiss. A shock of pleasure rippled through me as the demand of his lips grew. He wanted me — that was unmistakable.

"No." I stepped back, worked myself free from his embrace. "Not doing this again." Pushing against him, I took in his hurt expression and felt a wave of victory. I waited for him to say something, anything, but he only looked away. I left him there, looking dejected, and walked slowly to my room. At the door, I glanced back at him, lingering a second longer, giving him the chance to speak, but he remained silent. I slammed the door as hard as I could, using both hands. The sound, a bang that echoed through the bones of the condo, reflected my frustration. And yet, the undertow of shame smacked into me. How wrong for me to think that hurting Theo would solve anything. Stripping off my grungy sweats, I climbed into the shower. Underneath the hot water I pulled myself together. I couldn't pretend anymore. I was done denying I didn't want more. The risk he'd leave was always there, but I decided I had to tell him how I felt. If only he hadn't been drinking when he told me he loved me. Then I would've opened up to him. But it was time I stopped pushing him away.

I owed him an apology.

The kitchen was still lit up when I came back to make amends with Theo. He sat upright, his back to me. Only as I came around and called out his name did I realize he was asleep, head back, mouth open, snoring softly.

I put my hand on his arm, and he slumped toward me.

Finding my soft fleece throw, I covered him, kissed his cheek, and returned to my bed alone. As a peace offering, I left the door to my room opened wide. I hoped he'd wake up and accept my olive branch by joining me in bed.

The next morning I was jolted awake by someone pounding

at the front door. I stumbled out of bed and out to the living room. Theo and the blanket I left covering him were both gone. I glared with contempt at the vacant sofa, as I passed by, not ready for another day of uncertainty.

My stomach bumped the door as I peered through the peephole. I gasped and yanked the door open.

"Dad!"

"Wow!" He put his hands on my shoulders, leaning in to kiss my cheek. "You look fantastic!" He walked in, arms spread wide. "I love what you did to the place." He kept his eyes carefully diverted from my belly. Forever the realtor, he mentioned the updated light fixtures and the atmosphere created by the built-in bookshelves. "Your library is impressive." Dad had always been amused I shared his father's infatuation with books, and I'd always been amused the book obsession had skipped a generation.

"What are you doing here?" I peered out front, expecting Nina to waltz up and make her entrance.

"You can shut the door. I'm alone," he said with the tone parents use when there is more news to follow.

I shut the door. "What's going on?" I waited for the other shoe to drop.

Dad carried himself well, always a sharp dresser even when casual. Silver streaks infiltrated his thick, dark waves of hair. He slid his hands into the front pockets of his Levis and rocked back on his loafers. "Honey, I left Nina."

Whoa. When I was a little girl I prayed that he would leave her. I was considerate enough to vocalize the plea in high school, and by college I'd accepted that my father was entitled to love my evil stepmother even though for the life of me, I could never figure out why.

"What are you talking about?" I couldn't wrap my head around what he was saying. Dad was loyal to a fault.

He took a seat in the center of the walnut-hued Pottery Barn sofa, with arms outstretched across the twill cushion back.

"There's nothing to talk about. I wanted to come home."

"Dad, what's going on?" I asked again, crossing my arms over my belly. I could tell he was holding something back. "This isn't your home anymore. It's the baby, isn't it? Is that why you're here without Nina?"

"You're going to need help." He shrugged. "I want to be here for this."

"And Nina doesn't. I can't be the reason you left."

"Don't worry, honey. It's not you." He cleared his throat, leaned forward, and pressed the tips of his fingers together. "Look, I want to say she shouldn't have acted the way she did when she found out. You surprised us. We thought the whole thing was a joke."

I put my hand on my belly. "No joke, Dad. I'm sorry to embarrass you."

"Now that's nonsense," he said firmly. "Come sit with me. Meg, I'm proud of you. I'm proud of how you're handling this. And I, for one, can't wait to be a grandpa."

"But Nina is embarrassed." I went to my dad and fell against him, soothed by his solid presence, but disappointed that I could never please my stepmother.

"Nina is focused on work. She's very successful at what she does, but it's hard for her to see beyond the needs of the business."

"It'll be okay, Dad. She is who she is." Dazed, I shook my head. "I think you should go back."

"Family has always meant more to me than work. I worked hard to provide for my family. Now I'm going to be a grandpa, and I don't want anything to get in the way of that. Nina can't take her eyes off work. She's married to the real estate business, not me." Pain flickered in his eyes. He looked away. "It's okay. We'll figure it out one way or another. You get dressed, and I'll take you out for breakfast."

"I have to work today."

"I'm spending the day with you, honey. Let's eat, and then we'll go to the bookstore. I'm on your time now."

"Sure, Dad." I eased myself off the sofa to go get dressed,

but turned back. "Um, Dad, I've had a guy — well, he's a friend, staying here helping me out."

"Sounds like a good friend." His smile gave away that he knew more than I was telling. Still, I couldn't help but be relieved he didn't ask questions. Then I thought of something else. "Hey, are you really going to stay around for a while?"

"You bet. I'm bunking with Steve. I came in last night and shocked him and that girl of his."

"What girl?" Steve never brought anyone home. That would be against his code of conduct.

"Oh, I can't remember her name. We've met before."

"That can't be possible. He definitely hasn't dated anyone that long."

"You should have seen his face when I showed up. I'd have called first, but this visit is somewhat spur of the moment. Steve tried to give me the master bedroom back, but I insisted on taking his old room. I'm planning to help him fix the house up. Looking forward to it, actually."

"Wow, Dad, back at the old house. Nina's not going to be happy."

"Well, Nina can get over herself." He spoke casually enough, but then I saw his fists balled tight at his sides, the taut skin of his knuckles white, and the tension around his mouth. That was the closest he'd ever come to sounding angry with her.

But my dad was home, so I wasn't about to complain.

After breakfast, I reverted to little-girl status, sitting in the passenger seat of my dad's Lexus. It'd been years since the two of us had hung out alone. Sometime in the morning, he'd quit resisting, and after that, his eyes continued to drift to my belly, and he would smile with anticipation. I'd had no idea how happy the idea of becoming a grandfather would make him.

Having kids wasn't something I'd considered much before my unexpected pregnancy. Even though Bradley and I had been engaged, we'd never even spoken of starting a family. So much had changed in the past few months. I didn't care to dwell on my own mother, but as I grew accustomed to the changes with my body, questions about her continued to steal into my thoughts. Did she come to hate Steve and me before she made her escape? She couldn't possibly have left if she'd loved us.

When Dad pulled into traffic and his focus shifted to driving, I seized the moment. "Dad, why did she leave?"

He didn't speak for a while, but I knew he was thinking of her, thinking of the right way to explain. "Your mother was young."

Although he had a hard time talking about her, I pushed for more. "I'm young, Dad."

"She was younger. Things were different back then."

"She was my age when she left us. Did you even see it coming?"

"No, but I didn't want to believe she could leave. I thought everything was fine." I wasn't sure if he was defending himself or her as he explained. "I was naive in my happiness. All I wanted was a family. But for Candace, nothing was that simple."

"Do I remind you of her?"

"You'll do fine." He dodged my question. "You'll learn as you go—that's what I did. You know how to find your way around. You can navigate a kid. I'm sure of it." He looked at me and gave me the proud-dad smile, with a reassuring pat on the knee similar to when I was a teenager about to be dropped off at the mall. *Honey, I know you'll make good choices. I'll be back for you later.* He always said it that way, and I'd have to push away the memory that my mother never came back.

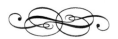

True to his word, Dad spent the day at The Book Stack. He walked the aisles, read the paper, mingled with the staff, and ate lunch in the café with Hazel, of all people. Just after noon, Steve strolled in, and once I got him out of Dad's line of vision, I cornered him in his office and shut the door. His office mirrored mine, but the walls were covered with Magma and anime posters, and the room smelled of coffee and stale pizza.

"Ding dong, the witch is dead." I grinned.

Steve grimaced. "Meg, you're awful."

"Oh come on, she bullies Dad."

"Dad always does what he wants." Steve sat at his desk and sipped his cup of coffee. "This is the first time he's ever gone against her."

"Whatever. Hey, you look tired. Late night? Who's the chick at your house?"

He blew into his steaming cup and yawned. "None of your business." He swiveled his chair, turning his back to me.

"No fair. Tell me. You can't shut me out." His game was getting old. "I kept one secret from you, and now you won't talk to me about anything."

"You have no room to speak, and I'm still not going to tell you."

I went for a different tactic. "Chicken."

"Ha! You're the one about to hatch an egg," he shot over his shoulder. "Confess your love to Theo yet?"

I mentally kicked myself for talking about love with Steve. "You cool with Dad staying with you?"

"Sure. We'll have fun until Nina comes and gets him."

"What if she doesn't?" I took a seat and slipped off my shoes.

Steve shifted to face me. "She will."

"She's really upset I'm pregnant."

"No, she's not." He shook his head. "She doesn't know how to be there for you, and you didn't invite her in anyhow. She wants to be happy for you, but she's hurt that you left her out."

"Oh, poor thing." I rolled my eyes. "This must be so hard for her."

"Well, she's also pissed Dad isn't trying to appease her. She's not comfortable having no control, but she'll figure it out. Will you?"

"I don't want to deal with Nina, but I don't want Dad to be alone."

"He's not alone. He's with me." Steve's long fingers drummed on his desk.

"It's all my fault."

"Get over it. They needed to have it out." He moved his mouse, pulling his computer out of sleep mode.

"How do you know?" Had I been so caught up in my world that I had no clue what transpired with the rest of my family? Even though Nina and I kept a cool distance, we still managed to have a relatively normal family, the four of us. But everything had changed, and I realized I was drifting away from the others. I didn't know what upset me more—that I was cast off, or that they were anchored to each other.

"Dad's been wanting to retire for some time, and she keeps pushing him out another year."

"How do you know?"

"Because he talks to me." Steve looked at me with raised eyebrows. "He knows I won't take the blame for what's wrong in his life."

"I asked him about Mom today," I said hesitantly.

He swiveled around in his chair. "Has he talked to her yet?"

"Not Nina... our mom."

"Oh, the lady who gave birth to us." He expression made it clear he didn't want to continue our conversation.

"She's our *real* mother."

"No, she's not," he snapped. "Our *real* mother married Dad when we were five. You were a flower girl and I was the ring bearer, remember? That other woman is simply a genetic component in our make-up."

"But she's still our mom. Don't you ever want to know, like *really know*, why she left?"

The muscles of his jaw flexed. "Nope. It doesn't matter. She could've stayed, but she didn't. That's all I need to know." He frowned at me, saw the wheels spinning. "Let it go, Meg. She wants no part of you. She's made that clear."

A plan formed in my mind. "But maybe she thinks we don't want to see her."

"I *don't* want to see her."

"Aren't you a little curious?" My words came out as a plea.

"No, not at all," he said. "Nina's the only mother we've ever had. Why don't you try and invest in your relationship with her?"

"Nina might have married Dad, but she's not a mother."

"She did the best she could. You didn't exactly make it easy for her."

"Hey, how did we end up on different sides?"

"We're not on different sides, Meg. Nina's on your side, too."

"Whatever. She dealt with us because we came with Dad, and that's the only reason why."

"That's more than the lady who gave birth to us ever did." His face was hard. "Look, I understand that you are under stress right now, but please do everyone a favor, and don't dredge up this shit from the past."

My brother's words wounded me. We'd been a team for so long; how could he not understand I needed a mom—a real mom?

"If you do, you're only going to hurt yourself and everyone who loves you. That includes Nina, whether you accept it or not." He spun back to his computer and tapped away at the keys, done with our conversation.

My brother, my twin. Opposite sides of the same coin and, no matter how we tried, unable to see the same view.

"I can't make that promise," I mumbled, slipping my swollen feet back in my shoes.

"Then you'll be alone with the consequences."

CHAPTER EIGHTEEN

I THOUGHT I WAS DREAMING WHEN I opened my eyes and Theo was standing at the foot of my bed. He watched me with a smile that reached his sparkling eyes. He looked recharged and animated, healthier than I'd seen him in many, many days.

"Are you ready?" He squeezed my ankle through the sheets.

I rolled onto my back and stretched.

He fell into bed next to me, pulled the covers back, and lifted my nightgown to expose my belly. His hands warm, his voice soft. "And are you ready, little baby? Today you will give us your secrets."

His joy proved too irresistible to ignore, and I laughed. "I can't believe you're here."

He raised an eyebrow. "I told you I would be. Today's our day."

I was drawn to the warmth of his body, so close to mine. Leaning into him, I placed my hand on his chest, feeling his heart race beneath my fingers.

His hand slid up to hold my cheek, his thumb brushing my lips. "I've missed this."

"I've been here," I whispered.

"I'm sorry I haven't." I looked into his clear, lively eyes. Maybe we'd turned a corner. He was truly present for the first time in weeks.

I wanted to ask if he was okay, but I also feared the answer. "Hey, don't be sorry," I told him. "It's okay. Everything is okay."

He rolled away from me. "Well then, get in gear, woman. Let's hit the road."

I showered and dressed for the appointment and found Theo in the kitchen with fruit salad, scrambled eggs, and biscuits. The fridge and pantry were stocked with so much food we wouldn't have to swing by the store for weeks.

"Why'd you get so much stuff?"

"I don't want to find you crying in your cereal again."

"Hmmm..." I checked the shelves of the pantry. "Cookies, donuts, potato chips. I think you're trying to make me fat!"

"Jake said that comfort food would pacify moody pregnant woman. He's bummed he's not allowed to give Ellie chocolate."

"If I get any more comfortable, I'm going to need bigger clothes again."

He came up behind me, slipping his arm around me. "You're getting more delicious," he growled lustfully in my ear. "But if you're worried, I can help you burn off extra calories."

Theo's enthusiasm continued to grow on the way to the doctor's office, until we arrived and he became quiet. Seven other pregnant women waited in the office, three of them with men by their sides. I did a quick ring check, discovering every woman in the room had one on their left ring finger, except me. A flash of guilt hit me, and I pushed it aside.

As people entered and left the waiting room, their stares would drift from me to Theo, to his missing limb, and away. I was amazed by the irony of people looking at what wasn't there. I took his hand in mine and wondered if he knew how protective I was of him.

He squeezed my hand and leaned in. "Are you nervous?"

I nodded, but my nerves had nothing to do with the ultrasound and everything to do with Theo. I couldn't wait to see my baby again. With all the other doubts floating around in my life, my love for my child kept me grounded.

A nurse called for me, and as Theo and I stood, the whole

room fell silent. Everyone watched Theo; even the nurse took an exaggerated step back, holding the door extra wide to accommodate Theo and his crutches. His eyes watched only me.

"Here we go." He winked.

I kept my focus on the nurse's shoes as we followed her to a room in the back.

"Hop up here." She waved to the table, and then she lugged a chair over for Theo. He thanked her.

"The technician will be in momentarily." She pulled the door shut.

I sat on the edge of the table and Theo stood between my knees. He framed my face with his hands and kissed me.

"I want to tell you what an honor it is for me to share this with you." He tucked a stray curl behind my ear.

"Theo—"

"I went from patrolling the streets of Baghdad to being a stranger in my own country. I returned to combat because if I didn't go to Afghanistan, I would've felt like I was shirking responsibility. Everything here seemed pointless. Over there I could *do* something and make a difference. The day we got blown up, I didn't just lose my leg. I lost the life I knew. The life I thought I wanted. But when I came home I found you. You make me want to be more."

"Theo, I love you," I blurted. I needed to say it. I needed him to hear it.

"I love you too, Meg."

The door opened and a woman in a lab coat walked in. She barely glanced at us as she moved around the table.

She got straight to business. "So we're here to see if the baby is going to cooperate with us today. Lie down for me." I did as I was told, never taking my eyes off of Theo, as she raised my shirt, tucked a small towel along the waist of my pants, and squeezed a glob of ultrasound jelly on me. While she tapped away at her machine, Theo stroked my hair away from my face. He tilted down to kiss me on my forehead.

"Thank you," he whispered. His tenderness moved me. I turned my head to kiss his palm. Oh my sweet, sweet Theo.

And then the magic started.

The technician put the device against my belly. "So today we're only doing a gender check?"

"Yes." *Come on, come on; let's go!*

Theo took my hand in both of his. "Hello, baby," he said to the screen.

"What is it?" I asked, looking from the woman to the screen.

The technician beamed. "There we go. You're having a girl. Congratulations."

Theo looked from the screen to me, his smile fierce. "A daughter."

"Oh," I inhaled with a sharp intake of breath. "Oh, baby girl." Tears slipped from my eyes, and Theo laughed as he wiped them away.

"She's beautiful," he murmured, his face close to mine.

"She's waving at us." I pointed to the screen. "Hi, baby."

"Look at her, look at her." Theo laced his fingers with mine.

My little girl took her foot with her hands and pulled it to her mouth. She spun around and wiggled and danced. I could feel her move as I watched. She was everything I never knew I wanted, and it was the best moment of my life. The whole world opened up before me.

The tech wiped my belly off and stood. While I sat up and fixed my shirt, she handed Theo a photo from the ultrasound. "Congratulations, Papa," she said, and his grin didn't even falter.

The door shut and he handed the photo to me. The image was of my daughter waving, and off to the side of her arm the tech had typed, "Hi, Mom & Dad."

CHAPTER NINETEEN

"WHO WOULD'VE GUESSED THAT THIS would become one of my favorite places to go?" Theo pulled into the parking lot of The Super Baby Depot.

"Why are we stopping here?"

"Because I want to do something I've never done before."

"And what is that?"

"I want to buy a doll." He got out of the car, slammed the door with too much force and came around to my side. He opened my door. "And a purse. A little girl needs a purse."

His enthusiasm was infectious, and I giggled. "She won't need one for quite some time, you know."

"Nonsense." He swept me to my feet and practically galloped across the parking lot on his crutches. He came back to me. "Come on woman, you can move faster than that." Theo circled around me and then walked alongside me to the door. He grabbed a cart, tossed one of his crutches in it, and took off down an aisle. He knew the layout of the store better than I did.

He led me to the baby toys and pulled a little doll with a pink dress and yellow hair off the shelf. He set it in the cart, looked at me funny, and then took an identical doll with brown hair off the shelf and placed it next to the first doll.

"Hey," he called to get my attention. "Pick something out for that little girl." He snapped his fingers and pointed at my belly and then at the rows of pink toys. At that moment, it clicked. We knew who we were shopping for. Looking around the store, the lights seemed brighter. I went to the wall, selected a soft flower rattle, and put it in the cart.

"Hey look." Theo held up a pink purse that had a fabric tube of lipstick and soft compact with it. "I told you so." He tossed it in the cart, laughed, and grabbed a pink toy cell phone. "She's going to need one of these."

"Oh, look at this," I said holding up a pink doctor kit.

"Get two—I want one for myself," Theo said with a wink.

We ended up with at least one of every pink item in the store. Pink was a color I'd never paid too much attention to, but now it screamed girl, girl, girl, with an anticipation I was only beginning to grasp. A daughter of my very own—how could I not be giddy? I picked out blankets and tiny jeans, and Theo found a dress he insisted we get and the sweetest little pair of booties.

I looked over our cart loaded with predominately pink and looked back, scanning the aisles.

"What'd we forget?" Theo asked. "Wait, I know. Come closer."

I stepped to his side, and he brushed the back of his hand against my cheek. I shivered, and he lowered his mouth to mine in a gentle kiss.

"I love you. I love this," he said. "What's the worried look for?"

I pointed at my belly. "What if she doesn't like pink?"

He let out a sharp bark of laughter, his smile going even wider. "You might be onto something. Let's go back and get one of those yellow trucks and a tool kit. We want to give her equal opportunities."

My heart swooned, and I hugged his arm. "Did I ever tell you how much fun you are?"

"You're not so shabby yourself," Theo said, and we headed back to the toy department.

The only dim spot in the day came when we stopped by

the baby carriers. Theo picked one up, and while attempting to try it on, he lost his balance. Catching himself on the cart, which wasn't strong enough to support his weight, he tipped sideways, slamming into the shelf with a loud bam. I caught the cart before it fell to the ground, and Theo steadied himself.

"Are you alright, sir?" a clerk asked loudly as he approached, arms out.

"Yeah, yeah." Theo spoke sharply, his face bright. He yanked off the carrier and chucked it on the shelf. "Come on, let's go," he barked.

He had hit the wall of fatigue. He didn't say anything as I handed his crutch to him, and he followed me silently to the cash register. His mood softened again when he joined me to put our things on the counter. He elbowed me out of the way when I went to pay.

"The next one's on you," he said and swiped his card.

"You've got to stop doing that."

"I'll do what I want—now, move over." He loaded the bags back in the cart before the cashier could help.

He whistled as we walked to the car, opened the door for me first, and then put the bags in the trunk. When Theo slid into the driver seat, he handed me a bag. I opened it to find the little blond- and brown-haired dolls.

He put his hand on my belly. "How's the little darling?"

I leaned into him, and we kissed a kiss that hit me like a sigh, until he pulled away and jammed the key in the ignition. "That's right, that's right, doctor's orders." With a fresh spark in his eyes, he threw the car in reverse, the tires squealing, and then turned the car around and took off for home.

Back at the condo, Theo made love to me. He fed me pancakes with sliced strawberries in bed. At some point, I caught the glaze in his eyes that gave away that he'd taken pain pills. But he made love to me again. We took a bath together and then lay in the dark whispering until we fell asleep in each other's arms. It truly was the best day of my life.

I woke up curved against Theo, his hand on my belly. The baby kicked, and Theo's hand moved.

"Hello," I said.

"Good morning." He kissed me behind the ear. "We've been hanging out together, waiting for you to wake up and join us."

Seven missed calls. I sat in the parking lot at work and scanned my phone. Ellie was the only call I made after the appointment. Two calls came from Steve, one from Chelsea, and the big surprise was the four calls from Nina. She knew nothing of the ultrasound and wasn't even checking up on me, although she inquired briefly at the end of her message. She wanted to make sure Dad was okay, mentioned she had mail for him, and asked how I was doing as an afterthought. I decided to wait to call her back. I had news to share.

I called Steve's house and Dad answered.

"Dad?"

"It's about time. You know we've been waiting, right?"

"I went to the doctor yesterday."

"And?" he asked.

"I hope you're okay with a granddaughter, because that's what the stork's bringing!"

"Well, that's perfect."

He hollered out the news to Steve, who responded with a whoop. I distinctly heard a woman's voice, hushed and mingled with his, in the background. I considered making a detour for a little recon mission. Who was he sharing my news with?

My phone rang.

"Hi Nina," I answered, in too good a mood to worry about her drama bringing me down.

"I know you're busy, but have you spoken to your father?" Nina's panicked tone stopped me in my tracks. She was never less than completely composed.

"Yes, I talked with him today. He's at Steve's."

"I know," she replied quickly. "I thought he'd be back by now."

"Is that what he said?"

"No, but he's never held a grudge this long before. He's being difficult."

A dull ache formed in my chest when I heard the desperation in her words. "Nina, I don't know what you want me to tell you."

"Oh, well. We'll work it out." Her voice took on a false bravado. "How is everything there?"

"I'm good. I found out I'm having a girl." I held my breath.

"How lovely. That's nice, dear. Your father must be thrilled." She sounded far off. "Look, don't tell him I called."

"Sure, I won't," I said, but she'd already hung up.

I unlocked the back door and headed to my office. I sat at my desk and stared at my phone. I had one more call to make about the baby. I contemplated whether he'd want to hear the news or not. My little girl gave a kick.

"He should know about you," I said and rubbed my belly. I dialed the number for the first time since I had called to tell him I was pregnant with his baby. He could turn his back again, but my daughter deserved to have her news shared with the man who had fathered her. I called him for her sake.

The phone rang once, I held my breath, and then it rang again. By the fourth ring I exhaled and decided I wouldn't leave a message.

He answered abruptly. "I've been wondering about you. How's everything?" His hushed words came out with a nervous inflection.

"Wonderful, Jason. I wanted to let you know I don't need anything, but I thought you had a right to know that it's a girl."
Silence.

And then the sound of children's voices filled the background. I heard him muffle the phone, mumble words to someone.

"Thank you for your call. That's good to hear. I'll be in touch. Goodbye, now." He hung up.

Stunned, I listened to the silence of the dead line.

I had no choice but to go on with my day. I did my part, and I willed myself to let Jason's reaction go. My thoughts kept returning to my dad and what he must've gone through when our mom disappeared. I'd never considered the dilemma he'd faced, having to explain that loss to us. I ached for my daughter. She would always long for the first man who decided she wasn't good enough to stick around for. I was going to have to figure it out. My daughter would not walk in a shadow of rejection.

I didn't let Nina bring me down, and I wasn't about to let Jason diffuse my joy either. As the store filled up and the news spread, the day turned into a celebration. Hazel brought out pink and white balloons from the story-time closet and filled them with helium. Dad and Steve rolled in shortly before lunch. Dad found the store aprons and put one on. Soon he was telling all the customers that his children owned the store, and his daughter was pregnant with his first granddaughter.

Hazel cornered me, sans filter, as usual, and asked if Bradley was excited.

"Hazel, this is not his baby," I snapped.

She gasped and covered her mouth with her hand.

"Humph, I better quit defending your honor then." She looked at me as though I'd betrayed her.

"Yes, that's not your job." I walked away, pleased I'd finally stood up to her. "And if you keep talking to me that way, you'll be defending your business in the unemployment line," I said over my shoulder.

Theo arrived for lunch and met Dad. We all trekked across the street to The Tavern. We sat at one of the larger tables, Dad and Steve across from Theo and me. Just as we were ordering, Hazel squeezed into the seat next to me.

"I'll have a Reuben and a Sprite-tini," she said to the waitress. "We're celebrating, so bring one for Meg, too—"

"Oh, no," I interrupted. "No, thank you."

"They're virgin." She put her hand over her mouth and giggled. "Just try one. Oh, and bring us a bowl of those green olives on the swords."

I glanced at Dad and took in his pleading look. "Fine, I'll drink a Sprite-tini with you."

Hazel put her cool hand on my arm when the waitress left with our order. "I'm sorry I said what I did about Bradley. I just thought you two were so good together."

I nodded. "Okay, just let it go."

Dad talked about the structure of The Tavern, and lunch was served. I absentmindedly sipped on my Sprite-tini and kept one hand on Theo's thigh. Just as we were leaving, Hazel pointed at my plate. There were six little plastic swords scattered on it. "I thought you might like those olives," she said with a gleam in her eye.

I looked at her questioningly.

"I have a way of diagnosing cravings," Hazel said, reminding me that she called herself the Mistress of Mystery for a reason. "Oh, and I knew you were having a girl because you're carrying that baby so high."

"Hazel, we work in a bookstore. Let's not get carried away with old wives' tales."

"Never mind, back to work." She grabbed her big purse and made a direct path to the door.

"What was that about?" I asked Dad.

He shrugged. "Ask her."

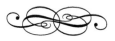

Theo blocked me in my office the minute we got back from lunch.

"What's on your mind?"

"What do you mean? I'm happy." Even I heard the unsaid *but...*

"Let it out. There's something rolling around up there, knocking up against you."

"I called Jason."

Theo's face got tight. "And?"

"He thanked me for letting him know."

"That's it?" he growled. "Why did you bother calling him?"

"Because he's the father," I said too quickly, and regretted my defensiveness. "Jason should know. I told him because that's the right thing to do."

"Don't talk about that guy and rightness in the same sentence. He's an ass for missing one minute of this with you. He hasn't checked in with you at all, has he?"

"No, and I wish he cared, *for her sake.*"

Theo pulled me to him. As he hugged me, his hand drifted to my belly. "This little girl will have everything she'll ever need without him."

"Will you be home when I get back?"

"Yeah, Cortez is going to stop by so we can finish up her room. Would you like to see the results tonight?"

"Yes!"

"We'll make tonight a night to remember," he promised, with a goodbye kiss.

CHAPTER TWENTY

THAT NIGHT I CAME HOME to find Theo and Cortez watching TV.

"You guys watch *Brooke and Bella?*" I asked when I recognized the reality show about two beautiful rich girls that go off to college, drop out, and end up in a halfway house battling addiction. At least that was the original premise of the show, but then Brooke got pregnant in rehab, and shortly after that, Bella did too. The show took off and became a megahit, with the draw of the grisliest train wreck. Millions of viewers tuned in each week as the girls' lives unraveled.

"We're hosting a book signing for them soon. Probably will be one of our biggest events this year."

Theo shot me a look. "Those dimwits wrote a book?"

"They had a ghost writer. Their management team had the idea they could put out self-help books, and the first one was an instant best seller. And actually, they have a second book coming out."

"Self-help? Seriously?" Theo shook his head, unable to take his eyes off the screen.

Cortez gave Theo the evil eye. "This isn't crap. Brooke and Bella are a couple of sophisticated babes. I don't care if they didn't actually write the book. I have to meet them," Cortez pleaded with me. "Will you introduce me?"

"Sure, come to the signing," I said.

Cortez glanced away while Brooke and Bella debated the merits of Manolos versus Louboutins. "Hey, wait! I almost forgot. The word on the street is our girl is having a girl." Theo's elbow shot out and jabbed him in the side. Cortez leaped away from him on the couch. "Hey man, watch it!"

Theo kept his eyes on the screen. "She's not our girl, and she's not your anything. She's my girl."

"No need to get in a pissing contest, man." Cortez looked back to me. "Congratulations on the good news. Sincerely."

"Thank you."

There came a sharp knock on the door, and Theo's eyes snapped up as if he could sense trouble on the other side.

Cortez laughed at the TV. "What's not to like about these two?"

I walked to the door, and opened it.

Jason.

He stepped in, eyes wide, mouth open, and put his hands on either side of my belly. "Would you look at that!" He slipped one arm around my neck, while the other hand continued to explore my stomach. Then he planted a kiss on my cheek.

I registered the rage in Theo's eyes. He pulled himself up on his crutches and made his way to us.

"Theo," I said calmly. "This is Jason."

"Get your hands off of her."

"Theo, it's okay."

Jason let go of me and extended his hand to Theo. Jason's smile froze as his eyes shifted down to take in Theo's leg situation, then Jason looked past Theo and cocked his head to the side, staring at Cortez's hook prosthetic, lying on the coffee table next to a beer.

"What's up?" Cortez stood and grinned.

Jason turned back to Theo just as Theo slammed a fist into his face. Stunned and reeling, Jason hit the floor, and I screamed. Blood splashed like scattered rose petals; brilliant drops of crimson arched out along the profile of his crumpled body. Jason cupped his nose gingerly, as blood continued to seep through his fingers. "You fucking animal," he said, his voice quivering.

Theo pressed the end of his crutch into Jason's chest.

"You don't come in here and put your hands on her."

"Okay, okay." Jason tried to push the crutch away, but it didn't budge.

"Theo, stop it." I went down on my knees to Jason. "Are you okay?"

"Call him off of me," he wailed. "Oh, you crushed my nose!"

I stood and put my hand on Theo's chest. "I said stop it. Get back from him."

Cortez moved to Theo. "Come on, man. Relax."

Theo took a step back, but his nostrils flared, and his breath hissed through his teeth.

"He's the *father*," I said to Theo, completely exasperated. "He has a *right* to check on her."

"He told you not to count on him, and that's the only promise he's kept."

"Hey, I'm here now." Jason shrugged. He looked at the blood on his hands. To Theo, he added, "I have a wife... and a family."

"Well, go take care of them. Meg doesn't need you."

"And she certainly doesn't need someone like you." Jason managed to put on an air of superiority, even sprawled out on the floor with blood dripping off his chin. Cortez sauntered back from the kitchen, tossing a dishtowel at Jason.

"What do you know about what she needs?" Theo snarled, lunging forward, only stopping when Cortez put his hand on Theo's shoulder.

"You're out of control," Jason said. "Meg's got a soft heart, but you can't be worth it."

"I would never hurt Meg. Damn you for suggesting she's not safe with me." He lunged at Jason again, and Cortez stepped between them.

"Stop, Theo," I snapped. "Cortez, get him out of here."

"Let's go, man," Cortez said.

"Meg!" Theo said in disbelief.

"I need to take Jason to the hospital," I said.

Theo's eyes darkened with anger. "I'll take him."

"No thanks, brother. I'm not getting in a car with you." Jason sneered at Theo. "Meg can take care of me."

"Unbelievable!" Theo roared with anger, but he moved when Cortez pushed him toward the door. Cortez gave me a slight nod and pulled it shut behind him.

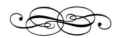

Jason and I sat in the waiting room of the Emergency Room and watched as people a lot worse off rolled through.

"Has it been hard?" he asked me. The words came out nasally, and he couldn't keep his hands off his nose. He had an ice pack in his lap, but instead of using it, he was busy poking at his nose and checking out his two black eyes with my Mac compact.

"Not as hard as I thought it would be."

"You think it's wise to have those guys hanging around? I know I don't have much to offer, but I still don't want to think of someone taking advantage of you. You said you'd call if you needed me."

"I don't need you, and those guys have been here for me. They've never wavered."

"Meg, I wish I didn't get you pregnant." He'd finally put the compact down and was watching me with a look that took me back to our shared youth.

"Don't say that now." Without a thought, my arms curved around our child, hidden under a curtain of fabric, protected by the layers of my flesh, thriving on the blood of my body. "I can't regret this anymore. This baby is wanted. I love her, Jason. I know this wasn't a plan, but I won't regret any of it. She is *not* a mistake in my life." I thought of Theo and all he'd done, all his excitement. I didn't need Jason. His friendly ways and charm kept me from getting angry with him, but the fact was, Jason never considered how his actions affected anyone but him. I had let him get away with everything, because he validated my secret fear that I didn't deserve to have someone love me with all his heart. Jason's actions gave proof that what I had to offer was not enough to make someone stick around.

"I'm glad. I'm glad for you. A part of me wants to go home and never come back. I know you don't need me. But that baby is mine." He shifted in his seat and stared at his shoes. Jason was better at leaving than staying. "I was hoping you'd be okay if I stopped in from time to time. You can tell the baby whatever you want. But I can't ignore that she came from me."

He was thinking of himself, not the baby. His ego kept him focused on what his needs might be and how he could fulfill them. The reality left a bitter taste. But I wouldn't erase Jason's existence from our child's life. She could form her own opinions of her father. Maybe she would deem him selfish, or possibly she would find him captivating, like I once did. But that would be her choice. For with every beat of my heart, knowing that the woman who brought me into the world was out there cultivating her own life with no desire to be a part of mine... It'd been devastating.

"We'll figure something out." I sighed, worn out from the highs and lows of my week. I forced optimism into my voice. "I don't want her to lose the chance to know you. Look, I'm sorry about your nose, but Theo's not going anywhere. You have no say in the matter."

Jason whipped his head up to glare at me, and his lip curled. "What could you possibly see in that guy?"

"He's amazing. He shouldn't have hit you, but you walked in, and you had your hands all over me. Imagine how you would feel." Even in the chill of the hospital waiting room, heat prickled my cheeks. I grabbed a battered copy of *Time* from the seat next to me and fanned my face.

"I didn't mean anything." Jason spoke in an insolent tone.

"When your wife was pregnant, how would you have reacted if an ex-lover came up and rubbed her belly?"

"Okay, you got me there. I'd want to kick his ass, but I wouldn't. We can't pretend we don't have a past."

"Doesn't mean anything."

"Really?"

"Come on, Jason. How many times have we walked away from each other? I want you to be a part of the baby's life. But when you come into *my* life you're a guest and nothing more."

"Ouch."

"Really. I've moved on. Cancun was as much my fault as yours. I shouldn't have slept with you, but I was still searching for answers from so long ago. I never got any closure, not with the way you left. I don't know why I still searched after all that time. It was stupid, stupid on my part."

"I'm sorry, Meg." He cradled his head in his hands and stared at the floor. He groaned. "My wife is going to kill me when she finds out about the baby."

"You haven't told her?"

"No, and I don't want to face it tonight. Can I crash at your place?"

"I'll be here when you get out," I promised, as the nurse came to take him back.

While Jason was getting fixed up, I called Steve and told him what happened.

"How do you always get yourself in a mess with that guy?" Steve asked.

"I don't know." And I really didn't. Was it Jason, or was I a magnet for trouble? As with every time before, I was certain I could make everything right for everyone. "So can he stay the night with you?" I asked. No way was I bringing him back with me.

"That's not a good idea, Meg."

"Please? I'll make it up to you."

"I do this, and you owe me, big time," Steve said.

"Fine. I have Theo at the condo, and Jason can't drive back to

Houston tonight. Once upon a time, you and Dad loved Jason. Just tap into that reservoir."

"Whatever." He covered the phone and mumbled to someone. At first I was surprised Dad would still be up so late, but then I heard the rustle of sheets and a woman's voice. Mystery girl was in his bed.

He came back on the line. "Sure, bring him by. But if you give me any attitude about anything when you get here, I'll kick you both out."

"Deal." I didn't care who he had in bed, other than looking forward to finally meeting her.

By the time Jason had his nose set and was ready to go, it was almost midnight. He looked nasty and probably felt worse. He wasn't too excited to crash at Steve's place. The last time they had seen each other was back in college when Jason and I were still an item, but their childhood friendship had already faded to dust.

Steve opened the door, wearing plaid pajama pants and nothing else. Behind him, in the plaid pajama top that came halfway down her thighs, stood Chelsea — my Chelsea — with bed-rumpled hair and a this-is-better-than-cake smile on her face.

"Chelsea? No, no, no." I turned back to Steve, and my brain snapped the missing pieces together. "Steve, how could you?" I stammered, looking from one to the other. "You are not allowed to sleep with my friends!"

"Keep your deal, or Jason's going back to your place." Steve took in Jason's appearance. "Man, you look like shit."

Chelsea threw a dispassionate glance at Jason, but rushed out on the porch to hug me. "Be happy for us," she murmured in my ear as she pulled me inside. "This is a good thing."

"Okay, okay. If it's so great, why didn't you tell me?" I scanned the front room, and the space seemed different. Dad's presence — his reading glasses on an end table, his shoes left under a chair, the newspaper folded haphazardly on the footstool — helped calm me.

"Because you expect everyone to follow your rules." Chelsea pulled my focus back on her. "And I didn't want to tell you. Anyway, *you* had secrets first." Her sweet voice sounded as childlike as the words she said. "This is between the two of us. We chose to see where this was headed before going public. Plus, all the hush hush of a secret lover—you're not the only one who gets off on that rush."

"Ew. Don't use the phrase 'getting off' when you're talking about Steve."

Chelsea rolled her eyes. "Come on back." She strutted down the hall to Steve's kitchen— the kitchen of my childhood— moving on tiptoe as if wearing invisible high heels, her bare legs sending me in a surreal flashback to when Nina moved in, before she married Dad. I flushed with a territorial heat, but the house I grew up in was no longer mine to claim.

"Don't be mad, Meg," Chelsea said when she looked back at me. I would never have placed my dark-haired, saucy friend with my blond jock of a brother. They didn't match in any way, and they had absolutely nothing in common.

"What do you see in him?" I didn't mean to imply Steve wasn't a catch, because he was. But I didn't think any of my friends were looking to reel him in. I wanted to see it from her angle.

"He's so sweet and funny and quite the romantic. Plus, he's amazing in the sack—"

"Stop!" I covered my ears.

"Fine. We'll talk about it when you're ready." Chelsea took my hands and squeezed them in hers. She spoke softly to me, "I make him happy. He's different with me than the other girls. You'll see." I stifled my groan but followed Chelsea back to the living room. I was done. The night had been long enough, and I was ready for a do-over.

Jason sat dazed on the couch next to a blanket and pillow. Since Dad was crashing in Steve's spare bed, Jason had to make do in the living room. His swollen face looked terrible, but from my experience with Theo and pills I could tell Jason was feeling no pain.

"See you later, Jason," I said on the way to the door.

He smiled at me and tipped over sideways onto the pillow, curling his feet behind him.

"It's late. Go home," Steve said. He put his hand on Chelsea's hip, pulling her close. "We'll take good care of him." He kissed the top of her head, before reluctantly letting her go and following me out into the starlit night.

"Did Theo cool off?" he asked.

"I don't know. He's not answering the phone." I shook my head. "I can't believe he broke Jason's nose."

Steve clutched his middle, laughing.

"What's funny?"

"I owe Theo a beer. I've been wanting to clock that guy good for years." Steve opened my car door. "I don't blame Theo. Go easy on him. He means well."

"I hope this means you'll be nicer to him."

"I've got nothing against the guy. I'm only looking out for you," Steve said.

"Well then, go convince Jason he deserved it, so he doesn't reconsider pressing charges against Theo."

"Don't worry about that. Jason will be put in his place in the morning. I'm very much looking forward to it."

Before I pulled out, Steve told me he'd drop Jason off at my condo in the morning, to get his car. I figured Jason would head home to his wife and weave some kind of story to explain the busted nose and black eyes. He needed to tell her everything, but I knew the truth could sometimes be so frightening you didn't know how or when to stop running from it. But those were his problems. I had issues of my own to contend with.

Driving along the quiet roads on my way home, I stopped at a red light and saw a man sleeping in the doorway of a church. He was filthy, his clothes stained with dirt and grime. He was somebody's baby. Where was his family? Why was he stranded?

His head rested on a backpack that I realized was identical to Theo's army pack. Theo had told me how many men came home from war to find out they had nothing worth holding onto. What an insult, to fight for your country—to be willing to give your life, a life surrendered to duty and honor—and after all the sacrifices, your world was you alone with your possessions only piling up high enough to rest your head on.

The man in the silver Volvo behind me honked, and I slammed my foot on the gas, jerking forward, my mind torn away from imagining an unknown man's desolation and back to the festering turmoil of my own drama.

Lost in my head, replaying the night while the rest of the drive home flashed by, I ended up parked in my lot, brooding. I finally left the car and walked across the lot with my eyes fixed on the condo door. My footsteps echoed, uncanny in the night.

I found Theo hunched over on the floor with a bucket of water, scrubbing away Jason's bloodstains. Five empty beer bottles lined the coffee table.

"Hi," I croaked, holding my breath, waiting for him to turn, wordlessly pleading with him to face me.

With a deep, shuddery breath, I edged around him and perched on the sofa to watch. How would we ever shake the gloom that settled all around? He scoured the floor, not daring a glance my way. Despite Theo's concentration on fixing the mess, his posture screamed of barely bottled rage. His jaw twitched. He clenched a bloodied cloth in his fist, drowning it in the steaming bucket, choking the excess water out of the limp rag, and he continued to scour.

"Theo..."

Pain etched his features, and his eyes slid shut.

I scooted a little closer to him. "You know, Jason has a right to know about the baby."

His eyes snapped open, and he gave me a curt nod.

"He's the baby's father, after all. It's only natural for him to be curious."

"*Absolutely,*" he said with an overly agreeable tone that sent the little hairs on the nape of my neck tingling. Still, he would not look at me.

"To be honest, I'm relieved Jason wants to be a part of her life." I was sure I could convince him—maybe even convince myself—that everything was fine. I looked down at my body, hugging my baby bump. "He *is* a part of her."

Theo dropped the rag in the bucket, wiped his hands on his shorts. "I'm very aware of that, Meg." Theo pushed the bucket and scrambled forward. He slid the bucket three feet across the floor and did a modified crawl to the bathroom with both hands on the ground, his single leg extended behind him. His crutches, propped against the sink, mocked us from ten feet away. Absentmindedly, I came up behind him and reached for the bucket.

"Don't you dare," he growled.

Stepping back, I cleared my throat and stared while he shuffled to his destination. He poured the rust-colored water into the toilet, tossed the rag in the trash, and sat on the edge of the tub to clean out the bucket. He reached for his crutches, pulled himself up, and washed his hands at the sink. After splashing water on his face, our eyes met in the mirror. I caught him soften for a beat, and then he seemed to look through me.

"Don't bother with the details." Theo toweled off. "I get it. He's the daddy."

"But that changes *nothing* between us," I said.

My mother's abandonment marred my childhood, my entire life. Not having my mother's love made it hard to believe I was worthy of anyone's love. I thought about telling Theo how it pulled me down and ripped me to shreds every time I spent the night at a friend's house or engaged in one of a billion activities that screamed: a mom should be there. But my mom was gone. How could I make Theo understand? This was my lot.

"Jason has nothing to do with you and me."

He looked at me as if I was crazy, moving past me to the laundry room. He scooped a load out of the dryer into a basket and kicked it across the room. Crutches forward, step, and kick basket onward. I followed him to the bedroom where his duffel bag loomed, half filled, on my bed.

"What is this?" I blurted, putting my hand to my head.

"I'm done with the baby's room. It's time for me to go. That was the plan." His words were spoken like a mantra; he hauled the basket of clothes up, dumping them in a pile on the bed.

Don't leave me.

"That was the plan?" My voice cracked, eyes burning, my vision blurred.

Finally, Theo touched me — he put his hand on my shoulder. "I lost control. I'm sorry... but I have to go."

"Put Jason behind us," I pleaded. "Don't go."

Theo gathered his folded boxers and tucked them in his bag. "He's behind me. His needs don't concern me, and I don't see why they concern you either."

"What about the baby's needs? She has a right to know the man she came from." My frustration flared, and I punched his arm so he would look at me. I needed him to see me. "I don't know what my mother looks like. I can't remember anything about her, and when I dream, I need to see her face. I want to know why — why she didn't love me enough to stay. I don't want my baby to have that kind of life."

"I know." Theo's exhaustion came through in his words. "I don't want that for her either." He continued to fold his shirts meticulously, filling out his bag.

"Don't do this." I touched his arm, and he flinched.

Don't leave me.

He moved to the bathroom with his travel bag in hand and loaded up his shaving cream, toothbrush, razor, and deodorant from the vanity. He zipped the bag and tossed it in his duffel bag. "Meg, I have to go. That's the way it is. I'm in the way, and if I stay, my demons will pull you down."

"That's not true!" I wailed, my throat raw. "I want you." I grabbed his arms, my fingers digging into his biceps, forcing him to look me in the eye. "I am not afraid of your demons — I am not afraid of you." And finally I let out what I always thought he knew. "I do not care about your leg!"

His face crumbled, his arms came around me, his head fell to my shoulder, breath quickening, deep gulps of air filling his lungs, and his chest heaved. "But I care." As though the words grounded him, he pulled back, composed. "You'll be fine." Theo's eyes filled with pain. "You're surrounded by people who care about you. If you need anything, go to Cortez."

"Where will you go?"

"I don't know yet."

"How can I get in touch with you?"

"I'll call you," he said. "Trust me — it's better this way. It will be harder the longer I stay."

"No Theo, don't do this to me. I love you. Don't leave."

He stopped and turned, took me in his arms, pressed his lips to my hair. I clung to him, scared at how fast he was slipping away. He pulled back. "I love you, too." He grabbed his bag and left me standing, broken, in the middle of the room.

I stared at the closed door for a minute, and then I went after him. I ran down the front walk. He reversed out of his parking spot, looking in the other direction, so he didn't see me rush toward him. He glanced my way as he took off toward the exit.

I stopped and cried out. "Wait!" But he picked up speed. Before he turned onto the main road, he looked into the rearview mirror. Our eyes connected, and then he pulled away.

CHAPTER TWENTY-ONE

W ITHOUT THEO, MY LIFE STILLED.
Days turned into weeks, with no word. If anyone
had contact with him, they didn't share. Relentlessly
aware of his absence, I was lost—disconnected. I walked by the
baby's room he promised he'd show me, never opening the
bags from our post-ultrasound shopping spree. I even avoided
driving past The Super Baby Depot. Without Theo everything,
other than the baby I carried, was a gaping void. He had to
come back to me. And at first, I believed he would.

Every few days Cortez would spring up. He'd appear at all
hours, never with any warning. Some days he brought food;
some days he simply came to talk. The days he hung out, not
giving or taking but simply being with me, helped the most.
Those times, I knew he ached too. Theo had been a constant
in his life. One day, Cortez admitted he knew where Theo had
gone but refused to tell me.

"How can you not tell me?" I asked, throwing our takeout
containers in the trash. "If I could talk to him—"

"No." Cortez crossed his one arm over his chest, his hook
hanging by his side.

"I can make him come back. I know you want that too."

"No," he repeated calmly. "You can't *make* Theo do anything."

"Okay." I nodded, tightness in my chest making my breath shallow. "Don't tell me next time."

"What?" Cortez's eyebrows shot up.

Finally, my safety net kicked in: I got pissed. People who walked away didn't come back. "Don't tell me about Theo." I stood a little taller. "If you hear from him again, I don't want to know."

Theo was gone. I had to carry on.

So I went through the motions of work, kept Ellie preoccupied, and masqueraded for my friends that all was well, that I had moved on. But alone in the dark—or even worse, when I first lifted my eyes at dawn—in those moments, my heart would detonate.

Theo's mother was the one person I didn't bother being strong around. She had that way with me. She continued to drop by every week with dishes from the church ladies, insisting the women wouldn't have it any other way. Splitting the meals—packaged in smaller portions—between the fridge and freezer, her presence gave me a taste of an affectionate mom. She took over, ready to nurture.

"We'll get you all stocked up," she said, both of us ignoring the fact I couldn't eat all that food by my lonesome. "When that baby gets here, you won't need to cook." She smiled sadly at me, her eyes glazed over, and she turned to fold the bag that held the meals.

"I don't know how to not miss him," I confessed. "But I'm so *mad* at him for giving up."

Melinda sat across the kitchen table from me. She folded her hands neatly on the table and leaned in. "You know, when I got that call, that call informing me Theo was hurt, they didn't have any details for me. I promised myself that as long as he was still Theo, we'd be okay. He's always been a fighter, Meg. All I needed was for him to still be my Theo, and we could figure out the rest. I was terrified for him. I went to see him. I paced the hospital before the plane got there. They said he'd been sedated for the trip home... he might not remember...

anything," Melinda sighed. "I was told he might not remember me, but when he opened his eyes and saw me, he mouthed 'Mom,' just once. Don't give up on Theo. He'll find his own way back to us."

She handed me a quilted baby blanket she had made with the softest of pink and yellow fabrics. She said she ached for her son and prayed for him, but she knew he was a man capable of taking care of himself. She gave me the note he'd sent her. It simply said, *Don't worry, I'm getting better.*

The note gave her hope, but all I saw was a man trying to comfort his mother with a fragile promise.

Jason became a steady presence in all our lives when he finally came clean to his wife about the baby. He hoped the broken nose surrounded by two black eyes would barter a reprieve from her outrage. No such luck. She packed him up and threw him out. Jason landed back at Steve's, garbage bags loaded down with balled-up clothes, hangdog expression on his face.

To my surprise, Steve allowed Jason to stay.

I couldn't stand the emptiness of my condo without Theo, and I gave in to the incessant invitations to gatherings at Steve's house.

Once, I drove up at the same time Jason's wife was loading the kids back in the car after a visit. She screeched her tires as she pulled away from the curb, giving me the finger, with her other hand pressed on the horn.

"Don't mind her," Jason said from the front porch where he watched, laughing. "That's for show. She's not as mean as she looks."

"Yeah, right," I muttered, looking over my shoulder to make sure she didn't circle back.

Jason whistled a happy tune to himself the rest of the afternoon, glowing with lifted spirits because of the brief, volatile visit from his wife. Jason and I got along great. But he thrived on the dose of crazy his wife flung around.

"Maybe you should invite her in sometime. Ask her to stay for dinner," I said.

His eyes lit up. "Too nice, as always. You know she'll eat you alive."

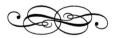

Later, at home, I found a message waiting on my answering machine. Upon hearing Nina's voice, I walked away without listening. I didn't want to be reminded that another day had passed without him calling.

I woke up too soon the next morning. I wasn't planning to go into work until later in the day, and I wasn't ready to face hours alone. Someone pounded on my door. I bolted up, hoping *he* might be home, but when I swung the door open, I stared into Nina's face. She looked every regal inch of her five-foot-nine height, in spiked crimson heels undoubtedly selected to accent her black Stella McCartney suit. Her white-blond hair was swept up in a tight twist, and she held an envelope clutch. Nina sashayed past me, moving with the grace of a giraffe.

"You're not ready?" She eyed the top of my rat's-nest hair then moved down to my unpolished toes. "Oh dear, you're a walking crisis. This is worse than I expected, even from *you*."

"Why are you here?" I was too shocked to be polite. I wanted to collapse onto the sofa, but that would be a vulnerable position with Nina in the room. As far as I knew, Nina only reclined for a massage. Even when she slept, she propped herself up — she'd never risk wrinkling her skin by resting her face against a pillow.

"Oh my word, you're enormous!" Nina stopped in her tracks. Her eyes took in my pregnancy, which she had not yet seen, and the look on her face was one of disgust. "Is that what you're wearing?" What she really meant was, that's *not* what you're wearing.

With no fight left in me, I stared at her.

"Don't you check your messages?" She handed me a sheet

of paper, and then she headed to a barstool, inspected the seat, and changed her mind about sitting.

Nina and I had scheduled a day of planning and shopping for the baby shower that Ellie and I would have together. Like always, Nina had managed to take over. She had offered to help Ellie do whatever she wanted, but that really meant whatever Nina wanted, which she'd then say was Ellie's idea. Whatever. I didn't care about the shower, didn't need the fuss, and only played along for Ellie's sake. The only thing—I had my day with Nina on the calendar for the next day.

"What's this?" Rubbing my eyes, I looked over the page she'd handed me.

"Our itinerary. We have much to cover if we're going to plan everything this weekend." The corners of her mouth pulled down. "I left you a message." She crossed her arms under her chest, causing her implants, the only part of her body that wasn't a hard line, to bulge up. "I told you I'd be here today. We're shopping. Go get ready." She started walking across the condo toward the baby's room. "I'll check out the nursery."

A wave of panic shot through me. "No!"

She stopped and turned with eyebrows raised.

"I don't want anyone to see it before it's ready." I pressed my lips together, facing her head-on. I couldn't even make myself look. I kept waiting for the urge to go in there, but it never came. Theo might have made the room for the baby, but the room was his. I couldn't bear to face the other side of that door without him. I wouldn't be able to go in there and not think of him. I crashed against thoughts of Theo with every breath of each day. I knew the other side of that door would be the place I'd lose my fight.

Nina studied my face for a minute. "I need to see the room to make sure whatever I buy coordinates."

"If it's pink it will match fine," I said automatically, although I had no clue if that was true.

She cocked her head to the side. "Are we talking salmon? Bubblegum? Fuchsia?"

I cleared my throat. "Pink... baby pink."

"I should've known you wouldn't go with something original for your baby's room. Don't be embarrassed." She gave a brittle smile. "I'll send my designer over to help."

"No—no. I want to do it my way." Not good words to use with someone whose sole purpose in life was to control people. I tugged at my sweat pants to draw her attention away from the baby's room. "How about I throw something on so we can get going?"

Nina looked me over again and grimaced. "There's no rush. Do what you need to do to pull yourself together."

"Everything doesn't have to be ready in the next two days," I said, looking over the micromanaged weekend she had plotted out for me. "We're going to a salon? What for?"

"Do you even own a mirror?" She all but snarled at me. "When people care enough about you to show up for an event in your honor—an event you're hosting with a dear friend—you have a responsibility to sparkle. I bet you don't even remember the last time you got a pedicure."

I did remember. About a month before Theo left, back when times weren't so prickly, he'd painted my toes early one morning. I'd wanted to wear sandals, but my polish was chipped. I could reach my toes, but only with effort.

"Give me those feet," he had said.

"You can't be serious," I'd replied, but he was. He took the polish from me. The bottle looked tiny in his oversized hands. He pulled my feet into his lap, spending time—too much time—on each toe. He was quiet, paying close attention to detail. I pictured him then, far off in a spectacular kind of hell, running toward the dying. He was gallant enough to try to save someone's life, but the fact that he'd done so while under attack was hard for me to absorb. He'd made it out alive, and I was lucky to know him, to have him holding my feet, painting my toes.

"How'd I do?" he'd asked when finished.

"Perfect. Ridiculously perfect."

Nina snapped at me. "Time's wasting. Go clean yourself up." She pulled her Blackberry out of her purse and disappeared into her own little world.

I almost made it to my room when she called me back. "Meg?"

I noted the hesitation in her voice. Nina was normally sure about everything. She tucked her purse back under her arm and held her compact up. Tilting her face in the light, she powdered her nose. "How's your father?"

"He's good." I watched her coat her red lips with another layer of lipstick. "Have you called him?"

She nodded, returning her makeup to her bag. She sat down on the edge of a chair and crossed her legs. Folding her long fingers together, she propped them on her knee. "He doesn't answer my calls. He doesn't call me back." Nina and defeat was not a mix I was familiar with. However, having a man not return phone calls was something I knew all too well.

"That sucks."

She met my eyes. "Yes, it does." She nodded her head. "It does suck." Her face puckered momentarily, and then her eyes lit up. "Let me do something at the bookstore."

"What do you want to do?" She'd never made an effort to visit us there, so I didn't trust her sudden interest.

"Well, if your dad's working there, I can too, right?" She stepped closer to me. "I'll do whatever you want. After all, it's a family business and I'm family, regardless of whether your father answers my calls or not."

Too tired to deal with her, I said the only thing I could think of. "Check with Steve. He's in charge of staffing."

She pulled out her phone, dialing, and I walked away.

Whenever I spent time with Nina, I always made sure to look my best. To her it mattered, and I never wanted to give her reason to put me down. But that morning, I was not so perky, and I didn't have it in me to put on a show. I pulled on maternity jeans and a roomy tee, threw my hair up into a bun, and slipped on flip-flops—a true footwear fashion crime. Nina's judgmental beat-down didn't scare me. I already felt like crap; I might as well spend the day with someone who would make it worse.

198

Inhaling, I rushed past Nina to the door, intent to get going, to get the mission over with, hoping she'd follow along. But she was not a follower.

"You ready?" Turning back to her, I was unable to read her. Another perk of the Botox—she had an effortless poker face. "What?" I asked, unable to wait out her stare.

"You look..."

Heat rushed to my face, a snappy reply ready on my lips.

"Quite gorgeous," she finished definitively.

The flush of anger washed out of me.

"What?" she asked. "I'm serious—women spend a fortune at the dermatologist to make their skin look as good as yours." Her eyes went to my belly again. I couldn't blame her; I was huge. "How fantastic to not have to hold it all in."

At those words, the giggles came. First mine, then Nina joined me, and for the first time in weeks, I felt light.

In my haste to get Nina to quit barking at me, I forgot to call Ellie to warn her. But with Ellie on extended bed rest, I spent so much time at her place that she was used to me stopping by unannounced. Jake was at work, so as usual I knocked and let myself in.

"Ellie, it's me," I yelled when I stepped in. "And Nina too."

Ellie's head popped around the corner from the kitchen. "Why are you here?" She looked strange out of bed. She looked guilty.

"Nina came a day early. What are you doing? You should be in bed." In the kitchen the fridge was opened wide, all the contents covered the table and counters. Refrigerator racks soaked in a steaming bubble bath in the sink. "Oh no, you don't want to make yourself go into labor," I said. Then it came together. "That's what you're trying to do, isn't it? Get back in bed!"

Nina stepped in then. "Ellie, you're gorgeous, dear. Show me your room—Meg will take care of this." To Nina's credit, Ellie listened and went with her.

I put everything away. Back in her room, Ellie lay propped

up in bed looking exhausted. Nina sat at the edge of the mattress, holding her hand, looking conspiratorial.

"We'll get through this," Nina said. I rolled my eyes at Ellie, but she smiled at Nina.

"Thank you," Ellie said to her. "It means so much to us."

"What's going on?" I asked.

"We decided I will throw the baby shower," Nina said. "For both of you. Email me your invitation list. Let me know where you registered, and I'll do the rest." Nina stood. "I know the perfect caterer. I'll contact my party planner. This will be the baby shower of all baby showers." She beamed. The woman clearly needed a project, and I was in no mood to plan a baby shower anyway. What a relief; for once my stepmother's control-freak ways paid off.

"I have to make some calls." Nina snatched her clutch off the bedside table. "Ellie, it was lovely to see you, as always. Meg, I'll be in the kitchen when you're ready to depart." She glanced at her watch. "We have to be at the salon in one hour." She strolled out of the room.

"Are you okay with that?" I asked, kicking off my shoes and slipping under the crisp, clean covers. Maybe I was relieved about the party, but Ellie loved to plan things, and she had nothing but time on her hands. Nina had that way of making people bow down to her demands, and I wasn't going to let her bully Ellie.

"Sure. It's not like I'm going to get anything done in bed."

"I know I've been wallowing about, but it's pretty pathetic when we're both feeling sorry for ourselves."

"I'm sick of sitting in bed, waiting."

I laughed.

"It's not funny."

"Oh yes it is," I said. "You're sick of waiting in bed, and all I want to do is hide in bed because that is the only place where I feel close to him. I'm sick of waiting too."

"He called."

Every muscle in my body tightened, and I bolted upright. "When?"

"This morning, early. I was going to tell you."

"Tell me what? Where is he? Is he back?"

"Meg, I don't know. Theo didn't give me details. He said he was busy, and he asked about you."

"That ass." I balled my fist tight, slammed them onto the comforter.

"I know."

"I miss him." My throat ached, and I pushed down the burn of tears that wanted to rip free. "I want him back."

"Meg, he was never really here. He's going through too much. You can't hold onto him." Ellie put her hand on my belly. "You have to focus on her."

"That ass."

"I know," Ellie said.

"What am I going to do with Nina? I don't want to hang with her all day."

"Surrender. Have a girl's day. She needs you, too, you know."

"Whatever."

"Seriously, cut her some slack," Ellie said. "She's troubled. I've never seen Nina lack direction like this."

"What are you talking about?"

"She looked sad, I think? Her face moved a little. She might have been frowning. Something's not right. She misses your dad, but it's more than that. She's not right."

"I'll figure out what's going on. It's going to be a long day. Promise you'll stay in bed?"

"Yeah, but come back later, so I can see how pretty your hair is."

"It's a deal."

Nina prattled on about the party and then about how Steve had told her she could help out with the upcoming Brooke and Bella event. Nina was a fan; who knew? She went on and on the whole way to the salon. I tuned her out and thought about

Theo's call to Ellie. I wanted to feel hopeful that someone had finally heard from him, but why didn't he call me? How could I have been so stupid as to think what we had was different, that I'd found a man who knew how to commit to a woman?

By the time we pulled into the salon, I was seething. My anger coiled inside me so tight I thought I'd shatter.

I sat on a sofa while Nina checked us in. When she sat down next to me, I grabbed a hair magazine and flipped the pages blindly.

"You're mad," Nina said.

"I am," I snapped back.

Nina pressed her fingertips into her temples. "I couldn't stop myself. I love taking over, but I should've stopped myself," she said quietly. "I'll apologize to Ellie. You girls do whatever you want. I'm sorry. I hope I'm still invited to the party."

"I'm not mad at *you*, Nina. I'm mad at myself."

"Tell me, Meg. I know I'm not a natural at this mom stuff, but I'll try." Her hands rested, neatly folded, in her lap. She sat rigid on the plush sofa, every joint stiff, shoulder back, head held high. "Plus you'll be confiding in the right person. I'm an expert at efficiently harboring self-inflicted hostility."

I looked at her. "It's this guy."

"Stop right there." She strolled across the salon to a bridal party sipping champagne as they had their wedding hair done. Nina stepped to the middle of the group and did a slow turn until she had everyone's attention. Soon the group was laughing with her. A minute later she walked back, a bottle in one hand, a glass in the other.

"Are you ladies ready to head back?" A thin woman with red and orange dreadlocks waved us down the dimly lit hall. She sat us at a station, and someone rushed over with a chair for Nina.

Nina gave explicit orders for what needed to be done with my hair, and someone brought me a glass of water with lemon and mint suspended in the ice. After making sure it was okay for the baby if I had color done, I was content to submit to my stepmother masterminding my makeover.

The stylist left to prepare our color, and Nina returned her focus to the champagne. "Go ahead and tell me about this guy." She popped the cork and filled her glass with bubbly. "Start at the beginning."

So I told her everything. I talked about holding onto Jason, and how I duped myself into thinking that by sleeping with him again I could prove to myself I'd moved on from the past and Bradley. I talked about standing by Bradley even though I was lost and alone in our relationship.

And then I told her about Theo.

"I wasn't going to fall for it again," I proclaimed to Nina. A hairstylist slathered chemicals onto strands of my hair and wrapped it in foil, while Nina downed her champagne. "I promised I wouldn't let it happen, but it did. I fell in love. When Theo came along, I couldn't resist."

"And he left you... like all the others did," Nina said.

"Well, first he backed away. He'd been pulling away for some time. But things got better after the ultrasound. I thought we'd make it. I believed in Theo."

"Do you think he wasn't that into you?"

"No, he said he loved me. He *showed* me he loved me. At first I thought he wouldn't get close to me because of his own problems, but his excitement about the baby was genuine. He did her room. He was about to reveal the room when Jason showed up." The stylist set a timer and wandered away. "Theo was pissed I'd called Jason with news about the baby."

"Well that's understandable," Nina said, placing her hand delicately over her mouth in an unsuccessful attempt to muffle a burp. "Theo can't pretend it's his baby if Jason is present. It's a reminder that you had a life before him."

"That's silly. We both had a life before."

"And what did he do before he met you?"

"He was on active duty in Afghanistan," I said.

"Being in the army is not a life you simply walk away from. He's probably living it on some level every day. He looks at you, and if he really cares for you, then it probably tears him up that baby is not his."

"How do you know so much? You and Dad have been together forever."

"Yes, but my mother got me a new daddy every two years," Nina said, and I realized she'd had way too much to drink. Nina, Mrs. Self-Possessed, sat relaxed. She was ready to open up.

With two tons of foil folded up on my head and miles of vinyl draped around me, I sat still. "You don't talk about your past," I said, a gentle reminder for her to keep it to herself.

"Well, it's not a beautiful story, more like one of those sinister fairy tales you're so into. Sometimes the men were nice enough. A few I got attached to." She sighed and extended her foot, inspecting her shoe. "I also had to deal with rotating siblings. I counted once. I've had eleven different stepbrothers and sisters. Not a single one I still talk to, not even the stepbrother I shared a bed with for six months in high school."

"Oh." I didn't know how to respond.

"Thankfully, my mother didn't reproduce after me. I was her one slip-up."

"I'm sure it wasn't like that," I said to reassure her, although I had no idea. Her mother died right after Nina moved in with us.

"Oh it was like that. She never let me forget how I ruined her body, how she had great plans before I came along." Nina downed the rest of the champagne in her glass and reached for the bottle. "But life is about learning, and my mother taught me many things." She filled her glass halfway, drank a few sips, and then added more before returning the bottle to the table. "Like, to stay calm when a man's interest fades."

"Dad loves you, Nina."

"He doesn't answer the phone when I call. He won't even say hello." She licked her lips really slowly. When she finally looked up at me again, she gave me a sad smile.

"I'm sorry." I said. "It's all my fault."

"It has nothing to do with you."

"But you're embarrassed about the baby. He wants to retire and move here, and you don't."

"Well, I *was* embarrassed you didn't tell me about the baby.

I'm embarrassed by my response to this..." She waved in the general direction of my midsection. "I don't know how I'm supposed to act."

"It's okay — nobody does."

"When I met your father... when I came to work for him, he was so good to me. I changed everything about myself because he deserved the best. He was always so happy with me. I did anything I could to make him proud. I was his advocate, his partner, but most of all I was his wife. I married the best man I'd ever met. Where I come from, it doesn't usually work that way."

"Dad's lucky to have you. You two are good together."

"The thing is, I worked so hard to create this life, this image, and I don't know who I'll be if I retire. I'm not ready to quit," Nina said. "I need to be in demand. And I love the rush of it all."

"So why not let him retire, and you keep working?"

"That would be fine, but my career is not here. He wants us to move. I'd have to start all over, and I don't know if I can do that. What if I don't make it on my own? And look at how I failed you as a mother. I'm not exactly grandmother material."

"You didn't fail me. Don't say that. I'm not mother material, so I know how you feel. Maybe we can figure this out together."

The stylist came by and checked under a sheet of foil. "Are you ready?"

I followed her to the sinks and reclined. While she washed my hair I thought about Nina. How strange to think of her as being a separate person from Dad. I knew Dad without Nina, but I never knew Nina without Dad, at least not in a good way.

After a cut and blowout, I was led to Nina, who was already at the nail station. Her eyes were glazed over, and she stared off into the distance. Her feet soaked in a tub of water. Nina saw me coming. "Have a seat." She pointed to the tub of steaming water waiting for me, next to her. "Amazing, your hair is gorgeous." She poured the remaining champagne into her glass.

"Thank you, you made my day," I said truthfully.

"The only thing better than retail therapy is a makeover."

With a wistful look she said, "Trust me, when I'm not working on work, I'm working on me."

"Things will come together with Dad."

"Well maybe things will work out with you and Theo, though after the pain he's caused you, I'm sure you can do better. You deserve to be cherished."

While my feet soaked, a nail technician sat on the floor in front of us and washed Nina's feet. I relaxed, and enjoyed relating to Nina for the first time. She wanted me to confide in her, so I did.

"I'm stuck, Nina. I'm in love with him. I want a life with him." I frowned. "Why do I do this? Why do I keep falling for men who don't want me?"

"Well, my shrink would say you seek out a variation of the imprint your mother left on you."

I considered what she'd said. "That's kooky, but what else would your shrink say?"

"She would say you choose men who hurt you because deep down you think you should be punished. Your mother neglected you and left you. You subconsciously believed you got what you deserved. Because you never worked through those feelings, you choose men who validate this belief. You buy into the lie that you're not worth it, because if you were, your mother would've stayed." She brought the glass to her mouth for another hefty sip. "I shouldn't drink this much. Loose lips will sink ships." She giggled and wiped her chin.

"No, keep going. I didn't know I could blame my mother for everything wrong in my life. I like your shrink. Why didn't I figure this out on my own?"

"Well, it's obvious, isn't it?" Nina asked.

I shook my head, a wave of nausea rolling through me.

"You have to vilify your mother to blame her. You can't do that. She's an angel—perfect, but you can't see her. You don't remember how she hurt your father. But by being loyal to her, you're hurting yourself. She left you. You have a right to get angry. It's the healthy thing to do."

"Whatever."

"See, you resist, but on some level you know it's true. Instead, you blame yourself, you make excuses for Steve's inability to commit, and you pity your father for being married to me."

"That's ridiculous," I said.

"And you project your anger and judgment on your evil stepmonster. I can accept it; I know my place, and I can take it. But if you want to be a good momma to this baby..." She poked me in the side of my belly. "If you want to have the life you deserve, then you should quit projecting all your pain in the wrong direction and put it where it belongs."

"What do you know? You've never been a mom." Nina didn't even flinch. Damn her for crossing the line. "My mother didn't neglect me."

"When was the last time she called to check up on you? Has she ever sent you a birthday present or even a note in the mail, just to say hi? That woman neglected you. My shrink would say you are in a world of denial. You must accept it to change."

"Boy, this was fun. You should play shrink more often." I dried my feet off and stood. "I have to pee." I stalked off.

She shouldn't trash my mom. She had no idea why Mom left. None of us did. I had let my guard down with Nina for one afternoon, and she ripped me apart. I splashed cold water on my face, considered that she might be right, and the truth tore through me. The bathroom door opened behind me, and Nina walked in barefoot.

"I just got a call," she said. "They're crowning me idiot of the year." She came up and hugged me. "I'm such a jerk—sorry."

Normally I would push her away, but for once I held on. "It hurts because you're right."

"If you think about it, we have a lot in common."

"Men we care about ditch us and don't respond to our calls?"

"Well, that, but it's our mothers. We survived women that couldn't show love. My relationships with men echoed that until I met your father." She went to the mirror and smoothed back her hair. "Marrying him was a victory over my past. I broke through the dark cloud my mother had left over me." She took out her compact and powdered her face, glancing back at me as she spoke. "But where I failed is, I couldn't figure out how to be a good mother to you guys because the only example I had hurt me. So I stopped trying."

"I'm sorry I said you're not a mom. You're the only mom I've ever had. We've had... moments."

"And I'm sorry I got carried away playing shrink. I didn't mean to cause you pain. I don't want you to hurt. Don't make the mistakes I did. Why don't I set you up an appointment with my therapist? She's a doll. I love the freedom of paying someone so I can talk about myself for a whole hour. It'll be good for you."

"No, no. You did a good enough job. I'm all shrinked out." I smiled. "Let's go get pretty."

After we had our nails done, Nina treated us to massages. I finished first and dressed, ready to go when they came to get me. Nina was asleep on the table, and they couldn't wake her. I found her keys in her purse and pulled the car up front. They helped get her loaded in. She snored all the way back to the hotel and came around enough to wobble to her room sandwiched between the doorman and me.

"Please stay with me. I'm tired of sleeping alone," Nina said.

"Don't worry — I'm here," I said, tucking her into the fluffy white comforter. I stretched out next to her. Comforted by the warmth of her, I fell into a deep sleep.

CHAPTER TWENTY-TWO

"WAKE UP, WAKE UP," NINA chirped. The sun sparkled bright in the room, creating a glowing halo around Nina's shiny blond hair. "Time to take you home, so I can head back to Houston."

"But you still haven't seen Dad." I sat on the edge of the bed in my rumpled, day-old clothes, but when I caught my reflection in the floor-to-ceiling mirror, I saw that my hair looked fantastic.

"He doesn't want to talk to me." Nina had her game face on. "C'est la vie! What's a girl to do?"

"I'll talk to him," I vowed.

"What's the point? He's tuning me out." She bowed her head and pinched the bridge of her nose. "Are you ready?"

Back at my place, Nina gracefully slid out of the car and came around to me.

"What are you doing?" I asked. "Do you need to come in?"

"No, I need a hug." She wrapped her thin arms around me, and her chin dug into my shoulder. "Thanks for staying with me last night."

"Sure. And thank you for taking over party plans for Ellie and me."

She gripped my arms and pulled back. "You sure about all that?"

"Of course! I wouldn't have it any other way." I forced a smile onto my face to sell my words, but truth be told, if not for Ellie, I'd have skipped the whole thing.

"Oh Meg, I will do right by you girls! Just wait... I can't wait!" She ran back to get in her car as fast as her tight pencil skirt and high heels would let her. "Bye dear! Take care of yourself!"

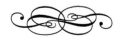

The smell of fresh coffee greeted me even before I entered Steve's office. "You'll never believe what happened yesterday." I pushed the half-open door.

Instead of Steve's smiling face, I discovered Dad and Hazel, sharing coffee and giggling. My father seemed plenty cozy with a woman who made my skin crawl. Disappointment at my sudden intrusion showed in their faces, and my instinct was to retreat, but Nina's resolve in the face of loneliness had given me a new empathy for her.

"So what happened?" Hazel asked eagerly.

"What are you doing in here?" I snapped.

"Meg—" My father's tone carried a warning. "We're having coffee, dear. Don't be rude."

And there I was, compromised between my dad telling me to be a good girl and my employee pushing boundaries. Pulling in a sharp breath, I told them both, "You're welcome to sit in the staff area, but I can't allow employees to sit in the management offices drinking coffee."

Dad opened his mouth, ready to give it to me, but Hazel put her hand on his knee. He smiled at her, reached for both cups, and said, "Why don't we take this to the bench out front and enjoy the fresh air."

"We need to talk, Dad."

"I'm with Hazel now. We'll talk later."

"Talk to her, Mike," Hazel said. "I'll go keep the bench warm." She left without giving Dad a chance to stop her.

"What's the problem, Meg?"

"What are you doing hanging out here and leaving Nina home alone?" I kept my voice level with effort. "At least give her a call."

"I'm not ready to go home yet. I'm having fun with my kids."

"At Nina's expense?" I didn't want to know the truth, but I couldn't drop it. "What's with all the attention on Hazel? She's ten years older than you."

"Hazel needs a friend. Being alone is hard."

"Like I don't know that!" I said.

"What is this really about? You have never been alone."

"Be careful, Dad. She's not your friend. She's my employee."

"She's both."

"Nina's alone."

"Listen up, little girl. Nina can take care of herself." He spoke softly, but when he called me "little girl," it only meant one thing: His temper was rising. "I've respected your privacy, Meg, and you will respect mine. You're being a hypocrite, pointing your finger at me with Hazel and questioning how I treat my wife. Let's talk about the mess surrounding you. Should I count the men I see? Have I asked you to explain?"

"Dad!"

"I don't ask, because I don't need to know. I'll call Nina. Don't trouble yourself with it." He pushed past me out of the office. "And don't be so hard on Hazel. She's a nice lady."

I went to the office and shut the door. What was my world coming to? Nina and I had bonded for the first time after twenty years together, and my dad was pissed off at me. No sooner did I sit down than my phone rang.

Ellie's number showed on the caller ID. "What's up?"

"Come over as soon as you can," she said in a rush, her tone light and giddy. "I have something to show you."

"Okay, on my way." I grabbed my purse. A visit with Ellie would ground me after all the craziness of the last twenty-four hours. Or so I thought.

Jake was home, so I knocked instead of letting myself in. A woman in a maid's costume opened the door. The tall woman, built like a refrigerator, wore a black, knee-length dress with puffy sleeves and a white apron. Her skin was the color of melted caramel and looked soft everywhere except on her pink, chapped hands.

"Can I help you, ma'am?" she asked.

"Yes, I'm here to see Ellie."

The woman pulled out a walkie-talkie. "Mrs. Ellie, you have company."

"Thank you, Marta. Send her back," Ellie's voice crackled through the walkie-talkie.

I followed the woman back. We passed the kitchen, where Jake sat reading the newspaper, toast in one hand, fork digging into an omelet in the other hand. I smiled at him, and he winked back.

"This breakfast rocks, Marta. Thank you," he said, waving his toast like the flag of victory.

"Yes, sir."

"Please call me Jake."

"Yes, sir," she said again.

After she left me with Ellie, I shut the door.

"Where did you find her?"

"Nina sent her! I told Marta she could wear sweats to work, but she insists she wants to wear the uniform. She's amazing! Can you believe Nina did that?"

"No way." How did Nina arrange it so fast?

"I called to thank her, and she made me promise to stay in bed. She said Marta will do all my nesting for me." Excitement pinked up Ellie's cheeks. "She's cooking for my Jake, too. I might never get out of bed again."

"Why is Nina nicer now that she's not with Dad?"

"It's a competitive thing. She's taking care of us, since she can't take care of him."

"Oh, you're right," I said. "I wish he'd quit being stupid and go home."

"You're tired of him?"

"No, Nina's a mess without him. This is all getting too weird."

"Soon it will be over." Ellie rubbed her belly.

"No, soon it will all begin," I replied and then added: "Did Theo call again?"

"No." Her smile faded. "But Jake talked with him."

"What'd he say?"

"Nothing, except that they talked," she said. "Don't ask him about it either. He didn't want me to tell you, but Jake knows we don't keep secrets."

"Why won't Theo call me?"

"He's trying to get better, Meg."

"Oh, and I guess I get in the way of that."

"That's not what I said."

"You don't have to. Why can't my heart hear what my brain is screaming? I won't ask about Theo again. He knows where to find me." I sighed with frustration. "I have to go get Jason. We have our first Lamaze class this afternoon."

"Oh, I'm so jealous of you."

"That's warped. I'm longing for a man who walked out on me, while I'm taking another woman's husband to Lamaze, and you're jealous."

"At least one of them is the baby's daddy," Ellie said.

"Don't remind me."

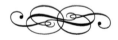

Jason got into Lamaze way more than I did. At the end of class, Jason pulled out his phone to switch the ringer back on. "Twenty-eight calls. Oh shit. Guess who's at Steve's house? She's dropping the kids off. Drive fast."

Jason called his wife and told her he was on the way, but it took us another eighteen minutes to get back to Steve's house. She'd kept everyone strapped into car seats with the air conditioner on full blast. Her black hair flew back from her face, which wore an angry expression.

She was at my door before I got the car into park. "You did this on purpose!" She screeched.

No one in his or her right mind would get out of a car with that bear scratching at the window.

"Jason, do something," I pleaded.

He was scared to get out of the car, too. "Babe, you kicked me out, remember?"

"I didn't say go bang your ex!" She charged around the car to his door and yanked it open, while he scrambled to lock it. She clawed at his shirt and dragged him out of the car. "I expected you to grovel your way back in, not romp around in your past!"

"I didn't mean to get her pregnant, babe," he said. "I love you, I miss you." Jason fell to his knees. "I'll grovel. Take me back." Then to my horror, he burst into tears, sobbing on her feet, his hands wrapping around her ankles.

"Get up—you make me sick! Get your kids out of the van, now!" She stomped away. "I need a break. I'll be back for them in a week… if you're lucky." She got in her seat, shut the door, and fired up the car. The kids filed out and scrambled for the porch. I got out of the car to help Jason. Pathetic and wrecked, he joined us on the porch.

As Jason's wife pulled away, she honked.

"Hey, Meg," she yelled.

I looked back.

"Your ass is huge!" She gave me the finger and burned rubber all the way down the street.

So much for all the years I'd spent imagining their fairy-tale romance.

In the house, the kids huddled in the living room. Jason was missing.

"Hi guys. I'm Meg."

Two rambunctious little boys moved around the room faster than cockroaches running from light.

"Are you replacing Mommy?" a pale, skinny girl with dark curls and a sharp chin asked.

"Shut up, Poppy," snapped the boy version of her.

"I'm a friend of your dad. Do you know where he went?" I wasn't about to march through his side of the drama on my own.

Poppy scrambled after her little brothers. The boys figured out that she was trying to herd them, and they split up, running in different directions.

"Jay, help me," Poppy demanded.

"Let them run." The oldest boy shrugged.

While Poppy went up the steps to grab the one little boy, I followed the other to the kitchen. Jason was at the table crying, with his head in his arms. The little boy charged him.

"Daddy! Daddy!" he cried. "Boo-boo, Daddy? Boo-boo? Kiss it, kiss it. Lemme kiss it, Daddy."

"Which one are you?" He pulled the little one onto his lap.

The child babbled an answer.

"Basil, Daddy's all better." Jason tousled the little boy's hair. "Daddy misses Basil."

The other three children stormed into the kitchen.

"Okay, here's my crew. You've met Basil." He pointed to the twin in the girl's arms. "That's Sage, with my daughter Poppy, and our oldest." He pointed to the gangly boy. "That's Jay. Give Daddy a hug."

The boy ignored him at first and then plunged into his dad's arms. Jay looked much younger than eight, sitting on his father's lap with his face buried into Jason's neck.

My brother called from the front door, and I excused myself.

"Steve," I said, coming out to the front room. Chelsea walked in behind him. "Oh, hi." I had to get used to her being with him all the time. The only way I had a minute alone with Steve was at work. "Jason's wife dropped off his kids for the week."

"A whole week?" Steve asked. "All four of them? Are you *kidding* me?"

"All four."

"This isn't going to work."

"Please, Steve? I'll help."

"It could be fun," Chelsea said, reminding me how she was a friend who would try almost anything in the name of a good time. She walked toward the kitchen, and they followed her like little baby ducks.

"Hello, hello," she called as she went through the door.

She caught the eye of one of the twins. "Shiny," he said.

"Mine," the other little boy said, and as they clamored to her, Chelsea sat on the floor taking them into her arms. They pulled on her necklaces and bracelets, and when one boy tugged on her chandelier earring, she removed it and handed it to him.

Poppy walked over and sat next to Chelsea, too.

"My name is Chelsea," she said, taking off a string of colorful beads and putting them on the girl. "Can we be friends?"

Poppy smiled. "You're pretty," she said, staring.

"You are too."

Steve watched Chelsea, and I knew he wasn't going to kick Jason and his kids out. He wasn't going to let Chelsea go, either. My brother was going to break out of his cycle, and I needed to do the same.

I missed Theo horribly, but I had to let go. I couldn't fix my relationship with Theo, but maybe I could help save the relationships around me. I needed to get Dad back with Nina, but first I needed to help Jason get home to his wife—not only for his kids, but for my daughter as well. There had to be some way to make it right for all of us.

"How about if I order pizza for dinner?" I stood in the corner, calling in the order, when Dad came in. He laughed as he walked through the door.

"Come on in," he said to someone behind me. I held my breath. Maybe I wouldn't have to intervene with him and Nina after all. But in walked Hazel.

CHAPTER TWENTY-THREE

"Y ou can't be here." I blocked her entrance. Once Hazel became entrenched in the house, we might never be able to get rid of her, like cockroaches.

"It's okay," Dad said. "I invited her to join us."

"No, absolutely not. This is a conflict of interest." It would be the end of the world if Dad and Hazel hooked up. The end of the world.

"Nonsense, Meg. Friends among family is not a conflict of interest."

One of the twins ran out and went straight for Hazel.

"Grandma!" he squealed and clutched her leg.

Jay barged out of the kitchen after the little guy. "That's not Grandma," he said as he removed his little brother from Hazel's leg. "Sorry."

Hazel's whole demeanor melted with the small child's attention. As far as I knew, she had no grandchildren—or children, for that matter. That was Hazel for you. I decided to cut her some slack.

"Well, you might as well stay, I guess. Dinner's on its way, and we'll have plenty."

"Thank you, Meg." Hazel seemed grateful, but then she turned back to Dad and slipped her arm around his waist.

Give Hazel an inch, she tries to do my father.

I waited for him to wiggle away, but he draped his arm casually across her shoulders. I wanted to throw up. I went back to hanging out with Jason's kids. His children were a part of my daughter's family. They carried secrets that my baby wouldn't reveal until birth.

After pizza, I found Steve alone in the kitchen. He stood peering out the window over the kitchen sink, drinking a beer. "What's up?" he asked, not looking at me.

"Did you really tell Nina she could help out with the Brooke and Bella event?" Watching Dad and Hazel get cozy was making my head spin. After the awkward bonding time Nina and I had shared, I didn't want to give Dad a chance to rub it in her face that he was moving on. Hazel had some kind of cougar spell over him.

Steve shrugged. "Sure. Nina's got connections, and the reality stars have sent us a list of what they expect to have available to them. Her offer to help couldn't have come at a better time. Have you reviewed the Brooke and Bella itinerary?"

Steve turned to face me and scowled at the blank look on my face.

"I hope you're keeping up with your end of things." He downed the rest of his beer and tossed it in the trash. "And here you are questioning whether we should accept help."

"Give me a freaking break! Can you not give me an ounce of compassion? I'm pregnant, and I'm tired, and I'm doing the best I can!"

He followed me as I stormed down the hall. Dad stood up, leaving Hazel still sitting on the sofa. "No, Dad, that's okay. You sit with Hazel. But could you please just call *your wife* back? She loves you, and quite frankly, you owe her a phone call."

I grabbed my purse and stumbled toward the door. "Wait, you know what?" I turned and faced Steve, Dad, Hazel, Chelsea, and Jason, giving them each a pointed look. "You are my people." My voice trembled. "I need your support right now. I need calm in my life. Can you guys respect what I'm going through without always passing judgment on me? Please?" I waddled out into the night.

"Wait!" Jason came after me. "Don't blame yourself, kid," he said, using his old nickname for me. "We'll get through this together." He placed a hand on my belly.

I pulled back. "Go home, and make things right with *your* wife."

He stuffed his hands in the front pockets of his well-worn jeans. "She won't forgive me. She's jealous of you."

"Me? But you left *me* for *her*. You chose her."

"Meg, I saw you both for a while. You didn't know, but she did." Finally, he told the truth. "I didn't break up with you until she told me she was pregnant. She's bitter I didn't end it sooner."

"Can you blame her?" I was so irritated with him. "Jason, she has to wonder who you'd be with if she hadn't gotten pregnant."

He sighed. "I still wonder the same thing."

"Oh God! You *are* stupid! Don't ever say that again. Call her, and tell her you'll do whatever she wants. Tell her she's always been your true love. Make her believe, if you want her to take you back. Now, if you'll excuse me, I'm going home, making some chamomile tea, and putting up my swollen feet."

I got in the car and slammed the door. Jason stood there, looking confused and dejected. If I'd asked him to come home with me, I bet he would have. I guessed that, for some people, the hardest part of making a choice was sticking with it. Then I thought of Theo. He didn't have any trouble sticking to his choices.

I headed for my home, and for once, I was glad it would be empty.

CHAPTER TWENTY-FOUR

THE DAY OF THE BABY shower rose hot and clear.

I followed Nina's instructions and showed up two hours early. She had a team of people decorating the house in pink and blue and yellow. When I walked into Ellie's bedroom, Ellie was mid-haircut and getting her toes painted at the same time.

Nina walked in, carrying two garment bags. "Wait till you see the dresses I picked for you girls."

The baby shower signaled the end of pregnancy, and my life was more unsettled than ever. I had yet to venture into the baby's room. I couldn't go in there. Once the baby came, I would have to look, but until then I had no reason to enter.

I took two steps back and ran my hands down the perfectly nice, black empire-waist dress I wore. Nina picked up on my reluctance to see the dress she'd brought me.

"I did everything I could to make this a big day for you," Nina whispered, tucking a lock of hair behind my ear. "I have a surprise for you, but first you should put this on." Nina unzipped the garment bag and pulled out a flowing, hot-pink dress. "Oh, try it on," she cooed. "If you don't want to wear it, I won't be mad." I took in her eager expression and confident smile.

"Thank you." I grabbed the dress and headed for the

bathroom. Hot pink was not my usual color, but when I put it on, I felt joy instantly. Yes, it screamed party dress, but it also hugged me in a way that said, "I love my body." And with the dress on, I did love my body. To Nina's credit, she had also picked out a delicate pair of flip-flops.

"Oh, wow!" Ellie gushed when I came out.

"What do you think?" Nina asked.

"You have an eye for clothes. It's perfect." I embraced Nina, and although she was angular and stiff, she made some odd movement that led me to believe she was hugging me back.

"Don't look so nervous, Meg," Ellie said. "I finally get to do something today, and we'll have fun." Ellie had permission to dress up and spend the day on the sofa, but at any sign of contraction, she had to return to bed. Doctor's orders. I sent everyone out of the room and helped Ellie put on the deep-violet dress Nina had chosen for her.

"I can't wait to get out there." Ellie raised her hand, and I gave her a high five followed by a fist bump.

"Let's do this," I said.

We traipsed down the hall from her bedroom, swinging our joined hands. Jake met us and took Ellie's other hand.

"Ladies, you look amazing." He kissed his wife's cheek and looked at her as though he wanted to take her back to the bedroom. Ellie ignored him, ready to see friends and family. She'd been cooped up too long.

A hush fell as we walked in. The room was packed, but everyone cleared the way for Ellie to make her way to the sofa. Very few people had seen Ellie since she had gone on bed rest. Now nearly everyone from Café Stay and The Book Stack was in her living room, plus Ellie's numerous friends, who'd missed her over the last few months. They all gathered around her, commenting on how wonderful she looked.

"Make way for my wife," Jake ordered as he led her through the room.

I fell back from the crowd. Hazel came out of nowhere and groped the pleated fabric of my dress. "I'm sorry about the other night."

I nodded absentmindedly, watching Ellie hug a man, her head resting on his shoulder.

Hazel talked in my ear, but I wasn't listening. Ellie stepped out of the hug and scanned the room. She found me at the same time the man did.

Theo.

He approached without crutches, steps not quite smooth, *but he was standing on his own.*

Nina sidled up to me. "Surprise! I found him." She rubbed my back. "For you."

"Uh-oh," Hazel said, and for once, she darted off in the other direction.

"You can thank me later," Nina whispered. She wandered away, and I was left in a room full of my closest friends, while the man I'd been missing for weeks *walked unaided* across the floor to me.

"Hello," Theo said.

I stood, immobilized. I couldn't breathe. I took a step back, trying to fill my lungs. I glanced around the room, measuring the distance to various escape routes. Focusing back on Theo, my whole body felt heavy with defeat. He wore a look of hope, but that look cut right through me, into the core of my loneliness.

"This was a mistake. I shouldn't have come," he said.

"No, you shouldn't have walked out on me." I glared at him. "But right now is a bad time to have this conversation. Everyone who has been by my side is in this room. I can't focus on you." I whirled around and walked off, keeping my eyes fixed forward.

I hunted down Nina to chew her out and found her huddled in the corner, talking with Dad. She sat at ease, beaming. I couldn't be mad at her.

My father had his arm draped around her, and he waved at me. "I'm sorry about the other night," he said.

I waved back, but didn't want to interrupt his moment with Nina.

Hazel appeared out of nowhere and put her hands on my belly. "You're so big, that baby will be here any day now."

I flinched, repulsed by her touch. "Not yet. I still have six weeks to go."

"Are they sure there's only one in there?" She cackled. "You poor thing, you're a house." She wandered off and made a beeline for my Dad. As she got close, he stood up, leaving Nina alone. Dad put his arm around Hazel and led her away. The smile he gave her made me sick. Nina didn't look too happy, herself. I went to her.

"I could fire Hazel," I suggested.

"That woman your father has befriended?"

"Yes, she's a real pain in the ass."

Nina frowned. "They are close. Did you see the way his face lit up? No, don't fire her. That will make her needier and probably more attractive to your father. I'm done." Nina didn't wear defeat well. "Tonight is about you. Let's go inside and enjoy the party."

"Everyone, can I have your attention?" Jake called out. "First, I want to thank you all for joining us today to celebrate Ellie and Meg becoming mothers. The baby games are about to begin, so any man that would like to bow out, join me out at the grill." Steve separated from Chelsea and joined the men outside.

Theo stayed. I wished he hadn't come to my party. I had finally gotten him out of my head. I had finally moved forward just enough to get through the day and sleep at night without torturing myself with questions of what I had done wrong. But he came back. He showed up at my baby shower, looking strong and sure, and I still didn't know what he wanted.

I took a seat next to Ellie.

"Are you okay?" She asked in a whisper.

"I don't know."

"It's good he came. We've all missed him."

"Did you know he was coming?" I asked.

"Nina checked with Jake first before she contacted Theo. Can you believe she found him?" Ellie smoothed her hands over her belly. "I didn't tell you because I didn't want to get your hopes up in case he didn't show. Don't be mad at me."

"I'm not." I took a shaky breath. "He looks good. I'm glad he's getting better. I wish he didn't have to leave me to do it. Is he leaving after today?"

"I don't know. You need to talk to him."

As the party went on, Nina slowly deflated. Once Ellie and I opened our gifts, Nina was itching to leave. "Don't pick up anything. The staff will take care of it all. Walk me to my car, Meg. I have one last thing for you." Her ominous tone gave me goose bumps. At her car, she told me to get in. I sat in the passenger seat, and she reached across me and popped open the glove box. She pulled out a large stack of envelopes wrapped with a heavy-duty rubber band.

Something about the way she held the bound paper gave warning that something big was about to happen.

"Your father doesn't know I have these," she began, and my desire to know what she held grew. "He'll be mad at me for giving them to you. It's not my place to do this, but you have a right to know. Your father avoids confrontation to the point of leaving everyone in the dark."

As she handed the stack to me, I could see my father's script on the top envelope, addressed to my mother. So he had known where she lived all along. I sorted through the envelopes, reading the postmarked stamps. At first, he sent letters almost monthly. Then it went to one letter a year until Steve and I graduated from high school. I read and reread her name to myself: Candace Adams. The few times Dad had spoken of her, he had referred to her as Candace.

"Now I know why I never found anything searching for Candace Michaels," I said.

"I didn't know you looked," Nina said. "But anyway, they never married." She turned in her seat to face me. "I checked it out for you. She's still living at that address."

"What are you suggesting?" Could Nina know I'd entertained this idea for years? "She doesn't want to see me."

"How can you be sure?"

"Return to sender," I read the words lettered in loopy scrawl. "She didn't even want to read what he had to say."

"You'll only know if you go. This is a chance for a relationship with your mother. Maybe she's waiting for you to take the first step." Nina's voice rose with excitement. "If nothing else, at least you'll get some answers. Who knows?"

I was tempted. I wanted to know. Although I wouldn't say it out loud, my whole life I'd deeply longed for the love and approval of the woman who'd walked out on me.

"What would your shrink say?"

Nina grinned. "Are you sure you want to know?"

"Give it to me straight."

"My shrink would say only you can decide if this is what you need to do." Nina lifted her chin. "But you must find a way to break the pattern of loving men who aren't available to you. You have to believe you deserve love. It will make a difference in your life, but more importantly, it will make a difference to your daughter. Otherwise, you'll be teaching her the lessons you don't want her to learn."

"Okay, I need to think."

"Let me know what you decide. I'm going to go home, pour a glass of wine, and drink it in bed."

"I can't convince you to stay?"

"No, I've appreciated the way you and Ellie have embraced me, but tonight I think I need to be alone. It's been too long since he looked at me with that same level of kindness and compassion. If he doesn't want to come home with me, then I'll go home alone."

"Are you sure you still want to help out with the Brooke and Bella event?" I asked, giving her a chance to bow out. "You know, Hazel and Dad will be there, too."

Nina put on her most professional smile. "Absolutely! I have it all planned out. Everything is ready. I can deal with your father."

"Ok." I hugged the letters to my chest. "Thank you, Nina."

I didn't want to bring the letters inside, so I went and stood next to my car. Once I read them, I would confront Dad. If Steve found out I had them, he would tell me not to open old wounds.

But I wasn't ready to let go. Nina was right. I had to confront my past before it tore me apart. Maybe she was also right about my mother waiting for me to take the first step. At first I put the collection of envelopes on the passenger seat, but then I decided to slip them under the driver's seat. Caught up in what I was doing, I didn't notice him approach my car. I pulled myself back up and locked the car. When I turned around I stumbled into Theo.

His arms came around me to steady me. "Hey there," he said. "I've looked all over for you. I thought you left."

I looked up to the cloudless sky and then back at him. "Gosh, that must've been hard for you." I tried to pull back, but he held me tighter.

"Wait," he whispered, staring into my eyes until I stilled against him. "I'm so sorry. I'm sorry I left you." He slid his hands up my back and held me against him. He buried his face in the curve of my neck, as if breathing strength off my skin. "I have some things to say to you."

I inhaled the familiar smell of a man I'd craved for weeks. My body gave in, relaxed against him.

Theo's cheek brushed against mine. His mouth blazed a hot path to my mouth. Once we connected in a kiss, time sped up, our lips sliding, tasting, hungry and hot for each other. Theo clung to me, devouring the moans that escaped my throat.

I thought the words before I said them out loud. "No, no." I pushed against him, and took a step back. "You can't do this to me again. I won't let you." I turned and walked on unsteady feet back to the house. Before I reached the porch I heard him start his truck and pull away. Relief washed over me, and I rested my head against the door for a minute.

I managed to pull it together and thank the guests as they departed. Wandering to the back of the house, I found Hazel and Dad rocking on a swing. They laughed, in on a private joke, lost in their moment. My fury flamed. How could he move on without Nina? I'd had enough.

I walked up to him. "Dad, why did you ignore Nina? She's

trying so hard to get you back, and you spend all your time with her." I pointed at Hazel.

"Meg, don't be rude." He placed his arm comfortingly around Hazel's shoulders.

"No, she's right. I should leave," Hazel said. She stood up from the swing and brushed the front of her pants.

"Hazel, don't leave. You belong here," Dad said.

"*Dad*," I said exasperated. "She's a store employee."

"Meg—"

"No, I need to say this. You do a great job, Hazel, but you have no boundaries. My life is none of your business. The hours I work are none of your business. My married father is none of your business, and if you insist on wiggling your way into our family, Steve and I will need to let you go." My chest rose and fell with the force of energy that surged from months of stuffing my outrage at her intrusiveness.

My father stood. "That's enough, Meg."

"She's right," Hazel said, ducking her head. "I have no business here."

Dad took her hand. "Yes, you do, Hazel. It's time. Tell Meg."

"Tell me what?" Acid churned in my stomach. I didn't care what she had to say; I knew from the look on my father's face that trouble was ahead.

"You tell her," Hazel whispered to my father.

"Meg," Dad said gruffly and raised Hazel's hand, gripped in his. "Meet your grandmother."

My mouth went dry. I looked from Hazel back to my father. "But your mother's dead."

"Hazel is your mother's mother."

I stepped back. "Why didn't you tell me?"

"That doesn't matter. She's here now, and she wants to get to know you and Steve better."

"She's here now?" I raised an eyebrow, looking from Hazel to my dad and back again. "That's really creepy. You... you've worked at the bookstore for over five years. I'm not doing this. I have to go."

I raced through the house. Jake had taken Ellie back to her bed. Everyone was gone except for Steve and Chelsea, who were lounging on the sofa.

"Hey, good party," Steve said. "I loaded everything in your car for you."

I thought of the letters hidden under my seat, and I could hardly breathe.

"Thanks, I have to go." My voice quivered. "Tell Ellie I'll call her later."

"I'm sorry about the other night," Steve added.

"Me, too," Chelsea echoed.

"That means a lot, thank you."

Chelsea hopped up and came to my side. "I'll walk you to your car." She grabbed my hand, pulling me along. "What's up now?"

"I can't tell you." I didn't look at her.

"You can tell me everything," Chelsea replied, squeezing my hand.

"I need to dump on someone. I need you to be my friend right now and not my brother's girlfriend."

"I'm both," she said. "One doesn't compromise the other."

"So can I speak in confidence?"

Her hands landed on my shoulders, shaking me. "Absolutely, spill it."

"Nina gave me letters my father's been sending to my mother for years, and I finally know where she lives."

"Oh goodie, I can't wait to read them." She bounced up and down, her boots crunching the gravel in the driveway. "Are you going to call her?"

I cringed. I didn't want to share the letters with anyone. I considered Chelsea's question. "I want to go see her." Once the words came out, I knew it was the only decision I could live with. "Hazel is her mother," I added.

"Hazel is whose mother?"

"Hazel is my mother's mother—she's my grandmother." The words tasted sour on my lips. "Oh, this is too weird."

"What?" Chelsea's mouth fell open. "Well, there you go! She can fill in all the blanks."

"I don't want to hear what she has to say. My grandfather hired her years ago, and she kept her identity from Steve and me. "

"So get to know her now."

"*No.*"

"That's plain stupid. You have a chance to fill in the blanks, and you want to stay in the dark. Sounds a little chicken to me."

"I'll think about it," I said, brushing her off. I couldn't tell her what I was going to do. That would be asking her to keep too much from Steve.

"Sleep on it," Chelsea said. "Everything will be clearer in the morning."

As it turned out, she was right. By morning my plane had landed in Atlanta. I was on my way to meet my mother.

CHAPTER TWENTY-FIVE

I READ THE FIRST LETTER FROM the bottom of the stack after takeoff.

Dear Candace,

Come home. Please. We miss you. The kids are fine, but they keep looking for you, asking for Mommy. You would make us all happy if you would only come back. I love you with all my heart and I only want good things for you. If you're not ready yet, just know I am always ready for you. Don't question that. I will never stop waiting for you, my love. We want you back.

Truly yours,
Mike

If I could've sent a letter to Theo in the days and weeks after he left, it would've been very similar to Dad's letter. Dad's pain, from all those years ago, cut into me.

The letters increased in urgency. Dad bared his soul, and my mom never opened a single envelope. How could she deny Dad's love? I was the first and only one to see inside his agony, and the ache in my chest grew until I felt like she was breaking my heart.

The letters changed about the time Nina came into his life. They became distant—simple updates about Steve and me. Then came a heart-wrenching letter:

Dear Candace,

I can't do this alone anymore. I've lied to myself, believing you'd return. No more. I've met someone new. The kids like her, and she loves us. I never wanted to give you an ultimatum, but I have to ask one last time. Come home. You are my heart. You are almost out of time—when I move on that's it for me. But still, I want you back, and the kids need you.

Truly yours,
Mike

By the time I got to baggage claim, my feet throbbed, my back ached, and my stomach growled, although I didn't want to eat. I'd planned only on a carry-on with enough for a few nights, but then I got wistful. I had packed my largest suitcase with scrapbooks, photo albums of me and Steve, my favorite books, my lucky shoes, and a pregnancy journal where I kept my sonogram images. I knew I might be setting myself up, but when I jumped in I tended to go feet first.

I sat in a blue, plastic-molded chair, pulled out the remaining four letters, and tuned out the swarm of people around me. I read until I reached the final one. It included a photograph of me and Steve wearing our gowns at our high school graduation.

Dear Candace,

This is the last letter I will send. They are all grown, and you've missed it all. You've missed all the beauty of their lives, the blessing of their growth; but most of all they've missed you. Through the years I held out hope you would come back to them. How could I have been so wrong?

Mike

"Excuse me, ma'am—is this yours?" an older guy asked, holding up my suitcase. "Are you alright, dear?"

I swiped away the tears that streaked down my face. "Yes, thank you."

I took a cab from the airport to a high-rise in Midtown Atlanta. The air was still and humid. Beads of sweat formed on my upper lip. I wiped them away and forced the thick air into my lungs.

A man with cropped gray hair and a neat uniform approached me in the lobby of the high-rise. "Ma'am, can I help you find somebody?"

"I'm visiting Candace in apartment 916." I forced myself to sound brave, confident, expected. Wanted. For all I knew she'd turn me away. But even with that risk, I had to see her.

He led me to the elevator in a well-lit alcove. "Good day, Ma'am," he said with a nod. Alone, I rode the elevator up to the ninth floor. I looked in the mirrored elevator doors and realized I was a little rough around the edges. I powdered my face, applied fresh pink lipstick, and ran my fingers through my hair. By the time the doors opened, my heart was pounding violently. I walked down the emerald-green-carpeted hall, reading the numbers, until I reached apartment 916.

I knocked, and right away, I heard movement on the other side. The door swung open. She smiled, and I had no doubt: I was looking into the eyes of my mother.

"Hello." I smiled back at her. "My name is Meg."

She made a squeal of delight and jumped toward me. "I always *knew* you'd come see me, one day." As she took me into a hug, I saw that her belly matched mine. My mother was pregnant.

CHAPTER TWENTY-SIX

"LOOK AT US." SHE STEPPED back. "We match! I guessed we looked about the same, but not this close. Come in. Oh honey, what a nice surprise. You're beautiful."

She looked like a fairy. Her tiny frame was petite everywhere except where a baby grew. Her long hair was a shade or two darker than my honey-blond, and it fell in waves all the way down to her waist. I knew she was almost forty-two, but she appeared years younger.

I followed her into the apartment, my head spinning from the way she acted as though she'd only seen me two weeks ago. My whole life, I'd thought about what I would say to her if given the chance. But she took control of the conversation.

"When are you due?" She sat on a faded plaid sofa, tucked her feet up under her exactly the way I always do, and patted the cushion next to her. "Sit, sit, sit. Tell me everything."

I dropped down next to her. "I'm due in six weeks," I said, rolling along with the freakish way she seemed completely at ease. "How about you? Do you have any other children?" It occurred to me for the first time that my family could be bigger than I thought.

"No, this is my first," she said, not catching her error.

"You're so lucky to be almost done. I have eleven weeks to go." She leaped off the sofa like a cat. "Let's go eat." She turned down a hall. "Don't you want to eat all the time? I can't stop myself anymore. I woke up in the middle of the night and made a pimento cheese sandwich. I've never touched the stuff before, but now it's like candy. Oh!" Her childish laugh was musical. "Get it? Like Candy! You can call me Candy."

Her hair swayed from side to side as she waddled down the hall. She was definitely more of a Candy than a Candace, and we'd both be weirded out if I called her "Mom." I followed her into the kitchen and watched as she pulled out bread and peanut butter. "Is this okay with you? I need to go to the store. I'm out of everything."

"Sure. Can I help?"

"No, I'm going to make you my specialty: happy baby sandwich." She pointed to a stool. "You talk while I cook. I don't see a ring. I guess you're not married either? It's good to be independent."

"No, I'm not married." I put my hand on my belly. "This wasn't planned. But I'm really excited now."

"Oh, hush." She pulled out two paper plates and put three slices of bread on each. "There are no such things as accidents," she said, reaching into a cabinet and pulling out a jar of green pimento olives. "I really believe that. This baby is my second chance. I didn't know I wanted that chance until Roger begged me to make him a papa." Her face twisted into a grimace. "He should be here soon. I'll tell him you're from my pregnancy yoga class. Anyway..." She smeared peanut butter on four slices of bread, then marshmallow fluff that she scooped out of a jar. Next, she sprinkled mini chocolate chips over the marshmallows. "This will make your baby dance. Oh, wait. I almost forgot the best part." She popped the jar of olives open and drained the entire jar in a salad spinner. Scooping out a handful, she dropped them on the side of my plate. "There — a bit of everything a girl needs."

"Thanks." A rush of nostalgia hit me, and tears burned

behind my eyes. My mom prepared a meal for me, and I ached for little girl me, who'd prepared most meals by herself. I smiled at the three-layer sandwich that towered in the middle of a paper plate surrounded by Doritos and olives. The meal would send Ellie into a diabetic coma. Then I took a bite. "Mmm..." I chewed the sugary fluff-peanut mixture and swallowed. "This is good."

She talked while we ate, and her easygoing nature relaxed me. Then I heard the front door open.

She frowned. "Shit. Don't tell Roger who you are. He has no idea."

"Okay." I dabbed at my mouth with a paper napkin, listening to the footsteps pounding toward us, dread tying my stomach into knotted ropes.

"Whose bag is out front?" His voice boomed.

Candy put her hand over mine. "It belongs to my friend. She stopped by on her way home from a trip. She wanted to see the baby's room." Candy stood up and picked up our plates. I was only half-done with my sandwich, but I couldn't eat any more—not that she asked. She dropped the plates in the trash. "Let's go see the room now."

"Get on with it, Candy. The Braves start at seven, and I told Mitch we'd be there early." He turned to me and scratched his head. "Ever notice how all pregnant women look alike?"

"Don't be silly." Candy giggled nervously and pulled me out of the kitchen.

Silly was the last word I'd use to describe the guy.

"Did you pack the cooler yet?" he called after us.

"Hold your horses, Roger. I'll get it done in a minute. Meg came all this way to see our baby room." We went down a dark hallway to a door. "Come here," she said to me. "You ready?" She smiled with pure excitement, waiting for me to reply.

"Yes." I nodded, my mouth dry.

She swung the door open, and we walked into a tiny room full of fluffy purple. The crib was white with soft lavender and yellow sheets. A baby doll lay on the pillow. The doll was the same blond doll that Theo picked out for my baby. I wondered if she had decorated a room for Steve and me.

"Don't you love it? I spend hours in here every day. I can't wait to bring her home."

Now was my chance. "Did you feel that way when you were pregnant with Steve and me?"

With my words, a shadow crossed her face, and she looked away. "I don't remember. I don't want to think about it." She crossed the room and busied herself sorting through baby outfits hanging in the closet. She chose a little dress. "Isn't this one adorable? Look at the little bloomers."

"I know I came with no warning."

"That's fine. This was a nice visit," she said. "But you should probably leave now. We have plans tonight."

"Okay. Can we get together again tomorrow? I'll find a hotel. You can come to me, or I'll meet you somewhere. I brought pictures of us growing up and some recent ones."

"I don't think that's a good idea. I'm glad you stopped by, though." Despite the kind words, her eyes took on a vacant look.

"I'm sorry, I have to ask you why you left us." The window for answers was closing, and I couldn't leave with nothing. "And why did you stay away? You could've at least dropped by from time to time."

She looked me square in the eye. "Sometimes loving someone means walking away. Your father was a good man. I knew he would give you the world. You were better off without me." She sniffled and glanced toward the door, rubbing her nose with her hand.

Roger's footsteps came down the hall. "Candy, we need to go if we're going to be seated by first pitch. Can't you ladies do this another time?"

I put my arms around her for a hug, but she pulled away. "It's okay. I'll go."

I looked at the floor as I passed Roger on my way out of their apartment. My bag was an unnecessary burden I dragged behind me as I wandered around the street until I came to a park. After pulling my luggage through the grass, I stopped under a great oak for shade. I sprawled out, resting my head on my suitcase, and watched clouds drift across the sky. I'd figured out nothing. I was still lost.

I booked a room at a Hilton and collapsed onto the plush, king-size bed, waiting and wishing for sleep to block out the day.

She'd had no warning I was coming, no time to prepare. I had to give her a chance to want me back. It wasn't ten yet, so I bargained that she and Roger might still be at the game, and I gave Candy a call.

"Hi, Candy, it's me," I said to the machine, and then for Roger's sake I added, "your friend Meg. I was happy to finally see you again today. If you want to contact me before I leave tomorrow, I am staying at the Hilton on Tenth Street. I hope to hear from you." I considered the message I needed to give her, wishing I could be direct. "Goodbye," I said instead, and hung up.

Then I called Ellie.

"Hey girl!" She answered on the first ring. Sheets rustled in the background. "Where are you? I've been calling all day. Theo stopped by again today."

"He did?" Only a day earlier, he'd kissed me in Ellie's front yard, but a lifetime had passed in those hours.

"Yes, and I think you should talk with him, Meg. You need to hear from him what he's been through, but it's really amazing."

"Now's not a good time."

"Oh come on. You've been waiting for good news." She sighed into the phone. "He had surgery to remove a bone spur and scar tissue. He's been weaned off most of his medications. Trust me, this time you should give him a break. He's been through so much, and he made mistakes, he knows that, but he's willing to do whatever it takes to make it right. Meg, this is what you've been waiting for."

"I can't think about him now. I found my mom in Atlanta."

"Now? You're in Atlanta, right now?"

"Yes, I flew out this morning."

"And you left without telling anyone? Are you crazy?" She made a scream of frustration. "It's kind of late in the game to be flying. What were you thinking?"

"It's not like getting on a roller coaster, where they stop pregnant women. I'm fine." I sighed. "I'll be back by lunchtime, tomorrow."

"Well, how did it go? This is surreal. Was she excited to see you?"

"No, she didn't care one way or another that I was there. Oh, and get this: she's pregnant too."

"No!"

"Yes. We look like sisters. She was only eighteen when she had us. She said this is her second chance, and she didn't care for the reminder of the last time she gave motherhood a shot." Talking with Ellie was making the whole thing seem less traumatizing. "I'm numb. Maybe a little shocked. I had this stupid illusion that she'd open the door, and I'd go 'ta-da!' and she'd collapse with tears of joy. It wasn't like that at all. Seeing her—her seeing me—didn't change anything."

"Oh, Meg. I'm so sorry. How are you, physically? You shouldn't be traveling, especially not alone."

She was right. I stopped and listened to my body. "I can't remember the last time the baby moved." I pressed my hand against the spot that usually caused her to kick me back. Nothing. I poked and prodded my belly, encouraging her to wiggle in protest, but still nothing.

"Drink some orange juice and lie down. The baby is probably as exhausted as you are."

"Okay, I'll call you when I get home."

I hung up the phone and went for my purse. I scooped up a handful of change from the bottom and went out to the vending machine and bought a Fanta Orange Soda. I made it halfway back to my room and went back to the machine for a Snickers bar. A bitter laugh escaped my mouth. I bet I considered walking away from that candy bar for longer than my mother did about leaving me. And I didn't last. I had to go back.

238

I waddled back to my room and propped my pillows to sit up in bed. I gulped half my soda and waited. No movement. Nothing.

"Come on, little girl," I said out loud. "Let me know you're there. I want you. I promise you, you will never question that. Move, little girl." I waited, but she was still. I tried to envision my life before I got pregnant, pretending the pregnancy had never happened and life had moved on. I couldn't see it. This baby wasn't my plan, but she was better than anything I'd imagined for myself. My mother hadn't planned on us, so at her first opportunity she disappeared. She hit the reset button on her life and started over.

I stroked my belly, waiting for my little girl to respond, and thought about my beautiful and detached mother. Soon I'd have a little sister that I would never know. But Candy wasn't going to call. I had to let go of that part of me. I fell asleep sitting up. I woke up at five and ate my Snickers bar by the light of the bathroom. Two bites in, and baby girl was kicking like mad. "You and I make a great team," I said to her. "You wait and see. Momma's gonna get her act together when we get back to Texas."

After I showered and dressed, I went down to the hotel's breakfast buffet and filled up on fruit and cereal. I wasn't worried about missing Candy's call. If she wanted to talk, she would have to make some effort, and I wasn't holding my breath. Baby needed to eat, so eat I did. Just as I cleared my table, Candy came through the sliding doors of the hotel lobby. She walked to the elevators before I could reach her.

I rushed to catch her before she got inside. "Candy!"

"Hi, there." Her eyes flickered to the exit. "I thought about you all night. I have something to tell you, but only if you promise to keep it a secret."

Her words sounded rehearsed, and she picked at the silver heart-shaped locket she wore around her neck.

"Can I tell Steve, at least?"

"No, you can't. See, the thing is, it's selfish for me to tell the truth. I want you to know so you'll think better of me, but it's better for everyone else if you keep quiet."

239

"Okay." I couldn't risk giving her an ultimatum. Steve had said he didn't want answers, but I did. I needed answers.

"So you'll keep my secret, even from your father?"

She was asking me to pick sides, but I wanted her secret—that secret from my past. "Absolutely. I won't say anything."

She backed me into the recess behind the elevators.

"I was in love with a man when I went to work for Mike," she began, her eyes going dark with the far-off memory. "Mike was a good man, he was always attracted to me, but he knew I had a boyfriend." She pinched the bridge of her nose, and I waited, afraid to interrupt. "Well, one night my boyfriend beat me up pretty bad. He told me not to come back until..." She gripped my hands in hers and leveled a fierce stare at me. She took a deep breath and continued. "Until I fixed my pregnancy. I didn't think I had a choice, so I went in to work to get my paycheck. When Mike saw me all busted and bruised, he took me home. He was kind to me. I couldn't tell him I was pregnant because I wanted to stay with him. He was so gentle. He was everything I needed. I fell in love with him, and he fell in love with me, but he still didn't know I was pregnant. I knew I had to tell him the truth, so about a month after I moved in, I broke down. I was terrified after what'd happened with my ex, but Mike was over the top. He never questioned whether or not he was the father. I loved him more each day, after that. He kept me safe. He fed me, he took me to the doctor, and that was when we found out there were two of you. He said twins ran in his family. He said he was the luckiest person in the world. I couldn't hurt him. I couldn't tell him the truth."

"Wait, no—" I took a step back, and she moved forward.

"Let me finish," she begged. "We were a family, we made a nice family. Every dream I ever had as a little girl for a normal life, Mike gave me. It didn't matter that you didn't come from him."

"He's my father."

"He is your father," she agreed.

"He's not our father?"

"No, that man is dead. And Mike doesn't need to know." She looked over her shoulder toward the entrance of the hotel. "The truth is no good. It would only hurt him."

"Why tell me, then?"

"Because I need you to know I left because I loved you. I left to protect Mike. To protect my babies."

"Protect us from what?" My voice sounded small. "We were all at the park one day, and my ex showed up. I saw how he looked at you and Steve. I told Mike to put you guys in the car. He didn't want me to talk to Danny, but I was afraid Danny knew. I was afraid of what he'd do."

"You should've left with Dad right then. He could've protected you."

"No, that would've been like petting a rabid dog. I couldn't have Danny follow us home. I pretended I wasn't shaken and went over to say hi to him. He recognized your father as my boss. First he accused me of cheating on him, and then he insisted he fathered you and your brother. I said I lost our baby after he beat me. I begged him to leave us alone. It had been over two years since we'd seen each other."

She was breathing heavily with the burden of the memory.

"Mike and I went home, but I knew my ex would be back. The next week, while Mike was at work, Danny surprised me. He cornered me at the mailbox. Wanted to come inside and visit with you guys. I told him to go away. He said he wouldn't have another man raising his babies. He said if he found out you were his, he'd take you both from me, and I'd never see you again. I was too naive to understand that it wouldn't be an easy thing for him to do. I lived in fear of the man. When I said the babies were Mike's, he grabbed me and kissed me. Something in me broke apart then. My beautiful life was a lie. Danny insisted the only way he'd believe me was if I ran away with him. I knew then if I made that choice, you would be free from him forever. I couldn't let him hurt you. I couldn't hurt Mike that way. So I went away with Danny."

"But Dad loved you. You should have read the letters he sent you. He would've forgiven you."

"I couldn't forgive *myself*. I didn't deserve Mike's love. I lied to him every day we were together."

"Dad would've understood."

"But Danny wouldn't have. I was frightened of what would happen to you if he got ahold of you. He harbored a vicious side, and I couldn't protect myself and protect you guys. He wouldn't have been any good as a father."

I wanted to hug her, but when I stepped forward, she stepped back.

She squeezed her locket and slid it back and forth along the chain. "He died four years ago, and then I met Roger." She smiled when she said his name. "He's a good one. He wanted to be a daddy, so I tossed my pills, and here I am."

Roger is the good one? What must my birth father have been like?

"We need to put away all these secrets," I said. "It's never too late to come clean."

"Well, what good would that do now? Here, take this." She reached into her bag and pulled out an envelope. "I've kept this hidden for years, too afraid to look and too afraid to let it go. You keep it." She stuffed the envelope in my hands. "Walking away from Mike and you kids was the hardest thing I ever did. That first letter he sent wore me down. I almost went home, but I had to stay strong. I couldn't risk reading another one. Each letter that passed through my hands was a blessing. A reminder that my babies had a home with love."

I was crying, and she took me in her arms. "Sshhh there," she crooned. "You're fine. See, everything worked out in the end." I sobbed harder. "Please, don't do this to me now," she moaned. "I want to do right by this baby. I have to forget the past."

"You're right." I pulled myself together, wiping away my tears.

She reached behind her neck and unclasped her necklace. "I want you to have this, too," she said. "Lift your hair, and I'll put it on for you."

I did as she asked. Her fingers grazed the back of my neck, and when she stepped back, the locket, still carrying the warmth of her skin, landed just below my collar bone.

I put my hand over the charm. "Thank you."

"Can you forgive me?" Candy asked, her eyes shiny with unshed tears.

"Yes, I do. Steve and I had a good life. Don't worry about us."

"And Mike?"

"Dad's happy. He's good."

"I can't make you keep my secret, but it's the only thing I've ever asked of you," she said. "Bringing up the past is not going to help anyone."

"I'll keep my promise. Thank you for telling me the truth." I held the envelope to my chest. A gift from my mother.

She put one hand on her belly and her other hand on my belly. "When I rock my baby to sleep, I'm going to think about you and your baby." A tear slipped from her eye. "You will be a good mother, Meg. All you need is in you." She took my hand and kissed it. "This visit was good for me. I hope it's been good for you." She released my hand and slipped into the crowd mingling around the lobby. Within ten seconds, she was out of sight.

I felt as if a bomb had exploded, and I didn't have time to survey the damage. I had to leave for the airport in order to catch my flight. Hurrying back to my room, I stuffed my belongings into my bag. In the cab on the way to the airport, I watched the city, gray with smog, speed past me. My mother had always loved me. She had always loved us. When I laughed, the cab driver asked if I was okay. I assured him I was fine. Poor guy had to drive a hysterical pregnant woman, one who laughed and cried at the same time, all the way to the airport.

I went through the motions and managed to get on the plane. After takeoff, I removed the chain from around my neck and spread it across my fingertips. It was a timeless silver rope with a heart-shaped locket. The heart had delicate flowers etched in perfect detail. I could have admired it for hours. I slipped my fingernail in the crease to open it. My eyes went directly to the photo of my mother's face — tiny, so tiny, but an image of her.

On the other side of the locket was a photo of Hazel. She

looked vacant, but I resisted the urge to pass judgment. I held a photo of my mother and grandmother, women who shared my blood but not my life. The one I wanted had moved on. The other one had lurked in my life unannounced until she was forced to speak up. The edge of Hazel's photo curled back slightly and another image was visible underneath.

Carefully, I separated the photos and found a baby picture of Steve. She'd kept our images in a safe place. I knew mine must be nestled under the other side, but I was too afraid to risk harming her photo by trying to look underneath it. I tucked the photos back the way I had found them.

About the time we were over Mississippi, I opened the envelope Candy had given me. Inside, I found a letter, just like the others from the stack. The only difference was that this one had been opened and handled. It was yellowed by time, its edges cracked.

Dear Candace-

I long for your body beside mine. You are my love, my life, the air I breathe. Why did you leave me? Our life so full, so beautiful, I never stopped to question your happiness. I know you. I know you were happy.

You are our sun. We are aimless without you. The babies call out to you all day and all night. Momma, Momma, Momma. Please come home. Where did I go wrong?

I know everything changed the day you saw him in the park. Whatever it is that upset you, we can work it out. If you are scared I will protect you. If you need me to come get you I will. I'll do anything for you.

We need you back. I love you.

Always yours-

Mike

Home. I longed for the safety and comfort of my home. My bed. My journey for closure exposed a history that lay tangled and bare before me. I was such a fool. I mourned for my mother, who despite everything, I loved even more. She had given up all she had, everything she wanted, to ensure Steve and I could have more. I wanted her back. I wanted to know her, but that was not what she needed. The pain shredded me to bits.

And when I thought about my father—the man who made me—I was at once relieved that he hadn't raised me and sorrowful for all the years he had kept Candy from us. I pondered the life Steve and I could've had.

The plane landed, and I moved slowly to baggage claim, but still arrived there before my suitcase did. Sitting in a chair, hands on baby shelf and ankles crossed, the truth hit me: I might never see her again. I would carry her secret, keeping it safe from everyone who loved me. I had to do it alone. What would it do to Dad to learn he didn't father us? Steve would be furious with me for digging this up. Candy had lifted her burden and placed it on me.

People swarmed all around me. I closed my eyes and felt myself start to crumble. I opened my eyes, startled to discover Theo, looking amazingly tall without his crutches, standing over me. He slid his hand across my back, sitting down and leaning into me. "Hi," he said, as if he had never left me. I pressed my face into his chest, and his other arm came around to cradle me in his embrace.

"It's okay," he whispered. "I've got you." I sagged against him while he held on. The noise of the airport drowned out my sobs as Theo rocked me.

"Can I offer any help?" I heard a woman's voice ask.

"No, no," Theo replied. "Thank you." I felt him reach for something, and then he handed me a tissue. I guess a pregnant woman bawling in baggage claim was an irresistible sight, because when I raised my eyes, reaching for composure, I saw people gawking at me.

"Let me take you home," Theo said.

"Why are you here?"

"I came for you," Theo said. "Ellie told me what happened. You don't have to go through this alone." His words sank in.

"You shouldn't have bothered." I stood. "I'm not doing this with you."

"It's okay, Meg. I'm not asking you for anything." He walked by my side to the baggage carousel. His gait was slightly off, but otherwise he moved with a captivating self-assurance. I waddled, clutching my purse with the letter tucked inside, my breath still uneven from crying. "I'll give you a ride home," Theo said.

"Okay," I replied, too tired to resist. When my bag got close, I reached for it.

"Here, I've got that." Theo plucked it off as it spun our way. "Is this it?"

"Yeah."

We went outside, where the dry Texas wind greeted us. As if my body knew I was close to home, my knees gave a little, legs stumbled, and Theo gripped my arm above the elbow to steady me. "Hang on, girl — we're almost there."

At his car, he helped me in and tossed my bag in the back. I hoped he wouldn't try making small talk during the ride. My head resting against the cool glass window, I watched the blurry landscape pass by. I had nothing left to search for. I wasn't going to get my mother back. Instead, I carried her secrets. The truth didn't release me, didn't clarify the reasoning that had led to bad choices in my life. All the truth did was make me reevaluate the need for secrets.

CHAPTER TWENTY-SEVEN

THEO'S BODY, SITTING CLOSE TO mine, held at bay the looping replay of the last twenty-four hours. I reached for the diversion his presence offered. I surveyed his profile out of the corner of my eye. "Why'd you come for me?" I asked.

"When I couldn't track you down, I went to Ellie. She told me what you were doing." With one arm resting on the window and his other hand casually hanging on the bottom of the steering wheel, he looked relaxed. Only the flexing of his jaw gave away his tension. "Not a good idea, considering how far along you are. I would've gone with you."

"I don't need a chaperone," I snapped back.

He chuckled softly, but the sound was brimming with bitterness. "Could've fooled me. Not enough people ready to let you down; you go on a search to find more. You looked lost in baggage claim."

"Stop picking on me."

"Why do you have to fight so hard to do everything on your own?"

"I was resting my feet for a minute, and anyway, you're a big, fat, full-of-it hypocrite!" With arms crossed over my chest, I looked out the window again. I should've snagged a cab.

Theo laughed hard.

"What do you think is so funny?" I shot him the dirtiest, most hate-filled look I could muster.

"Did you call me fat?" He laughed into the crook of his arm; his eyes left the road and glanced at my belly. "And I'm the hypocrite?"

My mouth dropped open, and heat rushed to my face. "I'm pregnant. Part of this is another human being. You can't call me fat."

He made no attempt to conceal his next laugh.

Outrage flashed through me; my hands trembled, and I failed to steady my voice. "You're a hypocrite because you tell me I should ask for help. I need someone to look out for me. I'm so helplessly pregnant. But you're the one who ran off instead of letting anyone be there for you. You weren't here to help me even if I did need you, and I'm not saying I did. Or if we needed each other, even. You didn't even have to lean on me. You could've turned to Jake, or your mom, or if you didn't want to go to your family, you could have trusted Cortez to be there for you." I realized I was yelling. "Instead, you push everyone away. You hurt every one of us when you ran away. Now you come back all better, and we're all supposed to pick up where you dropped us and carry on."

I tried to catch my breath while I waited for him to speak. He focused on the road ahead. He was no longer laughing at me. I'd hit a nerve.

"I'm not going to apologize to you because I'm right, and you know I'm right," I said.

Theo took a slow breath in and began. "I left because I was hurting you. I didn't want to hurt you anymore."

"That's crap."

"I wanted to get better, but nothing worked. My pain wasn't in my head, but when the diagnosis came back as 'phantom pain,' it was as if they were calling me crazy. I went into self-destruct mode. You kept me going—only you. And then I saw her." He reached over and put his hand on my belly. His touch was so memorable, so comforting that I longed for a simpler time where I could place my hand on his. I sat without responding, and Theo removed his hand from me in acknowledgment of my resistance.

His deep voice filled the car again. "When we went to the ultrasound together, and you told me you loved me, I knew I could have a better life than I'd ever dreamed. I wanted that life, Meg. I locked my eyes on it.

"When Jason showed up, I lost it," Theo said. "When he put his hands on you, I flipped out. I didn't think he had the right to walk into our lives and claim his part in this. I wanted him gone. After I hit him, when I saw your face, I knew how wrong I was. I shouldn't have put you through that. I blew it, not for the first time, and I'm sorry."

"I know, I know, it's okay," I said. "What's not okay is that you left. You left me. You said you loved me, and you went away to who knows where, and you didn't call me. I had no idea if you'd be back. That hurt me more than anything, Theo."

He reached out and grabbed my hand. "I didn't want to hurt you."

"But you did!" I pulled back from his grasp. "You could've told me what was going on. Called. Wrote. Emailed. Sent up smoke signals. I would have waited for you. I would have supported whatever you needed. I would have done anything for you! Didn't you think about what you were doing to me? Did you even care?"

"Yes. Yes, of course I did. All I thought about was you. But if I couldn't get better, I wouldn't have come home."

"What?" I jerked my head to the side to see if he really meant that. The look he gave me was harrowing. "You're selfish, Theo. If you think that would be best, then you are horribly selfish."

"Believe what you want, but I won't be a burden to you, Meg."

Theo turned into my complex. The tension in my body only tightened as we pulled up to my home. I wanted to go inside and lock the world, including Theo, out. The question was, would Theo try to follow me?

"It's not a burden when you love someone," I said. "The joy of having you by my side overshadowed everything else. All I wanted was you. If you don't see that, then not only are you selfish, but you're stupid too."

He laughed, a strangely sad sound. "I missed my feisty girl."

I let out a short bark of laughter. "I'm not yours to miss."

The second the car was in park, I swung my door open. Unfortunately, my physique no longer allowed a swift and graceful exit, so I heaved myself up by clutching either side of the car doorframe. Theo followed me, wheeling my suitcase behind him. I unlocked the door and turned to take the handle from him.

"Thanks for the lift. I've got it from here."

Hauling my bag inside I swung the door shut, but Theo's hand shot up, blocked the door from closing. "Wait. I'm coming in to talk. We can work this out."

"No." I forced myself to look him in the eye. I saw a storm there, pain and regret, longing and need. I felt exactly the same, but I had to — for once in my life — learn from experience. "You cannot come inside. You walked away from what we had. Now it's gone. Thanks for the ride, but goodbye."

He didn't move his hand from the door.

"I love you," he said. "Give me another chance." "Love is not enough to keep people from abandoning you. When people leave you, they never stay when they come back. You have to go. I won't take a risk with you again. I have to put the baby first. She's not going to have someone come into her life and leave her behind. Not if I can stop it."

He stared at me, seeming to weigh how to move forward.

"Just go," I pleaded. "Don't make this hard for me."

"Call me when you're ready to talk," he said, waiting.

I slammed the door, but immediately searched for him through the peephole. Finally, I'd gotten what I wanted. I'd explained my side and I'd put my foot down, and I expected to find relief. However it didn't come with his departure. My heart whispered: *Wait. Ask me again, and I'll say yes.* The pain threatened to crush me, but I had to make the right choice. For once in my life, I would listen to logic and not be ruled by my heart.

I would protect my little girl.

CHAPTER TWENTY-EIGHT

T HE BURDEN OF FRESH PROMISES kept me awake. I'd thought I could handle it, but I twisted and flopped about in bed, unable to find comfort, as unsettled as I was on the inside.

And then, I was sick with longing for Theo, for his warmth and companionship. Seeing him again had gutted me.

So when the knocking came and the clock on the nightstand read eleven fifteen, I leaped from my bed, hopeful that Theo had come back to me.

I glanced through the peephole — safety first — before opening the door. "Steve, what are you doing here? You should've called." I stepped back for him to enter.

He walked over to the sofa, dropping down onto it.

"What is it?" He'd been working his ass off to prepare for the Brooke and Bella event. "I'm sorry I missed a few days of work. I've slacked off, with all the extra help we've been getting from Dad and Nina. Are we ready for tomorrow?"

He gave me a withering look, and the beat of my heart picked up speed.

"You went to Atlanta to go see her," he said in a furious whisper. "And you couldn't even tell me first?"

"I'm so sorry, Steve." I lowered myself next to him, resting my hands on my belly. "I've tried to talk to you about her, and you keep shutting me down. When I found her, I didn't think it through. I—I just... went." The baby kicked, and Steve stood up. I cringed, realizing he didn't want to be close to me. He stuffed his hands deep in his pockets and walked back and forth in front of the bookshelves.

"You didn't think?" He swiveled to face me, threw his hands in the air. "Why can't you stop and think before you act? You're going to turn out just like her if you don't check yourself." He dragged his hands down his face, his eyes wild.

"How can you be so sure you don't want to know what she has to say?" I smacked the end table. "We've had the same experience. Don't you wonder at all? Don't you wish she could be a part of your life now?"

Steve crossed his arms and bowed over. "So what's her excuse for leaving?"

I hesitated, hearing her plea: *it's the only thing I ask of you.* I made a promise. I would keep it, even if it ate through my body in layers until I had a gaping hole through me, I would keep my promise. I'd justified my oath of silence with the knowledge Steve didn't want to know about the past. But still, he deserved the truth.

"Ha! She didn't have a good reason, did she?" He looked triumphant. What did he think he'd won?

"She loved us, Steve. I believe that now."

"Never mind. I don't want to hear about it." He came over and sat next to me again. He glared at me and then looked down at my belly, his attention caught by the sudden movement from a good, hard baby kick. "Oh, wow." His face relaxed a bit, the lines around his mouth softening. He reached out and ruffled my hair. "I couldn't believe it when Theo told me you flew out there."

"What? I thought Ellie told you."

"Again, I'm the last to know these things." He put his hands on his knees and stood up. "He didn't think you should go through this alone." Steve let out a bitter laugh. "He can't seem to get it that you do everything alone because it's easier than actually having faith in someone." Steve stopped at the door, his hand on the knob, and turned back. "We have a big day tomorrow, but after that, if you want to talk, I'm here. Or if you want to keep it all to yourself, then I guess that's your prerogative." He shut the door behind him with a slam.

CHAPTER TWENTY-NINE

THE DAY HAD ARRIVED, AND I had to be there for the biggest event ever scheduled at The Book Stack. I dragged myself—and the little one—out of the cocoon of the bed, splashed water on my face, ate cereal, and headed into work. My world was about to be dominated by Bella and Brooke. People were counting on me, and I would not let them down.

The girls' scheduled arrival was booked in at 12:00, with an appearance from 1:00 until 4:00, so we'd agreed to meet at the store at eight a.m. Steve and I pulled in our parking spots at the same time, but unlike me, he wasn't alone. Dad, Chelsea, and "Grandma" Hazel all piled out of the car, and with barely a nod, we all headed inside.

As we converged at the back entrance of the bookstore, Dad put his hand on my neck. "I need to have a word with you." So much for shuffling through the day in denial.

"Can we do this later? We have a tight agenda and family therapy is not on the list."

"So how was it?" he asked.

"Come on, Dad. Not now," I pleaded.

He stood with his hands on his hips, searching my eyes. Dressed impeccably as always, in ironed chinos and a crisp button-down, his calm demeanor was shadowed by the sadness that clouded his eyes. "How is she?"

"Dad." I stepped forward. "She's beautiful, energetic... captivating." My voice cracked and Dad looked over my shoulder, possibly imagining her as only he remembered her. "Her husband passed away." Dad's eyes filled with relief. "And she married a new guy, a better guy." I thought about my unofficial stepfather, Roger. "A better guy" was the best description I could give of him.

"Will she come visit?"

I looked down at Dad's feet, since I couldn't see my own. "Nah, she's got a new life and all." Dad put his arms around me. "It's okay. It's okay," I said. I pressed my face into his shirt. Our shared heartache gripped me. Damn my hormones and my inability to suppress emotions.

"Did she explain?"

I looked up at him. I had to decide which parent had my loyalty. Would I lie for my mother or betray her?

Dad spoke first. "Because there are things she didn't think I knew, but now I think it's better if we all did."

"Dad?" The word felt tight in my throat. I'd put so much weight on the bonds of a blood relative, but the person who'd have made any sacrifice for my well-being, the man who raised me as his own, had no genetic tie to me. "You know... You knew all along?"

"Honey, relationships are infinitely complicated. You make decisions as you go along, and sometimes it works out, and other times you make stupid mistakes. Back then I was stupid. She didn't want to tell me things, and I was afraid if I pushed her she'd leave me. I never pushed, but she left all the same."

"Do you know about the man she was with before you?"

He didn't answer, but I saw it on his face.

"You know you're not—"

He put his hand up. "It makes no difference. It changes nothing for me, nothing for you and Steve."

"Dad..."

"I'm your father. I wanted you before your birth, and I loved you every second since. I will be here for you all the days of my life. When I die I will watch over you. That's all."

"What about Steve?"

"He already knows," Dad said.

"What?"

"I told him after he came back from your place last night. He's worried about you. We shouldn't let the past shroud our lives anymore. You have Hazel to thank for that. She's made me realize our family is ready to bring all the secrets to light." He kissed the top of my head. "We have to make better choices for this baby."

The back door popped open, and Steve came out.

"Get in here, guys. Those darling divas are on the way. We'll hash out our family dramas later." He crossed the parking lot to me and hooked his arm around my neck. "You stirring the pot, again?"

"I am." I grinned at my brother. "I'll be good now, I promise. Let's do this."

Nina had outdone herself. The store sparkled, covered in pink, silver, and white balloons, and glitter confetti. Streamers decorated the roped-off area leading to the second floor, where the signing would take place. Dozens of young girls—plus a surprising number of men—already formed a line that traveled through the store and out the front entrance. People wore "Bella and Brooke" shirts or were decked out in the girls' over-the-top style. We opened shop, and the line moved in as customers purchased copies of *Brooke and Bella, Plus Babies*.

Nina arrived soon after we did and set the staging area for the girls. Thick drapes covered the floor-to-ceiling windows of the two classrooms on the second floor. Keeping with the color theme requested by the Brooke and Bella team, Nina had an elegant sofa and a pair of cozy chairs sent up to the room. The other room was set for the babies and nannies. The Bella and Brooke entourage included a security detail of five men, one make-up artist, a hairdresser, two personal assistants, and a handler, as well as the tag-along camera crew that continuously filmed Brooke's and Bella's life.

Nina had also hired The Tasty Tart to bring in the fruit and veggie trays the girls requested. Nina knew the security staff would starve on such fare, so she also had trays of roast beef and turkey club sandwiches delivered. Our employees had a strict warning to stay clear of the food in the break room.

But still, on my way to my office, I caught Hazel with a mini sandwich in each hand.

"Meg, wait," Hazel said as I moved past her. I wasn't surprised to see her doing exactly what we told the staff not to do.

"Sorry, can't chat now." I moved toward my office, but she blocked my path. A brownish-pink sliver of roast beef fell from her sandwich and landed between us. "I got it." I reached for a napkin, squatting down to clean the mess in spite of the ache in my back. When the signing was over, I planned to spend a week in bed. Everything was catching up with my body, the last thing I'd taken care of lately.

I pulled myself upright and stood face to face with Hazel, who was grinning madly, with soft bread squished between her coffee-stained teeth.

"You saw my Candy girl, did you?" she asked. Before I could respond, the grin slid off her face, and her eyes twitched and then watered.

"Yes, I did."

"The last time I saw her was the day she told me about you. Before that, it'd been two or three years. I was a terrible mother." Her eyes were wide as if the truth shocked her, too. "I dabbled on the dark side a little, back in the day... ended up in jail." She rubbed her nose with the back of her hand.

"I'm sorry," I said. She seemed to want me to say something more, but I had trouble connecting the woman in front of me to the woman I had met in Atlanta.

Hazel grabbed my arm.

"After I got sober, I tracked Candy down in Atlanta. She

told me to stay away. I begged her to forgive me—she was the only family I had. That's when she told me about you. She said if I wanted family, I could go find you and Steve. So here I am. I should have told you I was your grandma from the beginning, but I didn't want you to reject me, too."

"But you've worked here as long as I have." I couldn't remember a time when Hazel wasn't part of The Book Stack staff.

"I took this job when I found out your grandfather owned the place. I figured we could get to know each other. Anyhow, back then I was struggling to stay sober. My past is nothing to be proud of. I didn't want to embarrass you with the truth."

"It wouldn't have mattered."

"Oh, I don't know. You've never really liked me. I'm just the crazy old lady who works here." Her eyes lit up, and she grinned again. "Boy, did I fall in love with this place. I discovered that reading mysteries was my secret to staying sober. Those stories take me away from my problems better than the drugs ever did. Meg, you saved my life by leading me here, and you didn't even know it."

I smiled at her. Finally, something we could agree on. "Books saved me, too."

"Excuse me, miss?" In the doorway stood the largest man I'd ever seen, wearing a suit with a little black bow tie.

"Are you with the Brooke and Bella team?" I asked.

"Yes, ma'am. The ladies are prepared to enter the back door."

"It's through here." Hazel stepped aside, and the mountain reached the door before me. I thought he was mumbling to himself until I noticed his Bluetooth. His meaty hand flipped the latch and pushed the door open, revealing a cream-colored Cadillac SUV and four large men holding black sheets on either sides of the door to prevent anyone from photographing Bella and Brooke as they entered the store.

Brooke appeared first, leaping from the SUV in six-inch stilettos, black pants that fit like a second skin, and an equally tight, plunging-neckline top. She wore clothes in a way that made her seem naked. Her hair, a thick mane the exact color of cinnamon, flowed down her back. My fingers itched to touch it. I hated reality TV, but my job was to make her shine.

"Hi there." Her melodic voice hit me, and I was overwhelmed with a childlike urge to become her best friend.

Bella charged in next, her white blond hair bouncing in her trademark pigtails. "Wait, Brooke, we're supposed to walk in side by side. Don't you go stealing my thunder, girlfriend." She wore a pink skirt made with less fabric than my maternity panties. Her see-through blouse and plum bra that coordinated with her platform heels were nothing short of adorable and slutty, and the reason men were lined up for the signing.

On the show, Bella raced to catch up with Brooke. When Brooke had flunked out of college, Bella quit. When Brooke was forced into rehab, Bella showed up vowing sobriety, too. Finally when Brooke got knocked up at a posh halfway house, Bella scored a positive pregnancy test on the final episode six weeks later. Rumors spread that their babies shared the same daddy. Brooke was the only one who didn't seem to be aware of Bella's copycat syndrome. The ever-noble Brooke looked out for her best friend in all the ways she didn't look out for herself. The fangirls of the show looked up to Brooke, but the entire male species between the age of eight and ninety-eight fell in lust with Bella.

Bella staggered across the room and grabbed Brooke's hand. Looking me over, she squealed, "Oh, that thing's about to fall out!" She covered her mouth and erupted into giggles. "I'm so glad I'm not pregnant anymore." She hopped up and down, and I laughed with her, even though I wanted to tell her to sit down and hush.

My belly tightened, reminding me that I'd been pushing myself too hard. I made a mental note to stop and have a drink of water.

Steve walked in, arms held out in welcome. Gag me. "Wonderful! The girls are here." He introduced himself to each of them and to their crew, who had filled the room. I watched as the cameramen weaseled around, working different angles and distributing their microphones. Sweat trickled down my back, and I sighed, wondering how long the afternoon would stretch.

While Steve herded Brooke and Bella up the elevator to deliver them to the waiting crowd, I wandered around the store, checking up on the people in line. As word spread that the girls had arrived, the noise escalated. We had to be closing in on our maximum occupancy. I knew I was reaching my own limits. My head was throbbing with the noise volume, and the pain seemed to run down my back. When everyone was gone, I was going to have to rest on the floor of my office just to get enough energy to get home. I cursed myself for flying to Atlanta.

Nina and Chelsea kept me going. Chelsea worked the front of the line. Nina moved through the store, avoiding my father but showing up the moment I needed something as if she were in tune with my every thought. I waited forever for the elevator to come back down but finally gave up and wiggled my way up the stairs. At the top, a hand closed around my arm. I turned to look into the smooth, chocolate eyes of Cortez. "Hiya, doll," he said.

I should have responded, but I looked past him to Theo. "Why are you here? What makes you think it's your job to keep tabs on me?"

"We need to talk," he said. "They wouldn't let us in unless we bought the book." He held up a copy of *Bella and Brooke, Plus Babies*. It looked absurd in his hands.

Cortez had his copy pressed to his chest with his hook. "I'm here for the girls. I'm going to ask them out." He pursed his lips as though he had a delicious taste in his mouth.

Theo smacked him on the back of the head. "What's your plan, dumbass? To ask them both out in front of each other?"

Cortez jerked away from him. "Man, get off my back. Them girls do everything together. I can show them both a good time." He grinned at me and raised his eyebrows as if I knew what he was talking about. Okay, I knew what he was talking about but forced it from my brain.

Another guy in line turned around. "I heard they're looking for baby daddies."

"Aw, shucks, man. If that's what it takes! If that's what it takes!" He laughed, and the man gave him a high five, and then they bumped chests.

"You go," the stranger said. "You know it."

Theo was shaking his head. "Ignore these idiots. Are you okay? You look tired."

"I'm working. And I don't have anything to say to you, even if I had the time." I walked away.

When I passed the elevator I realized why it had never come back down. The shut-off button had been activated by one of the B&B security guys. The beefy man stood with legs spread, arms crossed, and sunglasses on. I didn't get the part about the sunglasses. Did he wear them to make himself more intimidating? The tattoo of a tiger biting his neck accomplished that. The man was scary. Scary enough I wasn't about to tell him to get out of my elevator. With the line on the stairs and the swarm throughout the store, I was having trouble catching my breath. My world was closing in on me.

Moving throughout the second floor of the store, I expected the crowd to be calm up there. Soon they'd be rewarded with the presence of the reality stars. No such luck. As we neared one o'clock, the girls had yet to make an appearance.

I located Steve at the front of the line. "What's the deal?" I asked.

He shrugged. "Girls. You know how they are." He nodded down the hall where Brooke and Bella had been holed up since their arrival. "You check it out. See if you can coax them out before this mob takes over."

"Okay, okay. Let's get this show started." I dashed toward the hall.

Just then, two girls who barely looked old enough to drive stormed the stairs. They could pass as Bella and Brooke back when their show first went on air, before the booze, pills and pregnancies. One girl was dressed as Brooke, in painted-on jeans and a minuscule white top. "Where are they? We've been here all night! Where are they?"

Beefcake with the tiger tat blocked them off at the top of the stairs. "No passage," he barked.

The Bella wannabe's lip quivered. She tugged on her bleach-fried pigtail. "But we have to meet them. We *have* to. Brooke!" she yelled around the wall of man. "Bella!"

Beefcake mumbled into his Bluetooth. "Ladies, we're getting you an escort."

"What's an escort?" She swung her head around so fast her pigtail, and the scent of mousse, smacked me in the face.

"He's getting us in to meet them." The girls clapped and jumped in unison.

A guy who could have been Beefcake's twin, only with ice-blue eyes, came up the stairs behind them. "Come on girls, let's go."

"Wait," the one with the pigtails said, putting her hands up. "I know they came up here. They're not down there."

"I'm removing you two from the property, for disorderly conduct."

"What?" Her friend's mouth dropped open, and tears sprang to her eyes. "You can't do that."

"I can, and I will. Walk, or I'll carry you out of here." He placed his hand on her back to usher her along.

"That's not necessary," Theo said. "Let the girls have their day. Give them a break." He took one exaggerated step out of line, with his arm out as though he was holding the space. "They can take our spots."

"Shut up, man," Cortez smacked Theo's shoulder. "They gotta go through the line, same as everyone else." He looked at the girls and sighed, shaking his head.

"We'll move to the back," Theo said.

The two girls slipped into Theo's spot. "Thank you, thank you," they squealed. Cortez rolled his eyes at Theo, but grinned at the girls. The guys trudged down the stairs, but I caught Theo turning to watch me.

"Thanks," I mouthed. His smile was so faint that, if I didn't know him, I might mistake it as hostile, but I knew what the look he gave me meant. As if to verify my thoughts, he winked. Right then, the wall of my grudge crumbled. But duty called. I marched down the hall to see what on earth those girls waited for. I could hear the giggling as I neared the room.

I tapped on the door, but no one answered. I turned the knob, pushing in a tad. "Hello? Brooke? Bella? We have a crowd waiting for you."

The door swung open and Bella, wineglass in hand, waved me in. "Would you care for some Pinot? Come in. Come in. We're settling our nerves before we head out."

She danced over to the bottle on the table, picked up a drinking glass sitting next to a pitcher of water with lemon slices floating in it—courtesy of Nina—and filled the glass with wine. "Drink up. Your nerves could use a drink too." She grinned and licked her lips.

"No thanks. I'd better not." I patted my tummy.

She pushed the glass in my hand. "Oh, no, it's good for the baby... in moderation." She winked at Brooke, who sat on the sofa, holding a wine glass and nursing a chubby, pajama-clad baby.

"I thought you girls didn't drink anymore."

Brooke took a sip. "We don't. Wine doesn't count."

Bella giggled. "Neither does prescription pills." She hauled up a purse so big it wouldn't pass as carry-on luggage. She rummaged through it and pulled out an orange bottle. "As long as you follow the directions on the label." She held the bottle up to the light. "Take one as needed for anxiety." She looked up to the sky and twisted her lips in thought. "Yep, it's needed. Hold this a sec." She pushed her drink into my hand, popped the lid off, and shook one, then another pill into her hand. "Oops!" She made a big O with her mouth, smacked her hand to her mouth and took the wine to chase it with. "Take that, anxiety!" She wiggled her shoulders with excitement.

"Come, sit over here," Brooke called to me. I followed her orders, pleased to get off my feet for a moment. I put Bella's wine on the table and settled in next to Brooke. "Are you planning on nursing?"

"Yes, yes I am," I answered. Her baby made eager gulping sounds, his fingers held tight in a fist as he sucked away. His eyes, wide open, watched Brooke, enthralled with his momma.

"It's the best," Brooke said. "I want to give him the best." She stroked his velvety head as she talked.

"Oh no, here she goes again." Bella rolled her eyes. "Olivia only gets the best, too, and the nicest part about formula is anyone can give it to her." She retrieved her phone from her purse and plopped onto the other white loveseat, humming to herself while she texted.

The girls needed to get out there to the waiting crowd. "How much longer do you expect it will be until you all are ready for the signing?" I asked.

Brooke looked at me over the rim of her wineglass and took a sip. "You should relax a little. Have a drink with us, and then we'll all go out together. It's fine at the end of pregnancy. Everyone in Europe does it, so you know it's a good thing." She winked, and that sealed the deal.

Why not? In all the books and magazines I'd perused over the last months, many said an occasional drink was fine.

I sipped the Pinot and moaned in delight.

"A toast," Bella said. "To new friends and good wine!" She came over to us and clinked glasses. The wine was fabulous. It'd been close to a year since I enjoyed a drink. My body relaxed into the seat, and I listened to their happy chattering debate on the best way to mother a child. They clearly knew more about the subject than I did. As it turned out, wine was exactly what I needed to take the edge off, and surprisingly, for once I didn't feel guilty indulging. After all, the Europeans do it, right?

CHAPTER THIRTY

AFTER BEING AS UPTIGHT AS I was, relaxation was a strange shift. Even when Hazel barged in, griping about getting the circus started, my body stayed languid, and I laughed along with my new buddies.

But Hazel was right.

"You heard the lady," I said, pulling myself up. "It's showtime!" No sooner did the words leave my lips, I heard a little pop, and I thought: *No!* But sure enough, as the nanny came from next door to get Brooke's baby, I felt wetness seeping between my legs.

The tight sensation surged again. "You guys head on out — I'll catch up with you." There was no need for me to panic; nobody could tell what was going on, and we had to get through the signing. But then the contraction peaked, and I braced the table for support, letting out a deep groan. I couldn't stop myself.

"Meg?" Hazel's hands flailed, as if seeking something to hold onto.

Both girls stared at me, and while Bella's face pulled back in disgust, Brooke, looking excited, pointed at the floor. "Hey look, your water broke!"

"Oh... *oh.*" Hazel stood with her mouth wide open.

"Hazel," I said and waited until her gaze wandered from

the floor to my face. "Can you find Nina for me?" Nina could handle anything—that, I was sure of—as long as she didn't get grossed out.

"Oh my gosh, oh my gosh!" Bella had her hands over her mouth, eye fluttering like a moth on a porch light.

My mouth fell open. "I'm sorry." I wanted to say more, but the pain surged, and I propped my arm on the table, curling inward as a tightening burned through me. The feeling was different from before. It was hard and fast, and I wanted to run from it. I lost myself in the contraction. It didn't matter that I was at work. All I knew was tearing pain seared through me, and I wanted it to stop.

Stop! Stop! Stop!

Then the hurt began to ease, and Brooke was by my side. She put her hands on my shoulders. "Don't be afraid. You're doing great. I can't believe you're going to have your baby today." She was grinning, all happy and excited, and all I could think was: *No!* Then another contraction came at me.

"I'm not ready," I moaned, trying to fight it. I rocked against the table.

Brooke rubbed my back. "You can do this. Your body was made ready to do this." When the pain eased, she led me to the sofa.

Bella paced. "We should get out there. Isn't someone going to come help you? Our fans are waiting." Her voice rose in pitch, and when the door swung open she cried out the same words I was thinking, "Thank God!"

Theo.

"How fast are the contractions coming?" he asked, but I was already losing it again, gripping the arm of the sofa as I perched, swaying, on the edge of the seat.

Brooke was next to me, holding my other hand. "They're coming really fast," she said. "She needs to get out of here. We can take her in our car. It's parked at the back door."

"*Brooke!*" Bella protested.

"Nah, that's not possible," Theo said. "All the cars in the lot are blocked in. It's too crowded out there. I called an ambulance. They're on their way." He cupped my cheeks in his palms, looking me in the eyes. "How you doing, sweetheart?" When I looked in his eyes, I knew then that I didn't want to make any more mistakes with my life. I loved Theo.

"I'm afraid," I confessed.

"There's nothing to be afraid of. I'm here with you."

"We're all here with you," Bella muttered from the corner.

"Shush!" Brooke hissed at her, moving to stand by the door.

"Look at me," Theo said. "I'm right here, by your side. I'm going to stay by your side."

Another contraction was building, but I had to tell him. "I'm afraid to love you, because I'm worried I'll never feel safe. Oh no!" I wrapped my arms around my belly, moaning as the pain took me again.

Theo held me against him murmuring, "It's okay," in my ear. As the pain moved back, he wiped the sweat off my brow. "I love you, Meg. I'll love you forever. I promise you, you're safe with me. I will never leave you again. You can trust me."

I believed him. His words rang true. And I also understood at that moment why they called the final stage of labor the ring of fire.

"Theo..."

"Yes?"

"I want to push." I clutched his arms, grinding my teeth. I fought the scream, but it fought me. I wasn't making it to a hospital.

The door opened. Hazel rushed in, with Nina and Cortez following. Cortez kneeled at my side, and then I saw the black bag he had with him. "Hey girl," he said as he opened the bag calmly, sifting through its contents. "I'm going to check you out." He pulled out a blood pressure cuff and slipped it on me.

Nina looked pale. "Ladies," she said to Brooke and Bella. "Hazel will take you out for the signing now. Sorry to keep you all waiting." And then to me she said, "I'm going to let Mike and Steve know you're okay. They're outside waiting for the ambulance." She turned her back to us and spoke into her walkie-talkie.

Bella headed to the door, but Brooke hung back. "Can I stay and help?" she asked.

"No, Brooke, come on. They're here for us. We have to go out there."

"Do the signing without me," Brooke said. "Unless you want me to leave?" She looked at me, but I couldn't speak. The pain returned, and I couldn't stop myself from bearing down with it.

"Stay," Theo said. "We could use an extra set of hands."

Everything happened really fast then. They helped me to the floor, and Theo lifted my dress and ripped my underpants to remove them. Not that I cared at that point, but Nina and Brooke focused on my eyes, encouraging me. Theo and Cortez switched into work mode. My head was in Nina's lap, and Brooke and Cortez were on each side of me.

"The baby's head is right there," Theo said.

An ambulance siren sounded off in the distance, but it wouldn't get to me in time.

At some point, Brooke and Cortez helped pull my legs back while Theo told me to push. The pain exploded from within, but even as I was being torn apart, every part of me screamed: *Push! Push! Push!*

And there on the floor of my bookstore, surrounded by my stepmom, two veteran amputees, and a reality star, I pushed my baby into the world. Theo placed her, all wet and screaming-mad, on my chest.

"She's perfect," he whispered to me.

A single tear slid from the corner of my eye. "She is."

CHAPTER THIRTY-ONE

TIME MOVED FAST ONCE THE baby was out. One second I stared in awe at the tiny baby in my arms, and the next, paramedics erupted into the room, men in uniforms bustling around and taking charge. They took my baby away. I could see two men working on her, but she was out of my reach. I wasn't going to panic, but I wanted her back in my arms. She was mine.

And she was wailing.

Theo stayed by my side. "They're making sure she's warm, that she's getting enough oxygen," he whispered while he stroked my hair back.

A man talked with Theo while inserting an IV into my arm. I ignored them, my eyes on the baby. "She's crying," I said. Her pink arms flailed, hands fisted, eyes clenched, mouth opened wide. The guys working on her offered no comfort. "She's upset. I want to hold her." Someone had placed a sheet over me, and a paramedic tended to my business down there. I didn't want to think about what he was doing. Maybe I was in mild shock. My body hurt, but I didn't care. I had a baby, and for once I could believe in those stories where a mother would lift a school bus with one hand to drag her child to safety. I wanted them to give my baby back.

I looked to Theo. "Why won't they give her to me? She wants me."

He was smiling at the baby, not worried at all. "It's good for her to cry. She's clearing her lungs." He smiled and peered down at me, his eyes glazed over. "She's got good lungs."

Two men rolled me onto a stretcher. I wanted to stand, but they wouldn't let me. They covered me with another sheet and strapped me down. My baby wailed.

"Give her to me," I said. Someone blocked my view. All I could see was the back of everyone. I struggled to sit upright, but bound to the stretcher, my mobility was hampered. And then she went silent. Her crying stopped.

Theo touched my shoulder. "Hang on. You'll have her in a minute."

"I can't see her," I said. Tears blurred my vision. My breath came in uneven gasps. "What's wrong?"

"Ma'am, I need you to try and calm down," the paramedic who had placed my IV said.

Theo lowered to my ear. "Hey now, don't cry. It's okay," he whispered. "Everything is okay. You want me to go see her?"

I nodded, afraid to speak.

He moved across the small room, around the paramedics that tended to my baby, and when he got to the other side of everyone I could see his face again. He looked down, and I could tell the minute he saw her. Like the sun rising, his face beamed. His joy gave me comfort. The men mumbled to each other. They shifted around, and for a moment, I lost sight of Theo. Then everyone parted, and he came to me. My baby was bundled in his arms. Swaddled in a blanket, she cooed. She peered at Theo with squinting eyes.

"Hello, beautiful," Theo said to her. "There is someone who can't wait to see you."

I reached for her, and he helped settle her in my arms. Someone told me to make sure I held onto her good. As if I'd ever let her go.

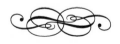

Chaos moved through the bookstore. The book signing was in full swing as we came out. In the hallway, Nina rushed to us.

"Oh, she's perfect, Meg," Nina said as she walked along with the stretcher. "I'm proud of you. You're amazing."

"I'm glad you're here," I said. "Really."

"Honey, it was an honor for me." Her eyes filled with tears, and she fanned at them, blinking fast. "Everyone knows. There's a news crew waiting outside." At the elevator, scary tat guy looked at me as though I was the scary one. He moved aside. "They came for the Brooke and Bella crowd, but they caught on when the ambulance arrived, and now they want to interview the woman whose baby was delivered by a reality star." The elevator was too small for Theo or Nina to fit. "Dad and Steve are outside trying to shoo them away. They're going to follow you to the hospital. I'll stay here and help out with the signing. Don't worry about anything." She took a step back, allowing the doors to roll shut.

"Wait, wait!" I called out.

Scary tat guy put his hand in the door, forcing it to open again, but Theo was gone.

Nina knew who I was looking for. She smiled. "He's on his way downstairs. I'll come to the hospital as soon as we're done here."

"Wait." I stopped her again. "Will you do me one favor?"

"Anything."

"Bring Hazel."

The doors shut, and when they opened again, Theo stood waiting for us.

"What? You didn't think I'd leave you, did you?" he asked, smiling.

With the commotion focused on the reality stars, we exited the store without too much notice.

"Can you ride with us?" I asked Theo. I held tight to the baby.

"I promise I won't leave your side."

The sun shone bright in the parking lot. I instinctively put my hand over the baby's face, but her eyes were closed. Already worn out from her first hour of life, she was asleep.

Dad and Steve stood, looking lost, at the back of the ambulance. Before we got to them, a woman with a microphone ran alongside me, the cameraman behind her. "Here she is, here she is. The owner of The Book Stack gave birth today in the bookstore during Brooke and Bella's highly anticipated book signing. How are you, Miss Michaels?"

Theo held up an arm to block her. "She's fine, stay back."

"One question," the reporter pleaded.

The paramedic slowed at the back of the ambulance, and the woman came closer with her microphone. "Will you name the baby after Brooke or Bella?" she asked.

Everyone froze and waited for me to respond, and I looked down at my daughter and thought of the one thing my life had been missing all along.

"Her name is Grace."

CHAPTER THIRTY-TWO

THE RIDE TO THE HOSPITAL passed in a blur. My baby was there. I stared at her face in disbelief, listening to Theo and the paramedic chatting like old buddies.

The ambulance pulled in at the Emergency Room doors on the ugly side of the hospital — no manicured bushes and flowerbeds like outside the maternity wing. A cop leaned across the desk to flirt with the nurse on duty. The lights pulsed bright.

A pale nurse with black fingernail polish took Grace from me. Theo held onto my hand.

"I'll check her vitals and get her washed up for you," the nurse said, holding Grace under her arm as if she were a football, until someone brought over a bassinet. "We'll bring her to your room once they get you admitted." She walked away with my whole world, or a large chunk of it.

"Stay with her, Theo," I said. "I don't want her to be alone. She knows your voice."

He leaned down and stroked my cheek. "Don't worry. I'll talk to her the whole time. She'll know I'm there." I watched him go to my daughter.

By the time they set me up in a room, a different nurse let me know visitors waited to see me.

"The bookstore is your favorite place in the world," Steve

said coming into my room. "But did you have to give birth there? You could've taken the day off if you had mentioned you were in labor." He laughed and grabbed my foot through the blanket. "Are you okay?"

"I didn't know." I shrugged and fiddled with my ID wristband. They said Grace had one to match around her ankle. "Believe me, I'm trying to live a more private life." I heated with the memory of moaning on the floor of the bookstore.

Dad stood with his hands on his hips, a little awkward and a whole lot proud. "Are you kidding? That reality star's your biggest fan. You made her day." He chuckled, and stuffed his hands in his pockets. "She's been sitting out there waiting to meet the baby with the rest of us."

"Really?"

"Really," Steve answered. "She only caught a glimpse of Grace before Nina ushered her out."

The door opened, and Steve and Dad moved out of the way as the nurse pushed the bassinet against my bed.

"Congratulations," Theo said, shaking hands with Steve first and then Dad.

"Thank you," Dad said, his voice wavering. "For helping Meg. You were there when she needed you."

"You can say that again," Steve said. "Oh, she's cute."

The nurse placed Grace in my arms and walked out as Nina and Hazel came in. Then Chelsea stuck her head in the door. "Knock, knock. Can we see, too?"

Steve ushered her in. "Come meet my niece."

And behind Chelsea, Cortez and Brooke squeezed in. Brooke waved at me, and I waved back. The noise in the room was growing louder, but Grace slept in my arms. Theo came to my side and leaned down. "Can I get you anything?" he asked.

"Sit with me," I whispered back, patting the bed next to me.

For over an hour, everyone took turns holding the baby and taking photos. Brooke retold the story of delivering Grace. Cortez stood by her side, filling in the parts she missed.

Steve left with Chelsea. Cortez and Brooke left together, too. Theo whispered in my ear, "Cortez got his date."

"Impressive," I said. I looked in Theo's eyes and shivered. We both waited for everyone to leave, so we could be alone. His love for me was vivid on his face. I promised myself in that moment never to hold back again.

I watched as Hazel cradled her great-granddaughter. "She looks like your mother," Hazel said and frowned. "You probably don't want to hear that."

"Yes, I do. You know so much that I don't know," I said. "Do you have any photos of my mom?"

A sad smile spread across Hazel's face. "Oh, sure I do. I can bring them to you."

"I'd like that. When I saw her, she gave me this." I pulled out the heart locket from under my hospital gown. "There's a picture of both of you in it."

Tears flooded Hazel's eyes. "I gave that to her." She wiped away a stray tear. "Thank you for allowing me to hold the baby." Grace opened her eyes and looked up at Hazel. "Oh, she's ready for you."

"Wait a sec," I said, before Hazel could give me the baby. "I need a picture of you two for the baby book."

Theo reached for the camera. "I'll take it. We'll get one of you girls all together."

Hazel giggled at Theo.

After he took the picture, he offered to walk Hazel to her car. They left, and I had a moment with Dad and Nina alone. Dad had stood by Nina's side since she'd arrived, talking and holding her hand. Something had changed between them; the tension had slipped away, and they were realigned to the way they were meant to be.

"Well," Dad said. "You made us grandparents."

Nina winked at him. "Hi, Grandpa."

Dad swung her arm. "Hello, Grandma."

Nina laughed out loud.

"You kids get out of here," I said. "I need to spend some time with my daughter."

"We're proud of you," Nina said. She came around and kissed my cheek. Her words meant more to me than I could say.

They left, and a nurse came in and helped me latch Grace on. I watched in awe as Grace nursed. I stroked her rosy cheek and opened up the blanket to see her tiny torso, little legs, and perfect feet.

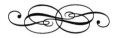

Over the next few hours, Theo brought me clothes from my condo and picked up dinner. He held Grace while I took a shower. I told him to go home and sleep, but he didn't want to leave us. While I was nursing Grace, he dozed off in the chair watching us. I called Jason to tell him the baby was born.

"Does she resemble me?" he asked.

"Not at all," I said, laughing because Jason always thought of himself first.

"That's probably a good thing," he whispered into the phone. "Tell me about her."

"She has wise eyes. She looks at me as if we're old friends and she knows all my secrets. Her skin is the purest pink I've ever seen." I smiled, looking at my daughter. "She has light hair. A tiny little tuft of it. And cheeks. You should see these cheeks."

"She sounds divine. I'm happy it all worked out." He cleared his throat. "I'm hiding in the garage. I better get back in the house before she notices I'm out here. But thanks for letting me know."

I sighed. I had so much I wanted to say to him about everything we'd been through. I looked at Grace and let it all go. "Okay, bye."

"You'll be fine. You don't need me."

"You're right, I don't." I hung up the phone. Theo slept in the chair next to me, his arms hugging his chest. He had delivered my baby and stayed by my side. We both had been through so much in the past year. His eyes opened.

"I love you," I said.

He smiled. "And I love you."

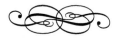

The next afternoon, Theo opened the door to the condo, carrying my bag and a vase full of flowers. "You never said what you thought of the baby's room," he said. "If you don't like it, I'll change it however you want."

Grace was asleep in the carrier car seat, and I set her on the floor. "I haven't seen it yet."

Theo put the flowers on the coffee table and turned to me. "Not even a peek?"

"I promised you I wouldn't look until you showed it to me."

Theo took my hand. "Let's have a look." He took me to the door I hadn't entered since those first days he stayed with me, before he moved into my bed. I swallowed the lump in my throat as he turned the knob.

The room was as enchanting as a fairy tale. In soft, muted colors he had painted a castle and a whimsical bridge by a beautiful garden. The mural covered every wall. On a hill, a weeping willow bent in the breeze, surrounded by butterflies, and just past that was a dark and inviting magical forest. From the ceiling hung origami stars made of printed paper.

"Is that what I think it is?" I asked, pointing at the stars.

"If you think I folded stars out of the actual pages of a fairy tale, you'd be correct. I found the discards from the print collection in your office."

"Theo, this room..." I turned around slowly. "This room is perfect." I sat down in the glider and picked up the e. e. cummings book he had left there. "Your book." I held it up for him.

"It's for Grace."

Not exactly bedtime reading for a child, but I knew the book had special meaning for Theo. "Thank you," I said, and when I flipped it open I saw he had drawn in nearly every margin. Sketches of me sleeping, my hand draped across my pregnant belly. One of me standing in a doorway, with a slight smile on my lips. A drawing of Theo and me laughing together. Another of me in bed, reading. Theo had created his own love story between the lines. Tears filled my eyes as I turned the pages. "I can't believe this was here all along and I had no idea." I looked up at him.

"Remember the night I bought the book, and you traced your hand on a poem? You showed me a part of you, of your love of books, and how you don't put boundaries on that love. And Meg, I know sometimes you doubt yourself, doubt your ability to be a mother, but when you love, you are fierce in that love. Grace is a very lucky little girl. Come here." He pulled me into his arms and kissed the side of my face. "We talked when you were in labor, but I have a few more things I need to say."

He tilted my head, framing my face with his hands, smoothing my hair back.

"I love you," he said. "I want to be with you forever." He shifted and reached into his pocket, and pulled out a little box. Theo opened the box and removed a vintage solitaire engagement ring. "Will you marry me?"

I inhaled, ready to respond.

"Before you answer, I need you to know I'm ready to be your husband, and I'm ready to be Grace's father." I stood very still, overcome with emotion, as he took my hand and kissed it. "Let's share this life together."

I threw my arms around him. "Yes, I will marry you, Theo."

He put the ring on my finger and we kissed. That was when I was sure that my happily ever after had already begun.

ACKNOWLEDGMENTS

Writing a book is a long journey, and I arrived here with love, support, and faith from some very awesome people.

First, a huge thanks to my girl, Kim Aleman. You were with me from day one, always ready to have a serious conversation about these people living in my head. Sure, you kept refilling my glass of wine, but you always took me seriously, so thank you.

Next, my heart goes to everyone at Red Adept Publishing for believing in Meg and Theo's story. Special thanks to my brilliant editors, Michelle Rever and Sarah Carleton, for seeing my vision and leading me there.

Thank you to my fabulous sisterhood of writers, Brenda Hummel and Elizabeth Buhmann, for reading and rereading my pages. Thank you for helping me tear it down and build it back up. And thank you, Kate Moretti, for your guidance along the way. I am a better person and a better writer for having you all in my life.

Thank you, Steve Kozeniewski, for letting me pick your brain endlessly. You might've helped with a few things in this book.

To Alex Horton, you captivated me with your Army of Dude blog. Thank you for taking my call, Alex, and sharing your journey home with me. You are an inspiration.

Throughout the writing of this book, I came across many

stories of survival. After reading Bryan Anderson's *No Turning Back* and his articles in *Esquire* and watching his HBO Documentary, I felt as if I knew him. One day, I hit a point where I had a few questions that I couldn't find the answers to on my own. I contacted Bryan, and he replied as if we were old friends. Thank you, Bryan, for answering my most intimate questions. You are amazing.

Thank you, Lois and Amy, for your unwavering love, and thanks to Don and Edith for believing in me. I love you all.

To my husband and the wild monkeys: you are my everything.

And finally, to the one person I have to thank twice: Brenda, I wouldn't be here if it wasn't for you. You kept me going every step of the way.

ABOUT THE AUTHOR

Claire Ashby was born and raised in the heart of Atlanta. At a young age, she began keeping journals and over time embellished the details of her quiet days. Eventually, she let go of writing reality altogether and delved completely into the world of fiction.

When she's not reading or writing, she spends her time watching extreme survival shows and taking long walks after nightfall. She has an unnatural love of high places, but still regrets the time she skydived solo. She believes some things are better left to the imagination. She resides in Austin with her family and a pack of wild dogs.

CPSIA information can be obtained
at www.ICGtesting.com
Printed in the USA
LVOW11s1518240117

522002LV00007B/1180/P